We hope you enjoy this book. Please return or renew it by the due date.

You can renew it at www.norfolk.gov.uk/libraries or by using our free library app.

Otherwise you can phone 0344 800 8020 - please have your library card and PIN ready.

You can sign up for email reminders too.

NORFOLK ITEM

30129 086 648 301

NORFOLK COUNTY COUNCIL
LIBRARY AND INFORMATION SERVICE

D1143023

Fiona Watson is a medieval historian and writer. She is the author of *A History of Scotland's Landscapes*, *Scotland from Prehistory to the Present*, and, with Birlinn/John Donald, *Under the Hammer: Edward I and Scotland*. She was the presenter of the BBC TV series *In Search of Scotland*. Fiona lives in rural Perthshire.

Dark Hunter

F. J. Watson

Polygon

First published in 2022 by Polygon,
an imprint of Birlinn Ltd.

Birlinn Ltd
West Newington House
10 Newington Road
Edinburgh
EH9 1QS

www.polygonbooks.co.uk

1

ISBN 978 1 84697 611 7
eBook ISBN 978 1 78885 495 5

British Library Cataloguing-in-Publication Data
A catalogue record for this book is available on request
from the British Library.

Typeset by 3btype.com

To Nick, who sustains,
and Finn, who inspires

Evil is spread widely abroad these days and
he knows what he did was evil too.
But he is sure it was the lesser of the two.

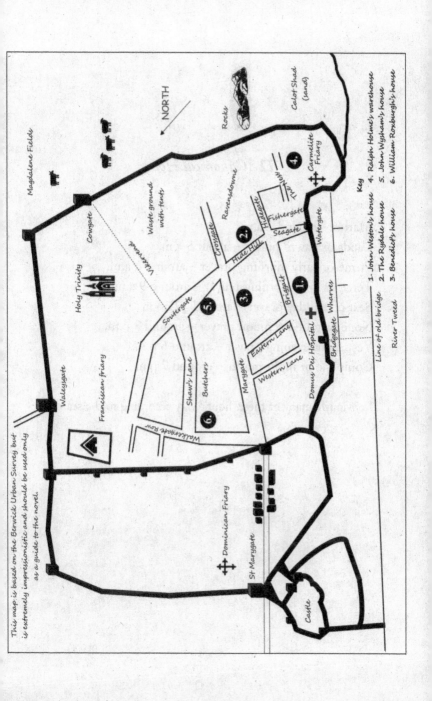

This map is based on the Berwick Urban Survey but is extremely impressionistic and should be used only as a guide to the novel.

NORTH

Magdalene Fields

Holy Trinity

Walleygate

Franciscan friary

Crosgate

Waste ground with tents

Viewgang

Soutergate

Crossgate

Ravensdowne

Hidegate

Fishergate

Seagate

Rocks

Calot Shad (sand)

Carmelite Friary

Hae Hill

The Ness

Watergate

Briggait

Wharves

Bridgegate

Eastern Lane

Western Lane

Domus Dei Hospital

Line of old bridge

River Tweed

Shewly Lane

Butchery

Marygate

Walkergate Row

Dominican Friary

St Marygate

Castle

Key

1. John Weston's house
2. The Rydale house
3. Benedict's house
4. Ralph Holme's warehouse
5. John Wytham's house
6. William Roxburgh's house

The Canonical Hours

Matins – around 2 a.m.
Lauds or dawn* prayer – about 5 a.m.
Prime or early morning prayer – around 6 a.m.
Terce or mid-morning prayer – around 9 a.m.
Sext or midday prayer – around 12 noon
None or mid-afternoon prayer – around 3 p.m.
Vespers or evening prayer – around 6 p.m.
Compline or night prayer – around 7 p.m.

* obviously many of these 'hours' vary according to the season

Chapter 1

1 May 1317

The land lies beneath a heavy darkness, the moon but a sharp sliver in the western sky. The man moves slowly, bent like a yew beneath a heavy sack, his face lost under the brim of his great hat. He is afraid the sack will betray him, its bare patches threatening to reveal the terrible thing he has done. That he had to do. But it is too late to remedy that now. He must trust to the darkness and the fear he means to sow.

He glances towards the mighty gate set in the town's walls, still closed to keep Berwick's inhabitants safe from the marauding Scots outside even as dawn approaches. Fixing his mind on the next step, he tells himself he must not speak more than necessary.

'Who is it?' A shape shifts on the wall.

'Richard Heron.'

The shape comes down a few steps, taking on the form of a

man with a spear. 'And who's Richard Heron, and what's he doing breaking curfew?'

'I work for Ralph Holme.'

'What? I can't hear you.'

'Ralph Holme.' He pushes the sack further on to his shoulders. 'I have a mad dog in here.'

'Ralph Holme, did you say?'

'Yes. I have a mad dog . . .'

Another man, much broader, rushes to join the first. 'Then get it out of here.'

The first man scuttles down, averting his gaze, as if that will protect him. He removes the great wooden bar holding the gate in place and pushes it away from him with a grunt.

The man with the sack smiles, still bent low. He moves carefully, one step, then another, muttering his thanks. He knows they will remember he went out very early beyond Berwick's walls. They might even remember his name. But they will not know who he was. The great gate bangs shut behind him.

He has many hard steps ahead of him under the weight of the sack. It is a burden he was willing to take as soon as he knew what needed to be done. Evil is spread widely abroad these days, and he knows what he did was evil too. But he is sure it was the lesser of the two.

One month earlier . . .

'God's teeth, will you stop singing!' Sir Edmund twists in his saddle to growl at me, the tip of his nose livid in the frigid air. I hadn't realised I was singing out loud, for I know how much it irks him, but it helps to coax a little cheerfulness out of the day. The cold moves through me, taking root. I can barely feel my fingers clutching the reins, but I risk a sharp slap across the cheek if I cannot stop my teeth from chattering in time to the music in my head.

'Useless,' Will mouths at me.

I feel the weight of my stupidity like a millstone round my neck. But I will not let them see it.

Though this is England, it is our enemies the Scots who are most at home here. It is whispered they are devils who can move from valley to valley in an instant, trailing the smell of sulphur behind them. And they do not need to coax fire, like honest men. One glance from the Black Douglas and a house or barn will glow with a white heat. But these are just peasant superstitions and I know better.

A heron rises with a terrible screeching from the river to our left, and my heart shudders long after I see what it is. We enter a wood, the grass studded with violets and stitchwort and I am thinking it would make a nice bed for a weary traveller when Sir Edmund raises a hand. After a moment we trot on, our mounts fretful. The wagon toils behind us, Ade the driver keeping his curses to himself for once.

The silent oaks and skittish birches huddle close now, pushing away the light. In a small clearing, a young deer with a stub of antlers lifts its head and darts away, the light touch of his hooves smothered by a heavy thunder. And then we see them, riders snapping branches, cleaving the air with their cries. I struggle with my scabbard, jerking my sword free as Morial lifts his head, pulling at the reins. I pull back, pressing my calves hard into his flanks, and he settles with a sharp whinny.

Like a tide, they are upon us. I see only the front rider, black curls jerking against pale skin, glittering fire in his dark eyes. Someone shouts 'England!' but all else is the clang of steel on steel. Raising my sword, I feel a blade scrape the air beneath my armpit and then the riders are through in a great breath of wind. 'A Douglas, A Douglas,' they cry. I see now they are only three fighting men, the same as us.

'Don't let them get around!' Sir Edmund is screaming, but I don't know what he wants me to do. I turn Morial, but another rider is almost upon me. I swing my sword up and it flies out of frozen fingers, curving away with serene grace. The world shatters into an insistent throbbing in my ears as I wait for Death to claim me.

The rider drops his blade arm with a scream as blood spatters my face. 'Damned fool!' Sir Edmund's blade runs as red as his face turned furiously towards me.

The riders head towards the wagon, slicing at the canvas. The pale man with black hair seizes a flagon of wine, jerks out the stopper with his teeth and drinks deep as they gallop off. We sit entirely still. Then Sir Edmund draws his arm back and hits me so hard I am thrown off my horse. I lie on the soft ground and imagine the flowers coiling around me, their fragrance lulling me to sleep.

'Get up.' Sir Edmund looms above me before spurring on his horse.

I pull out my sword from a foul-smelling morass and wish I were dead, just to spite them.

Some hours later we sit before a much bigger river running black and deep. I want to ask Sir Edmund about the man with the pale face and burning eyes, but by the look on his face, I risk another blow if I venture any questions. The wagon lurches down the slope and on into the river, Ade's arm rising and falling with his whip, the oxen's flanks trembling. 'Go, go, go!' cries Sir Edmund, jerking his red face at Will and me. 'Or are you waiting for a Scottish blade up your arses?'

Will leaps into the river with a triumphant 'Ha', his horse kicking up great plumes of water. Morial tosses his head as I dig my heels into his flanks. The water is freezing cold, but there is something exhilarating about driving through it. In only a few moments we scramble up the far bank, grins on our faces, horses shaking and stamping. Companies of reeds along the riverbank shiver in an icy breeze, but otherwise all is quiet, distant fields lifeless under a pallid sun. The good Lord knows there should be more signs of spring, but we are now in Scotland, a sinful, forsaken place.

The others ride on. I linger a moment to watch the ducks return to the rushing waters of this river they call the Tweed. A dipper flits on to a rock and disappears below the surface. With a sigh, I stroke Morial's black head and urge him on.

In truth, this Scotland is little different to the country we have toiled through since leaving Sir Edmund's lands in Yorkshire. All is bleak and mournful, full of wild mountains, its people as sodden and filthy as the ground they till. The very air feels thin, as if intent on conserving what little strength it possesses. I try to conjure up black-thorns frothing with white blossom, or woods carpeted with celandine gold back home in Lincolnshire. But they seem no more real than the gardens of Jerusalem or Araby.

A shout goes up as riders gallop towards us from the east, still an agitated clump at this distance. We sit, set to stone, as they become faces and limbs. Sir Edmund spits on the ground. 'It's Wysham. That's his banner.'

The company draws up in front of us, Sir John Wysham – captain of the Berwick garrison – at its head. 'Do you have news of Arundel?' He greets Sir Edmund with a kiss. 'I thought he was going to cut down the great forest at Jedburgh and flush Douglas out.' He is pale and thin, with a reedy voice that makes him sound peevish. I suppose he has no reason to feel cheerful. Though the old king – father of the Edward who rules us now – conquered all of Scotland when its fiendish inhabitants rebelled some twenty years ago, God has seen fit to deprive England of all but Berwick, which means we must have sinned most grievously.

Sir Edmund frowns. 'You haven't heard? Arundel crossed the border more than a week ago.' We met the earl's company by chance on his way south, as we rode north. It was not a happy meeting.

Sir John grunts. 'What goes on even half a day's ride from Berwick is a mystery to us.'

'Then I have bad news. A few boys in Arundel's army decided to surprise Douglas at his house at Lintalee.

But that devil's scouts saw them coming, and he left the door wide open and a feast ready for eating. So that's just what they did.'

Sir John's eyelids flutter. 'What?'

'They sat down and ate. But the Scots came back. Killed more than a score of them.'

Sir John slumps into his saddle like an empty sack.

'Arundel was still back towards the border.' Sir Edmund sighs. 'Douglas didn't run away, of course he didn't. It was a trap. Those fools set no guard and he had them like rats in a barrel. And then he came for the main company. I don't think Arundel even knew he was there.' His eyes narrow. 'We met Douglas ourselves . . .'

Sir John's face twitches. 'Where?'

'Just beyond Ford.'

'What was he doing? There should be no raids till the end of the truce.'

Sir Edmund shrugs. 'There were only three of them. Perhaps he has a whore nearby.'

Sir John gives a tight smile and turns his horse around. 'Let's get out of here.'

Now I know that the pale man with black curls really was the Black Douglas, a fiend just like his master, Robert Bruce, who calls himself King of Scotland. We climb a long, tedious hill, the river out of sight. The sky seems altogether vast but quite empty, as if God and the saints have left the heavens.

Will stirs at my side. 'He should have let that Scottish dog have you, Book Boy. You're as much use with a sword as a girl.'

'God will strike you down, just you wait. He will come when you least expect it and He will leave you in torment for the rest of your days.' I sound exactly like Brother Arnold berating the novices.

Will snorts. 'No, He won't.'

'Yes, He will.'

'God's teeth!' Sir Edmund turns and shakes his head, thankfully too far ahead to hit either one of us. 'I've met cockerels with more wit than you two.'

I shut my eyes and imagine myself back in Gloucester Abbey, the 'Deum Verum' rising and falling like a silken tide against the quiet stonework. I mouth the words, searching for the touch of God's infinite mercy to soothe my wretched heart in such barbarous company.

The river catches up with us and at last we glimpse a pale tower and the roofs of houses crouched behind a wall of stone and timber, all that will keep us safe from the savages outside. 'Shut us up tight now,' Sir John says to the men guarding a huge gateway. We pass through, the great wooden doors scraping the ground before closing with a mighty thud. Our journey is over, for better or worse.

We trot through a mess of houses on either side, pass beneath another great gateway and are finally in the town. I have heard that Berwick is a noble port, for all it is in the north, and much wealth sails in and out of it. In a broad street Sir John calls Marygate, we pass some fine, well-plastered houses two or three storeys high, their timbers in recent repair. But just as many are collapsed like old cripples, with gaping windows and holes in the roofs, gardens growing plentiful crops of decaying carts and piles of rope and broken pieces of wood. We stop in front of a large three-storey building, a patchwork of plaster giving it a rough look. An archway leads into a cobbled yard and the wagon trundles in. Leaving Will to gather Sir Edmund's gear from behind his saddle, I retrieve our master's chest from the wagon.

As I struggle up to the first floor, a dumpy little man with flailing arms tells me he is our steward and points me up another staircase. In a low-ceilinged chamber at the top of the stairs, I put the chest down beneath the little window. Several panes are stuffed with rags and the wooden panelling on the walls is most ill-used, but it is a comfortable room, even if the fire seems almost bereft of coals. I find the bottle of vinegar in the chest and quickly clean Sir Edmund's sword, which lies over a stool. I can do no more without a candle or proper daylight. Putting it back in the scabbard, I spit on the leather to loosen the mud and the blood, scratching at it with my thumb.

Sir Edmund thrusts the door open and strides in. 'Where's Will? I need food.'

'Here I am.' Will is behind him, all smiles and carrying a large bowl of water. He rushes over to Sir Edmund, water sloshing dangerously near the edge of the bowl, and casts a disdainful look at me. 'You still have your boots on.'

'Leave Benedict be. I've only just come in.' Sir Edmund sits down in the chair by the fire. 'I saw you hanging round the kitchen, cooing at that girl. You don't waste any time, do you?'

I grin, but now he turns his great boulder of a face on me. 'And you've nothing to feel clever about. Go and fetch your chest. The steward wants it out of the way.'

I run out, cheeks on fire, but can see nothing in the dark courtyard. After much searching, I find my chest abandoned in the shadows near the back door and drag it upstairs. The others have already gone to eat, and I follow them down to the hall on the floor below. Will has finished serving and sits towards the middle of a long table. Opposite him is a dark-haired fellow, plump and sweating. Sir Edmund is at the end, leaning his great head towards a handsome man of middle years who is telling him something that has him in his grip.

I slip into the seat next to Will, who turns a cold shoulder. A skinny boy ladles some broth into a piece of bread and I slurp it down, happy to be left to eat, even if there is little to taste. The dark-haired youth follows my every bite with his eyes. I pick up the remains of my bread and he sighs. 'Do you want it?' I hold it out.

He grabs it like a fat pigeon and begins to crunch and chew with his mouth half-open. I try the wine and nearly spew it out, it's so bitter. The handsome man is still talking with violent hand gestures. I tap Will on the shoulder. 'Who's that?'

His shoulders convulse in an extravagant sigh, but he turns to me, as I knew he would, for he likes to know things I don't. 'That, Book Boy, is Sir Anthony Lucy.'

'A very fine knight,' says the youth opposite, mouth crammed full.

'A very fine knight who was captured at Bannockburn,' Will says quickly. 'But not in the battle . . .'

'Was he?' I look at Sir Anthony again, the narrow set of his shoulders, the delicate cut of his jaw, but can find nothing there marking out such a terrible ordeal.

The plump fellow leans towards me, crumbs flying. 'It was in some castle with a Scottish dog in charge of it. He let them in after the battle and took them all prisoner. I'm Stephen. I suppose you're Benedict?'

I nod, trying to stay out of spitting distance.

'Sir Anthony is my master.' Stephen stares hard at me. 'Will says you're not a proper squire.' Will sniggers.

'I am now, whether I like it or not.'

'Well, you won't like it. Nobody does. There's nothing to do but stand on the walls, and the food's heinous.' Stephen belches, patting his stomach. 'We'll not stay long, I reckon. We're better off nearer home, in case there's trouble.'

My sister Elizabeth springs into my mind, bringing a chill to my guts, for his words remind me that the man my mother is married to now can do no more to protect them than wring his wizened hands. I already pray for Sir Edmund to find some proper occupation with regular pay back in Yorkshire, which is not so far from our lands in Lincolnshire. If I cannot return to the abbey, I might at least be nearer Lizzie.

Will slaps the table, glowering at Stephen. 'What kind

of cowardly talk is that! We're here to strike at the accursed Scots before they drive us into the sea. It's every Englishman's duty to fight and . . . and to . . . to . . .'

Stephen starts back as if he'd been whipped. I hold my breath, trying to think of something to say to bring harmony, as Master Aquinas teaches us, for his shoulders are shaking. And yet I see now it is not anger but mirth that has a hold of him. He laughs until tears dapple his cheeks. 'You're going to save England, are you? Well, I'm sure we'll all sleep soundly in our beds now.' He sits back. 'But I doubt your master is as foolish as you. Most of the knights here are either desperate for money or needing the king's pardon for some sin or other.'

I nod, speaking softly since I do not wish to be heard at the top of the table. 'I'm sure you're right. There is . . .' I hesitate, for I would not wish to be disloyal to my master. 'There's a good reason why Sir Edmund thought it prudent to enter the king's service.'

'Have you finished telling tales, Book Boy?' Will's loyalties are simple. But I suppose, since he has served Sir Edmund as page and squire, it is his affections that rule him, not his mind. I have been Sir Edmund's squire only this last, long half-year and can see things as they are.

The scraping of wood alerts us to the rising of our masters. They settle on chairs drawn around a dying fire and Sir Edmund waves us onto the floor beside them. A deerhound lying there like an unkempt carpet turns onto its back and Sir Anthony strokes its belly with his foot. 'How long do you think you'll stay?' he asks Sir Edmund.

I lean forward, not breathing. Our safe-conducts last until Midsummer, some two months away. I have prayed every day we will not stay longer.

'It depends what Arundel decides to do now. He needs to find a way to push Douglas back so we've a chance of taking Roxburgh once the truce is over. I don't want to sit here on my arse waiting for those dogs to creep up on us, but I need the money.'

Sir Anthony snorts. 'Don't we all! I've a ransom to pay.'

'Surely the king is bringing an army to Scotland, sir?' I do not mean to speak, but the question bursts out of me.

Sir Anthony gives me a long look. 'The king is always bringing an army north. Every year he orders a muster, and every year he cancels it. He has no money, not without parliament giving him a tax, and he won't do what they want to get it. We're on our own, and that's the truth of it.' He takes a long swig from his goblet. 'Have you served the king before?'

I shake my head. 'I am newly come to soldiering, sir.'

'How so?'

I hear Will snigger again, and Sir Edmund kicks him.

'I was supposed to be a clerk. To Sir William Martin.'

'The king's Justice in Wales?'

I nod.

'Then your family has good connections. Surely they could keep you away from here?'

'Sir William wished to honour a debt to my father for saving his life. He paid for me to go to school and my older brother Peter became his squire. But Peter . . . he went swimming last year and drowned.' I swallow violent feelings. 'So, I had to take on his responsibilities. Sir William thought he'd done enough, and Sir Edmund is . . . very good to have me with so little training.' I sound ungrateful, I know. No one else would take me.

'Swimming,' Sir Anthony pronounces, standing up, 'is a very foolish thing to do. Forgive me – I was on third watch last night and am weary. But I'm glad you're here. We need more men-at-arms, not the tailors and shoemakers they've got up on the walls these days. Weston would have Percival up there if I let him.' He fondles the dog's ears. 'God help us if there's any fighting to be done.'

I am confused. 'I thought Sir John had charge of the garrison. Who's Weston, sir?'

'He's a John, too, but this one's a clerk, even if he calls himself Chamberlain of Scotland. That's the man with the money.' Sir Anthony strides away, still talking over his shoulder. 'Not that there is any. Forget Wysham. He only has eyes for Alice Rydale and the road out of here. It's Weston you should keep in with. But don't trust him and keep a close tally of what you're owed and what you get.' With this torrent of advice, he and his dog step swiftly through the door, Stephen running to catch up.

Sir Edmund stares after him. 'I hate clerks.' It's true. His own clerk, Thomas Fleet, made it only as far as Newcastle before succumbing to a violent ague that left his huge frame quivering like an old oak in a storm. My master looks at me and plucks his lower lip. 'I'll need one, though, till Thomas gets his fat arse up here. Someone good at all that bookish drivel. You can do it.

Go to this Weston in the morning and don't leave till you're sure I'll be paid.' He stretches. 'I'm going to bed. Will, you can help me.'

Will smirks past and I let them leave. Stepping into the courtyard, I am assailed by the night's chill and hurry to the stables to bury myself in Morial's flanks. *Into your hands, O Lord.* I wait. An owl murmurs a nocturnal greeting nearby and I sense he is speaking to me, but not what message he brings. For I do not understand why the Lord has cast me into a life I do not want, and for which I am entirely unprepared.

Chapter 2

The dawn edges into a heavy sky as we head east along Marygate, bells ringing for Mass. Passing the market cross, we turn left into a narrow street that staggers up a gentle incline and is called Soutergate. The houses loom over our heads like giants, their timber upper storeys almost touching the ones opposite. We pass a baker's, alive with light and heat and the scurrying of men and boys and even women. The marvellous smell of bread vexes our bellies until we turn right into a narrow lane that Stephen tells us is called Vikerwende. The Church of the Holy Trinity sits on barren ground above it and we pick our way through slumbering graves to reach its main door.

Inside, the building is narrow, with three great windows on each side and a handsome hammerbeam roof. We worshippers gather like chessmen on the stone flagstones this side of the rood screen with protracted yawns most do not try to conceal. I bow my head, but there is no peace amidst the jostling and coughing. Will seems to have made friends with Stephen, and they whisper loudly about what they would like to do to the pretty kitchen girl.

But now they fall silent and I follow their eyes to a small procession parting the company. At its head glides a matriarch, plump as a fattened goose, her face sweetly proportioned. At her side, a small dark creature rocks and shuffles. But they are not the ones drawing every man's gaze. Eyes fixed ahead, a girl in a gown of apple green walks like a queen through her courtiers. Her skin is as pale as the lily-flower, with a bright flush on her cheeks, her mouth a glistening cherry-red.

I have never seen a girl as lovely. Knights and merchants move out of the way, smiles leaping to faces that were crumpled and creased only moments ago. Will starts forward, lips moist, but already this little parade has stopped beside Sir John Wysham, who takes the girl's arm, leaning close to whisper in her ear. Her mother watches like a contented Madonna.

The priest emerges through a door on the other side of the screen flanked by two acolytes waving the incense. I sing softly, closing my eyes and letting the psalms flood my heart, which is still gripped by the girl in the green dress. Alice, wasn't that the name Sir Anthony gave her? Alice Rydale. I want to look at her, though I know I should be thinking of our Lord's painful sacrifice. But that is impossible, too, with Will and Stephen chattering behind their hands.

We retrace our steps, raindrops stoning our faces so that I must grasp the hood of my cloak tight at my throat.

Will speaks endlessly about how he wishes to steal the beautiful girl from under Wysham's nose. He is handsome enough to do it, but that is all, and I am tired of his chatter long before we pass into our courtyard and tramp up the stairs to the hall.

Accosting the steward to discuss our keep, Sir Edmund roars his displeasure across the room at what he is expected to pay. But the steward, for all his diminished stature, stands firm. Sir Edmund stamps his foot and barks at Will to come with him to see Sir John and tells me to go and do my best with Master arsesmart Weston, the arsesmart chamberlain, or I'll feel the back of his hand.

I force my mind on to Master Weston. It pleases me to have been given a task Will could not manage this year or next. But I don't understand why Sir Anthony thinks we must keep a close watch on a man so trusted by the king. And surely Sir Edmund must account for what he is paid and what he spends anyway? He is always moaning about how much everything costs, and that God surely jests if He thinks he can live on a few acres of land, what with the bad harvests and the cattle disease.

Chills slither down my back, for no one has told me where the chamberlain can be found. I run back into the hall, which is empty but for a bow-backed crone sweeping the floor. She jumps as I pass and mutters something I'm glad I do not understand.

I tarry by the screen that separates the hall from the kitchen, hoping the steward comes back. It is noisy and full of smoke in here, with a cloying stench of raw meat. The cook stands adorned with a red hat, examining a small array of dead animals laid out on a well-scrubbed table. A pretty girl with apple cheeks and sweat on her brow carries an armful of wood towards the great fire in the middle of the room, where an older woman turns the spit. Others clean pots or cut vegetables, and I imagine they are happy there, in the warmth, with each other for company.

A lad with long brown hair faces the cook across the table, twisting his cap vigorously in his hands, apron smeared with rusty streaks. He must be the butcher's boy who brought the meat. The cook nods and the boy's shoulders soften and drop. He stuffs his hat on his head, picks up his basket, then turns and runs straight into me. I yelp as his bony shoulder drives into my arm.

'I's not seeing you, sir.' He wrinkles his nose, as if the fault is mine.

'Is Wat bothering you?' the cook asks.

'Not at all. No harm done.' The boy's face-pulling makes me smile. 'Perhaps you should slow down.' I speak gently, for fear I will startle him off.

'My master be expecting me, sir.'

'You are a butcher?'

He bobs his head down, to hide a smile. 'Apprentice, sir.'

'Of course.' And if this lad delivers his master's meat, he'll know who lives where. 'Tell me . . . Wat, is it?' He nods slowly, as if this were dangerous information. 'Do you know where Master Weston lives?'

He nods again most gravely.

'Excellent. Perhaps you might accompany me there? I am new to Berwick and cannot yet find my way.' I fish inside my pouch and hold up a ha'penny.

His eyes gleam. 'Will you be quick, sir?'

'As quick as you.' But already Wat has scuttled through the kitchen and out of the door. I follow him at a trot across the courtyard and down the lane to the left of our house, which is narrow and muddy but pleasant, with a small wood rising behind a wall. We seem to be moving towards the river, a sharp smell of salt and seaweed thrust into my face by the wind.

Wat turns left again into a broad street, its large buildings made entirely of stone. Opposite is a fine house, a woman kneeling to scrub the entranceway with a gentle rhythm. Wat bobs up and down, pointing at the house, and I throw him the ha'penny. He grins and runs on along the road, apron buffeting skinny legs.

I slide past the woman, two men in tight-fitting gowns not troubling to glance at me as they pass on their way out. Climbing a short set of steps, I enter a wood-panelled hall, a fire snapping brightly in a metal brazier in the middle. A young man in sombre tunic and hose bustles up to demand my business. He goes back to a desk set beneath two windows and writes something down. Then he tells me to wait on a stool some feet away.

I watch him write in a great leather-bound book. He seems to be copying the contents of a pile of papers into this ledger, and I am surprised to find I do not envy him a task that once might have been mine. He glances up and catches me, so I give him a fulsome smile, as if I am a dull-witted youth who struggles to write the shortest of love letters.

I look out of the window, a milky glow of light throwing soft shadows. Two men emerge from a door to my left. One is tall, with a sharp nose and greying hair, his pale blue gown set off by the tawny fur lining it. The other is, like the clerk, dressed in dark colours, but the brown velvet is plush and unmarked, the matching fur as glossy as the man's raven hair. 'So, when should we expect you back?' this one asks the other in soft southern tones.

'God willing, we should be home around Midsummer. And I will save the best Bordeaux for you, John.'

The chamberlain smiles. 'You say that, Walter, but I haven't forgotten the odious stuff you tried to sell me last time.'

'Never send your son to do your business.'

Weston pats him on the arm and they part. I stand up, but the chamberlain is already turning back into his room, and the clerk makes no move to follow him. I go over to his desk. 'Master Weston is a busy man,' he says without looking up.

'Sir Edmund expects . . .'

'Then your Sir Edmund will have to wait. Just like you.'

The sky grows darker, rain streaking the window. A boy runs in, splashing droplets across the stone flags. He spills out a rumour that the Scots have captured a Berwick ship coming back from England with supplies. The clerk jumps up, raps on his master's door and enters. They reappear and follow the boy out.

I sigh. On the side away from the street, the slumbering remains of a garden stretch towards the town wall. An orchard of fruit trees is still half-naked, shivering in the wind. Only the cherry gives any hint of spring's tentative approach. Passing the clerk's desk, I look down for lack of anything better to do. The piece of parchment he was copying lies across the ledger alongside a torn scrap on which he has scribbled numerous reckonings. I hop to the other side of the desk.

I was always skilled at making numbers add up. But I cannot make sense of those written in various hands on the originals and the copy in the ledger, for none match. They are clearly quantities of grain, wine and other foodstuffs, the descriptions tallying in both. But the numbers on the copy are always higher. I take myself on a march around the hall, thankfully before the clerk hurries back through the door and returns to his desk.

Playing with the numbers in my head, I see they form a regular pattern, the higher number on the copy around one-tenth more than the original. But what do they mean? Distant church bells ring for Sext and I feel the agony of this waiting, for Sir Edmund will be angry if I tarry or if I return without success. The clerk flings down his quill and gathers up the pile he has been working from. Sailing past me, he throws them on to the fire, which briefly erupts with a great burst of light. He closes the ledger and gives a little smile to himself before disappearing through a door at the other end of the hall.

I look out at the blustery day. It matters not one jot that these numbers danced to my tune if I don't know why the clerk changed them. I hum 'Puer natus in Bethlehem', eventually letting the words spill out as I cast about for an answer.

'What do you want?' It is not said unkindly, but I spin round in agitation. Master Weston stands with his back to the fire, hands thrust inside voluminous sleeves. Whipping off my cap, I bow low. 'Benedict Russell, sir. We are newly come from Yorkshire. In the garrison. Sir Edmund Darel is my master.' I wonder if disturbed thoughts are easily read on my face. I must remember why I'm here.

'Ah, yes. Step this way.' He sweeps back into his room, whose walls are adorned with pictures of saints set against a dark ,blue background edged with clouds of golden stars. I look with joy at St Ambrose, bees buzzing around his halo, for he was the first to set choirs singing responses to one another.

Master Weston sits down behind his desk. 'So, you are dressed like a squire, but sing like a scholar. Which is it?'

'Both, I suppose. Sir Edmund's clerk is at Newcastle. With an ague.'

'I see. You have a fine voice. Where did you learn?'

'Gloucester Abbey, sir.'

He leans back. 'You're a long way from there, Benedict Russell. But we must go where God chooses, must we not?' He rummages on his desk and finds a well-thumbed manuscript. 'Write down the names of Sir Edmund's company and I will start his account once I have ascertained the terms of his service with Sir John.'

He motions me over to a table furnished with quills and ink and I write quickly, eager now to tell Sir Edmund of my discovery. Outside the clerk has returned, ignoring me entirely. But he has no reason to feel superior.

Sir Edmund rubs his forehead vigorously. 'So, every payment that goes into Master Weston's ledger is for more than what's on the documents they're copied from?'

'Yes.'

'It's not a mistake?'

'No.'

'And what was this scoundrel copying?'

'I think they're bills for supplies, probably for the garrison. Grain and wine, that sort of thing.'

Will yawns loudly.

Sir Edmund throws an almond at him. 'But then he burnt them, which shows he was up to something.'

And now I understand and wonder how I did not before. 'Sweet Jesu! He'll be charging us what's in the copy, won't he? I mean, for the food you buy us out of the king's wages.'

'The thieving dog!' Clasping my shoulder, he squeezes hard. 'Good work.'

I feel a warm glow even as my belly aches, for what if I'm mistaken? I cannot imagine why the chamberlain should deliberately deceive the king's own men. 'But there's nothing we can do about it, is there?'

He frowns. 'We must speak to Wysham. He must not allow it. But first you must get proof.' He scratches the rough surface of his ponderous chin.

I feel as if he has punched me in the stomach. 'But how can I do that?'

'You're a clever lad. You'll think of something. But we've got more important things to do now. Where did Wysham say we could practise the sword, Will? Mary Fields, was it?

No, Magdalene. Go out the Cowgate, wherever that is.'

I groan to myself. Peter and I trained together when we were boys, but that is many years ago and I have not proved an able pupil despite Sir Edmund's efforts to teach me, setting me against Will time and again these last months. Will has dealt me many a scratch, for he feints and parries well, dancing in and out while I lumber around trying to get near him.

We walk up towards the church, the sharp, foul smell of the sea catching the back of my throat even here. An easterly wind cuts through the gaps between the houses, sending the townsfolk scurrying about their business, heads down, cloaks wrapped tight to the body like armour. I have rarely seen faces so pale, as if this northern climate sucks the blood from a man as effectively as any leach. I wonder if it will happen to me and how I can endure this constant, pinching cold.

We walk past the church and across a wasteland full of the foundations of houses, where thorn bushes have knitted themselves into stone and timber. And yet people must live here, for canvas tents droop and flutter within the foundations, clothes drying in the bushes and fires spluttering in the damp air. The Cowgate stands open ahead of us, a couple of soldiers leaning on spears.

'Whose tents are those?' I ask them.

A small man with a bulbous nose and shocking red hair pulls a face. 'Nobody you'd want to know. Beggars and thieves, to a man. If they give you some noisy lament about the terrible deeds done to them, you just come to me and I'll give them a good kicking.'

We go through the gate, walking between rows of conical hives. The yellow blossom on nearby tangles of gorse quiver and buzz with armies of bees guzzling at the nectar. Beyond, small flocks of woolly cows and scrawny sheep graze intently on a grassy meadow, the sea showing white skirts in the distance. Two old women shuffle towards us, one nodding so often she seems to be in constant agreement with her companion. They smile and remark that it has turned out a fine day and, what with all the nodding, we can scarcely disagree.

I place my left hand at the mid-point on my sword – which belonged to Peter and, before him, our father – trying to feel its weight so it could sit unaided on my palm. I think I am ready to pounce and escape at the same time, but there's already a fog inside my head. Will comes close, his blade a dull flash before it deals me a blow to my side. Sir Edmund throws up his arms, face glowing. 'Satan's arse. No!' He grabs me and tries to put me how he wants. But I doubt I will ever be in the right place.

Sir Edmund and Will have gone to see about a new saddle in the Ness, a part of town where, according to Sir Anthony, you can buy a pair of Christ's sandals if you so desire. It is hard to fill the long hours even now we've been assigned to the watch, and the day stretches endlessly ahead of me with nothing to do but practise my sword. At Gloucester, where I would spend hours reading in the peace of the cloisters or working in the garden, feeling the warm soil gather life to it, I did not know the freedom I had. For all the times I cried for my mother, for the pain and humiliation of Brother Sextus's cane burning my fingers for fumbled Latin, for the nights I shivered beneath a threadbare blanket, I would endure it all a thousand times if I did not have to stay another minute here, where even our horses whinny and complain for lack of decent food and exercise.

What I really yearn to do is sit somewhere in perfect tranquillity. Alas, I cannot ask Stephen where to find such a place, for he will certainly tell Will, who will mock me without mercy. But I have an ally in Wat, the butcher's boy, whose cheerful face I see almost every day and who is always happy to answer questions without comment. The monks at Gloucester were Benedictines, but he tells me there are no Black Monks here, only Franciscan Grey Friars, whose house lies in the northern part of town. After one shower has stormed past, I hasten to the top end of Soutergate before the next one blows in over the walls.

Standing at Berwick's northernmost point, I am drawn to stand beneath the Waleysgate, as if a siren is singing to me from outside. It is surely the very edge of the known world. Beyond, the land lies quietly, coils of smoke from a few distant dwellings smudging the heavy sky. But like deadly serpents concealed beneath a pile of autumn leaves, I imagine an infinite army of Scots rising from beneath the soil, sweeping like locusts across the sleeping fields and over the town wall, into every house, every barn and workshop and on across the Tweed, destroying everything until the English nation is driven into the sea.

I shiver, the wind bringing a tear to my eyes. To my left, the top half of a church keeps watch over the friary wall. I knock on a small wooden door, the gate-keeper wheezing through my request to gain admittance. Entering the cloisters, I pause to breathe in the contented harmony of the place. But a commotion behind me drives me quickly into the church.

I stand, adjusting my eyes to the gloom. The nave is mean and narrow, crammed between two aisles along which a few columns rise. I move further in, the screen to my right and the choir beyond. An image of St Francis, dove on one hand and tiny tree in the other, rises out of the gloom on the far wall. He looks straight at me, keeping me in his gaze when I move. I smile and settle behind a column near him. I feel as if I have spent long days in the desert and have an urgent, aching thirst, for I have scarcely looked at any scripture since I left Gloucester.

I want to feel the joy that comes from sending song up towards the heavens: *I will bless the Lord at all times; praise shall be always in my mouth. I sought the Lord, who answered me, delivered me from all my fears.*

But that is no longer true, for He has sent me here.

A sharp rush of wind alerts me to the church door opening, and I peer round to see who is coming into the gloom. A great, black bird lurches from side to side across the floor. I shrink behind my pillar, studying it closely for sharp claws. It comes closer still and I hear it muttering:

'Sir Gawain is a *knight*. He wields a sword with *bite*. He loves his lady *dear*. For him she sheds a *tear*.'

It is a girl. A strange misshapen creature but a girl, nonetheless. Her face is sharply pointed, skin paler than the grave, with hair of midnight black cloaking her face. She stands no higher than a child of ten, but her face is somewhat older.

I shrink further behind the pillar. There is a shuffling and grunting, then silence. I have seen her before, with her mother and gentle Alice in the Church of the Holy Trinity. I do not care to sit here any longer, for she has scattered any peace that might have descended upon me. Standing up, I see she lies on her front, hair hanging like a curtain as she examines something in her hands. Immediately her head jerks up, two large eyes gleaming like moonstone. With surprising strength, she sweeps something off the floor and pushes herself up with her arms until she sits, half-collapsed, in front of me. 'What did you do that for?' she asks fiercely. 'You frightened me.'

'I wanted to leave but couldn't without disturbing you.'

'So, it's my fault, is it?'

'I didn't say that.'

She turns her face away, nose pointing towards the door. 'Well, go now.'

'I'll go when I please.' I speak loudly, for she is surely as weak in her mind as she is in body. 'What do you have in your hands?'

'Why do you want to know?'

I see I must be firm. 'Tell me.'

She brings her hands out of her lap and there, carefully cushioned, is a tiny wren.

'Oh!' I cannot help myself. 'What are you doing to it?'

She sighs. 'I'm trying to mend its wing, but I'll need sticks and strips of cloth.'

I see she has tied a red ribbon round the little creature to stop it flapping. I sit down. 'May I see?'

'Will you be careful?'

'Of course.'

'There's no "of course" about it.' But she places her hands over mine, releasing the wren gently.

I can feel its heart beating. 'Where did you find it?'

She almost smiles. 'On the ground beneath the rowan at the door.'

'Are you by yourself?'

'Of course not. Mother is with Brother Leonard. We sell the friars what supplies they do not receive in alms.'

I blink. 'Your mother has a shop?'

She tuts. 'My mother is a merchant. As was my father before he died.'

I look down at the wren, struggling against its bond, and wonder if Alice is here too.

'Give her back before you hurt her.'

I do not like the way she speaks to me but am afraid for the wren. She reaches for the bird, and I put my hands around hers, feeling the softness above and below.

'I am Lucy Rydale. Do you have a name?'

'Me?'

She grins like a demon. 'Is there someone else here?'

'Benedict Russell.'

'And why are *you* here, Benedict Russell?'

'I am in Berwick because I am squire to a knight in the garrison. And I am in the church because I am used to them and like them.'

'How so?' Someone shouts outside and the girl looks up with a frown. She thrusts the wren into a pocket and pulls herself slowly upright.

'Lucy! For pity's sake, where are you?' The voice seems to be coming nearer to the church. It is Alice, I'm sure of it.

The girl has just begun her ungainly shuddering across the nave when the door flies open, framing two figures against the light outside. One has the girth of a fattened pig, the other is as graceful as a willow. I wonder that these three should be so close in blood.

Alice runs to her sister and tries to gather her up. 'I said she'd be here.'

The girl pushes at the encircling arms most churlishly. 'Let go! I don't need your help.'

'Come now, don't quarrel,' their mother entreats, holding out a hand to her disagreeable younger daughter, who takes it with a little sigh. 'My head hurts from Brother Leonard's wheedling. He forgets I have mouths of my own to feed.'

The girl tugs at her mother's sleeves and says something in a low voice. I see them glance towards where I'm standing in the shadow of the pillar. Surely this Lucy is about to call me over to make lovely Alice's acquaintance and I think I will at least dwell happy knowing she is aware I exist. But it seems the girl does not have the manners to bring me to their notice and I would feel foolish bursting upon them like some rustic dolt.

'What have you been doing, Lucy?' The maiden's voice is the murmur of a river.

'Counting sheep and making a profit. Other than that, nothing at all.'

I see Lucy Rydale laugh as they turn and walk away without even a backward glance, leaving me angry and bereft.

Next morning, I am in our room working hard to remove any lingering traces of Scottish blood from Sir Edmund's sword and trying to think of a way to extract some of Master Weston's papers to serve as proof of his wrong-doing. There is a knock on the door and the little steward puts his head around it. Sir Edmund and Will are playing dice, but neither look up. 'Sir John would like a word, sir.'

That gains Sir Edmund's attention. 'O-ho. Maybe he's thinking of going after Douglas.'

I put the sword away carefully. 'What about the truce?'

'We can still show those damned Scots we're not here to look at the view. Take something of theirs for a change.'

'Coward!' Will mouths at me as he puts the dice back in Sir Edmund's chest. It is his favourite word. I nudge him roughly and he spills them all over the floor. Sir Edmund cuffs us both.

Sir John lives in Soutergate, towards the church but on the other side of the road and almost opposite the bakery, which must be a constant temptation. It is a small house compared to ours, but well kept, with no panes of glass missing and the timbers sturdy and neatly hewn. His men live next door, which is far less comfortable, great holes in the thatch gathering rooks. We join a small group of knights in Sir John's hall. In less than two months' time the truce will end, and Douglas will surely ride out again to wreak havoc on the villages and farms beyond our walls and far into England.

Sir Edmund leans forward in his chair. 'Arundel's gone back to Newcastle. Are we to let those devils go unpunished?'

Sir John breathes deeply. 'The earl has sent word he means to send five ships to attack Scotland.' Everyone talks at once. 'I know.' His thin, fretful voice struggles to be heard. 'I cannot see what good will come of it either. We're still waiting to hear if Bruce is sailing back from Ireland. There may yet be another truce.'

Voices hurtle up the stairs and the door flies open. For a brief moment, no one enters, and we begin to look at one another. But then the fat matron, Alice's mother, flies through the open door as if the Devil himself had pushed her, followed by a bearded man of medium build and one of Wysham's servants wringing his hands.

Sir John springs to his feet. 'Eleanor! Shall I come to you this afternoon?'

She is in a terrible state, her hair nesting on her head, coif lurching to one side. It is as if some demonic creature has made away with the careful, seemly matron and left behind a sluttish imitation. She stands there before us all, mouth opening and shutting, and nothing said.

The bearded man pats her arm. 'Madam. You must speak.'

She nods, swallows. 'Yes. I must speak.' She places her hands flat across the silken expanse of her stomach and stares at Sir John, as if she did not expect him to be there. Or is it that she hoped he might not be, which is very strange indeed? 'Please forgive me.' Now a hand floats to the pearls at her throat. 'I . . . You have always been a good friend to us. But these are strange times. Strange times indeed.' She breaks off, searches the wood panelling above Wysham's head, mouth wide open. I hear Sir Edmund snort, scarcely troubling to hide his laughter.

And still she gasps for breath, and I think I cannot endure much more of this. 'Youwillbeleaving soon . . . We cannot . . . Itisnotrightthatweshouldleave . . . I cannot . . . Alice . . . Youmustnotmarry. I beg your pardon. I will pay, of course.' She stops, looks around, blinking at us all in turn.

Sir John blinks, too, his body held taut against the tide of words. He raises a hand slowly, puts it down again. 'Woman, do not jest with me. It is agreed that Alice and I will marry. God's bones, it's what you wanted, to leave this accursed place. "We will be safe in your care," you said. "No Scots to worry about."'

'I crave your forgiveness, sir.' She attempts a winsome smile that merely looks ghastly, stretched across her flaccid, twisted features. 'You are a worthy husband, but I can no longer allow it.'

Sir John lifts his hand and throws it towards the door. 'Be gone and we will speak of this later. I can only think you have lost your mind.'

She picks up her skirts and runs away like a rat caught in the corn. The bearded man bows low to Sir John and shrugs his shoulders a little, as if he cannot understand it either.

But I have, and I wonder if it is wrong to give thanks to God for what is surely a miracle.

But once the door closes, Sir John sits back and smiles. 'I would ask you not to speak of this abroad, but I confess I am most relieved. Alice is beautiful, an ornament in her person, without a doubt. But she is a merchant's daughter all the same and I have been dreading taking her back to Clifton. You might think me foolish but I have been relieved of a great burden and will extract a pretty penny from Dame Eleanor to boot. 'Tis a very good day indeed.'

Sir Edmund stands up, patting Sir John's shoulder. 'Quite right. Pretty looks quickly fade and soon enough you find yourself in bed with her mother.'

I find Wysham odious, to think only of money and position. The Rydales are rich, and Sir John has no more than a few manors to rub together, so surely he had already struck a better bargain than he has any right to. I don't know how any man could resist capturing so great a prize. But at least now I can dream of Alice at my side, even if I have no more reason to imagine I might marry her than I did before.

Chapter 3

I go often to the friary church to wrap myself in my own thoughts, which is a marvellous freedom after the rough talk on the walls. I was restless at first, always hoping Alice would step inside. I wanted to drink my fill of the way her hair tumbles in silken waves of gold down her back, thin tendrils of it framing her forehead. I wanted to sing psalms to the delicate curve of her chin and nose and the way her arms lie modestly folded over her belly even when she walks. There is a generosity to her slender figure that I find far more pleasing than her sister's awkward angles. I do not want to see Lucy Rydale again, for she is surely a changeling who can do no good. But, alas, I doubt I will see one without the other.

I confessed this dreadful longing to the priest of the Holy Trinity, but he just sighed and told me not to be a fool. I begged him to absolve me, and he told me to be gone, for he had no time to waste on all the men in Berwick with the same thoughts. That did not please me at all.

And yet I find that already I have grown tired of such imaginings, which have the lustre of a faerie tale and no real substance. My mind lingers now on Lucy Rydale's impertinent remarks and the feather weight of the wren in my hand. That was real and those moments holding the tiny bird brought me to a pitch of happiness I had not experienced for a long time. I felt our Lord's love once more, not just flowing to me, but from me. That is surely blasphemy, but I do not wish to confess it.

I know I should not be dwelling on such things when I cannot think of any reasonable way of gaining entry to Master Weston's house and staying there long enough, without anyone watching what I do, to go through the clerk's reckonings and take those that prove what I'm sure I saw. I conjure up all manner of foolish ideas as I walk back down Soutergate from the friary as evening approaches, past the empty plot where the goats graze, their bells tinkling merrily, and the broken-down house where a woman hanged herself and her unborn child when Sir John Segrave had the keeping of the town.

A moon-faced youth dressed in black hurries towards me, hat pulled down almost to his eyes. I move out of the way, but he stops before me. 'Are you Benedict Russell?'

I nod.

'My master asks that you sing for him.'

I am astounded. 'Who asks?'

'The chamberlain.'

And then I wonder at God's mysterious ways. 'When would it please him?'

'If you are at liberty, you could come with me now.'
He smiles and I fall into step beside him.

As we approach Marygate, the streets are still thronged
with people from this morning's market, their talk loud
and boisterous, nourished by drink. It is hard work to pass
them by and avoid all the detritus littering the streets, the
stench of rotting meat mingling with the faeces and piss
deposited in every out-of-the-way corner. But down in
the Briggait, all is quiet behind the chamberlain's stone
walls. I pause a moment before climbing the stairs to the
first floor, wiping my sweating palms down the side of my
cloak. I am going to sing, that is all.

The youth holds open the door into the empty hall.
He smiles again and I feel like a thief, sternly reminding
myself that it is not me doing the thieving. I smile back
and he places my cloak carefully over a stool. The clerk's
quills are put away and his desk is most neat, the ledger
to one side and two piles of paper carefully stacked beside
it. That suggests he is in the middle of transferring his
figures and gives me hope I might find what I need,
providing I am left alone long enough to search for it.

The servant disappears through the door to Master
Weston's room. I edge nearer to the clerk's desk, but he
reappears almost immediately. 'You are to wait here. May
I bring you some wine?' I nod, rejoicing inside. He
disappears through the door at the other end, and I slip
towards the desk.

I open the ledger, for otherwise I cannot tell which
pile is already written into it. My heart beats so loudly it
almost drowns out the bells for Vespers, but if He has

given me this opportunity, I must not waste it. I find the most recent page and study the last few entries. Quickly closing it, I look to see if I recognise any of them in the first pile. Nothing. Scarcely breathing, I try the second and find what I'm looking for.

But how many receipts should I take? I need enough to show that the false entries are no mistake when compared with those in Master Weston's great ledger, but not so many that the clerk will notice. I realise I'm being presumptuous, to think that the chamberlain will allow any such comparison, can be forced to show his fraudulent figures. But Sir Edmund is so sure the king will not countenance such appalling treatment of his men that I dare to believe he is right. I take five from the bottom of the pile, checking that they are already in the ledger, before moving swiftly away from the desk, my back to the door through which the servant will return. All I need do now is squeeze them into my pouch. I hear his footsteps beyond the door. The papers keep catching but at last they slide in, and I cough to hide my discomfiture.

'Here.' The youth hands me the wine.

I drink it in great gulps, scarcely tasting any of it. 'Thank you,' I stutter. He smiles and returns to stand with his hands behind his back beside the door to the entrance stairs. I wish most heartily that I could leave now, that I need not face Master Weston with the key to his ruin lying next to my skin.

But even as I think this, the chamberlain emerges from his room and bids me come to him with arms spread wide. He drapes one around my shoulders. 'You must sing the "Magnificat" for me. Will you do that?' He draws me into his room.

I am confronted by a group of men, their long robes beautifully furred and their hair curled. But it is the one sat with legs thrust apart nearest the fire who draws the eye. This one does not look at me but studies a hand well-studded with rings. 'Is this another one of your strays, John?' he asks.

'Hush, Ralph. Benedict has come to save us. He's one of Wysham's new recruits.'

'I see. How reassuring. And he sings as well.'

For all the room's great heat, I feel as if a north wind blows through me. I am sure they can see through my tunic and shirt to the pouch beneath.

'Come, Benedict,' Master Weston says gently. 'My friends are not as terrifying as they look.'

'*I* am,' says Ralph, whose surname I soon learn is Holme. They all laugh.

'Where would you have me stand?' I whisper to Master Weston. He gestures towards the window, away from the seated men. The sun is setting in wondrous hues of rose and gold. I pause, eyes closed, feeling the glory of the dying day, of the Lord's mercy and infinite wisdom in which I must trust. I begin to sing the words of the Holy Mother, her joy in carrying our Lord, knowing what He would bring to this sinful world. I wonder if these pompous merchants know that He came to scatter their pride.

I hear them talk as I sing and know they care nothing for these beautiful Latin words. Perhaps they have no notion what they mean. But when I am finished, I open my eyes and see the chamberlain has his closed, a smile on his lips. Of course, he is educated while they have little learning beyond what they need, but he is a curious man all the same. 'Beautiful,' he breathes, and I cannot help but feel pleased. 'Sing some more. Forget these heathens! Sing for me.'

I am still there long after night falls, and it is as if there is only Master Weston and me. And yet when I am finished, it is Ralph Holme who holds my attention. As I sip on a smooth Bordeaux that pleases my tongue and warms my belly, I come to understand he has been mayor of this place and is its richest merchant. And I see that the others defer to him, at least until they have had enough of his boasting and jests, which are coarse and cruel. I feel like a pet dog and, sure enough, they have their fill of me too. 'You must come again,' Master Weston says with a smile. I am most vexed this cannot be.

I slip out into the street and gulp down some fresh air, patting my chest to hear the crinkle of parchment. I feel lighter than air, carried by the ecstasy of knowing I have done what Sir Edmund asked of me. And yet, a part of me struggles to understand what kind of a world I have come to, where a good man can commit a heinous crime and still feel the love of God.

Last night, going to throw water out into the courtyard, I saw Will pull Edith, the kitchen girl, into the shadows on the ground floor. She didn't want to go with him, trying to wriggle free of his arm around her waist, but he kept saying: 'Just one kiss.' I heard him thrashing and grunting when I came back in. I heard her, too, whimpering like some wounded creature. This morning her eyes are red, and she has lost the flush to her cheeks, even in the heat of the kitchen. Will does not throw her even one glance as we sit at table.

Sir Edmund reaches for more bread. Since I brought him the documents, he has taken to looking at me and shaking his head, as if I am some kind of miraculous being he cannot possibly fathom. 'We'll tell Wysham your story tomorrow. He's going up to see Horsley in the castle today.'

'What if he does nothing?'

'Men like Weston should be roasted on a spit. He thinks he doesn't answer to anyone in a place like this, and I hope to God he's wrong or I'll not stay. But that's enough talking. Take my armour downstairs and give it a good clean.'

I am heartened by his words as I carry his padding downstairs into the yard, returning for the armour itself. The air has a softness to it, the skies filled with birds diving like missiles as they hunt on the wing. I scrub and patch and polish until long after the bells for Nones, thinking about the May Days of my childhood, the evergreen boughs tied to doors and the wreaths of flowers Mother made for us. I would kneel at the window at dawn to watch the maidens and their lads cross the meadow, dipping to wash their faces in the dew before they searched the woods for blossoms. I can still smell the sweetness hanging in the air, the sound of bells and laughter.

There can be only one Queen of May here.

Next morning, the sun pushes through a grey sky edged with angry red as we stumble to Mass. There are more people on the street than usual, but for all it is May Day, they seem fearful, arms clasped tightly round their children, murmuring in tight little knots.

There is no sign of Alice or even Dame Eleanor. But the low murmuring and worried faces have followed us to church and Sir Edmund strides over to a group of towns-men. He comes back with a pinched mouth. 'Someone took a mad dog out of the Cowgate this morning.'

'Was it dead?' Will asks.

'Christ's balls, of course it was dead! The question is whether there are more.'

I shiver. 'That was a brave man who took it away. I suppose he killed it too.'

Sir Edmund nods. 'One of Ralph Holme's men, they said, whoever he is.'

I remember Ralph Holme from Master Weston's house.

Since it is a holy day, most people have nothing to do but spread rumours of the mad dog. That it arrived on a ship. Or was found in a warehouse. That the man who took it away was bent double under the weight of it. That another was seen foaming at the mouth in the Western Lane. But some of the girls and their swains still slip off towards the Cowgate, hand in hand.

We walk back down Soutergate with Sir John, whose nose drips from its red tip. He seems even more grey and furrowed than usual. 'They say men are gathering across the north of England to take matters into their own hands if the king doesn't come.'

'There's always one or two willing to make trouble.'

'This isn't one or two, Edmund.' We reach his hall. 'How can I help?'

Sir Edmund hands over the parchment and I tell my story.

Sir John looks from me to the parchment to Sir Edmund. 'I'm not sure I understand.'

I feel my palms grow clammy. 'You will need to ask to see Master Weston's ledger. The entries will be under the date given here ...' I stab at the parchment. 'But you will see that what is written in his book is exactly the same except for the amounts, which will be more than they should be. More than was paid and recorded here.'

Sir John strokes his bottom lip. 'You are certain of this?'

I nod vigorously, placing a hand on my heart. 'On my life.'

He looks away, kneads the back of his neck. 'I knew we were ill-fed and paying dearly for it. But I thought it was the bad harvests. Not that ... that Master Weston ... You have done well, Benedict, to work it out, and so quickly.'

I smile, lowering my eyes.

Sir Edmund thumps the side of his thigh. 'So, what now?'

'I will write to the king, never fear, Edmund. He will get to the heart of the matter. Other than that . . .'

A door slams and someone rushes up the stairs. A young man runs in looking as if he's seen the Black Douglas himself. 'Sir John!' He whips off his cap, kneading it violently. 'It's Alice Rydale.'

Sir John frowns. 'What of her?'

'She's dead.'

I fall to the bottom of the ocean.

Sir John stares at him. 'You jest.'

'I do not, sir, I swear. We were walking out towards Lamberton. I know we're not supposed to go that far, but it's such a lovely day . . .' He bites his lip.

'What in God's name is she doing out there?'

The youth lowers his head. 'She's been stabbed. Many times.'

Sir John's face is so red, I think he must have a fever. He is on his feet and pacing the room. 'Does her mother know?'

'I came to you first.'

'I see. Good. I'll go now. Myself. To tell Dame Eleanor.'

'I'll come with you.' Sir Edmund pushes himself violently up out of his chair.

Sir John nods before shaking his head in melancholy wonder.

We walk down Soutergate and on into Hide Hill, stopping at a grand house of three storeys on the left, its tiled roof reaching up towards the sky. A freckled youth with some of his front teeth missing sits on the bottom of the inside stairs, head in hands, and I wonder if they know already. But he rises with hope leaping on to his face. 'Is she found, sir?'

Sir John pushes on up the stairs to the main chamber. It is the first time I have been inside a home with a family living in it since I came to Berwick, and this one is very fine indeed. Though some of the windows still have wooden shutters, those facing south have glass in them and handsome curtains that sweep almost from the ceiling to the floor. The candlesticks and sconces are so well polished they are like eyes all over the room reflecting everything they see. Perhaps that is a pleasant thing in ordinary times. But these are not ordinary times and the flames dancing in them seem hellish. A pair of tapestries, one depicting a dance and the other a hunt, seem to mock us with the cheerfulness of their antics.

Dame Eleanor reclines in a great cushioned chair, her robes as loose as her hair, the bearded man I see now must be her steward beside her, hands behind his back. She grips the arms of the chair so tightly, her knuckles are become entirely bloodless. Sir John's face is a book anyone can read.

'I' – Sir John coughs – 'I have news about Alice.'

Dame Eleanor closes her eyes.

'Pray forgive me, but she is dead.'

There is a cry from the window, and I see Lucy Rydale curled on a seat there.

Dame Eleanor takes a long, shuddering breath. 'She did not come home yesterday. We have waited all night.'

'And you didn't send word to me?' Sir John throws his words at her.

She takes a deep breath, eyes glistening. 'Forgive me. We thought she would come. I did not imagine . . .' Her whole body convulses, and she stuffs a kerchief into her mouth. A strange low moaning escapes her all the same.

'When was the last time you saw her?'

Dame Eleanor rocks back and forth in her chair, the moaning incessant now. It is Lucy who turns awkwardly towards us, her face a rigid mask, eyes grown huge. 'We went out to the Fields yesterday afternoon to gather blossoms for May Day. Then I . . . I was tired, and Ellie Maynard brought me back.' She looks up at the steward. 'We saw you in the cart, didn't we, Edward, leaving for Lamberton to get meat?' He nods, and I think him brave to venture out there, so near to the Scots, even for a May Day feast. 'We did not expect Alice to be much longer but when the gates closed, we didn't know what had become of her.'

'Those murdering devils!' Sir Edmund grips his dagger.

Sir John whirls round. 'The Scots, you mean?'

Sir Edmund nods. Lucy Rydale lifts a hand, but Sir John has already turned away. 'I will bring her home.'

The steward stirs. 'Let me do it, sir. I confess I was drinking with friends for much of the night, not knowing Alice was . . . and Dame Eleanor . . .' He waves a hand towards his mistress, who laments to herself without heed to anyone else. 'Anyway, it would ease my conscience greatly if I could attend to her.'

'I care not which of us fetches her, but you're not riding alone. No one is to go beyond sight of the walls unless it's strictly necessary and not without an escort.' Sir John puts his hand to the door, does not look at those wounded faces. 'I'll get my men together. Come with me if you want, Edward.'

We ride out of the Waleysgate in the north of the town, people gathering on the walls as the news spreads. Edward rides near me, face taut, though he is not nearly as old as I first imagined. Perhaps he has known Alice all her life, for I do not know how long he has served the family.

I see where she lies long before we get there, a huddle of girls cradling her head in their laps. 'Fools,' Sir Edmund mutters, but I am glad Alice was not left all alone, as she must have been during the long night. Sir John jumps down to walk the last stretch holding his horse's bridle.

I did not imagine such a great wound in her chest. The blood has long since dried, staining her clothes and skin. It is not Alice who lies there, but some creature from Hell.

The girls stand up. I thought they would be covered in gore, but they have little to show for their bloody vigil. I thought, too, that Alice . . . that the Scots would have violated her, that she would be . . . dishevelled. But her clothing seems intact, apart from the terrible stains. We lift her into the cart, hair falling in stiff clumps, and

I am glad when her empty face is covered by a mantle. Only her stained, slippered feet remain to be seen. What is she doing so far from the places she might easily find May Day blossoms? And where are her overshoes?

We make our sombre way back into town, pursued by the irreverent twitterings of small birds, and convey her to the chapel of the Maison Dieu hospital next to the river where she is to lie overnight before being buried beside her father in the graveyard there. The physician has promised to wash her wounds, but there's no need to bind them.

Sir John also asks him to examine her for evidence of evil-doing. His rage is quiet but venomous as he orders the arrest of all Scotsmen living in Berwick, the meaner sort to be placed in various secure places throughout the town, and the better sort to stay in their homes. I hear him say to Sir Anthony that he is minded to expel them altogether, which I believe would be a terrible thing since many have sought refuge here from Bruce and his band of murderers.

We return to Marygate in silence. There is nothing to say, for those who butchered this innocent girl will surely not be punished, however much they will suffer in the next life.

The next morning, I go to the friary to say prayers for Alice's soul. It seems only a moment since I saw her standing in the church doorway and I cannot believe such beauty is gone for ever. Walking back down Soutergate buffeted by a chilling wind, I pass a group of men standing outside Sir John's house. They nudge each other, looking at me, and I feel my mouth dry up. I keep walking.

'Are you the clever lad who found out Weston?'

I turn to stare at the soldier, scarcely comprehending. I nod slowly. Sir John did write to the king. But Sir Anthony told us Master Weston has sent a flurry of letters south to confuse and contradict my story, for the chamberlain is still a powerful man with even more powerful friends. Sir Edmund draws himself up into a fearful rage almost every evening over it, for only King Edward can command answers from his own officials. But he is so very far away, with so many important matters to contend with.

Nevertheless, it is true that I did find Master Weston out and perhaps I should be satisfied with that. Certainly, the men crowding round me now seem to be most pleased with my endeavours, patting me on the back and filling me with a surge of warmth in the pit of my stomach. 'Come and let me buy you some ale,' says one.

'Gladly, sirs,' I reply. 'But my master expects me immediately.' That isn't true, but I am unused to such goodwill from other men and do not really know what to do with it. Blushing at all this ill-founded approval all the way home, I have no sooner taken off my cloak than Stephen puts his head round the door of our chamber. 'You've to go to Sir John's. Sir Edmund's there already.'

Will is crossing the courtyard and scowls at me. I stick out my tongue at him, well pleased at the thought he is jealous. Racing back up Soutergate, I smile at the men still gathered outside Sir John's house and climb the stairs once more. What astonishes me this time is the presence of Lucy Rydale.

'Where in God's name have you been?' Sir Edmund's fists are furled tight on his great thighs.

'I . . . At the . . .' I look from him to Sir John before turning my gaze on Lucy standing near the window. I wonder they do not give her a seat, for I can see the dark imprint of weariness digging deep into her face and pointing out the strange curve of her body.

Sir John picks up his dagger, turns it over and over in his hands. 'Lucy has come to tell us something' – he sighs – 'something that changes everything. I confess I don't know what to make of it. But you will understand, I'm sure.'

I turn to Lucy and she captures me in a gaze that ignores everything else. 'I saw her the night she died.'

'Who?'

'Alice.'

I almost laugh at yet another of her strange assertions, but I see I must attempt to divine what she means. 'You were outside the walls, too?'

'I thought you were supposed to be clever. No, I mean I saw her here, inside our walls.'

'She can't have been. You must be mistaken.'

'I have been over and over it and I know what I saw.'

I take off my cap, run my hand through the tangled length of my hair. 'Where was she?'

'Running up Hide Hill. As if to get away from something. Someone. To get home. I was up in the solar on the top floor, looking down Hide Hill, waiting for her. It was nearly dark, so I couldn't see everything, but there was a moon. It was Alice, I know it was.' Her gaze does not falter.

I look out of the window, the world twisted and thrown into disarray through the diamond-shaped panes. 'So, she may not have died where we found her outside the walls?'

'I'm sure of it. Someone came running out of the shadows, from up the hill. I could not see him. He wore a big cloak and a hat with a brim right down over his face. He struck at her here' – she feigns stabbing herself in the chest – 'and she fell into him and they disappeared.'

'When was this?' I want to wander about, the better to compose my thoughts, but imagine Sir Edmund will cuff me and tell me to stop, which I would not like him to do in front of Lucy Rydale.

She takes a moment to reply. 'I had already heard the bells for Compline. It was a little after that.'

I feel the weight of eyes upon me. And then I wonder, turning to Sir John, 'What is it you want from me?'

He presses his hands together, eyes murky. 'If Alice was killed in Berwick then her murder becomes a very different matter. An important one. Perhaps you have not had time to notice yet, but there is much suspicion and apprehension here already. The thought that it was one of us . . .' He frowns deeply, the lines on his face like scores on tree bark. 'The murderer must be found and quickly. What you did with Master Weston's reckonings was remarkable – I cannot think of anyone else who could have done it. And I need you to solve this mystery just as swiftly.'

'Me?' I think the world has gone completely mad.

'You will do as he asks.' Sir Edmund pushes himself up, wincing at some ache or other.

Sir John gently strokes the arm of his chair. 'She came to see me, you know. On the day she died. I wish now I'd been at home. My steward said she was . . . that she seemed very troubled. She' – his chest rises and falls, and I think I see tears shimmer, but he does not let them fall – 'she said she would come back the next morning. That I should wait for her, if it were convenient, after Mass.'

Lucy's eyes open wide. 'So that's where she went. She told us she would find us on the Fields, that she had something important to do first.'

For reasons I cannot fathom, I feel a brief tug of pleasurable agitation as I listen to her speak, but it is immediately smothered by frustration. 'But she did not tell you what it was?'

Lucy sighs gently. 'No. She did not.'

I wish to ask her more, but Sir Edmund is already striding away. Lucy lurches alongside me and we almost collide in the doorway. I let her pass and, just as I'm wondering if she will be able to manage the stairs, I see from the set of her jaw that some strange force has a hold of her. She turns and touches my arm. 'You will help us?' She draws a deep breath to expel the next word. 'Please.'

Yet again, a strange pleasurable agitation leaps from the back of my neck to my heels. 'I don't know. I mean, I don't expect we'll be here very long.'

She leans on the wall, closes her eyes for a moment. 'My mother has been talking about how you discovered Master Weston's false reckonings.'

'Oh!' That again. I don't know why I'm disappointed.

The ghost of a smile settles on her lips. 'And you were kind, that day in the church. Most people wouldn't have spoken to me. They think they'll catch something.' Her sharp little chin drives straight at my chest. 'I'm sure you'll think of the questions to ask to find this fiend.'

'So, I'm clever, am I?'

'Did I say that?' A little colour rises to smudge her cheeks as she continues her unwieldy descent.

I smile. But then I chide myself for my foolish pride. Death haunts us closely enough from beyond our walls without the Dark Hunter stalking the streets within them too. I have no doubt that when this news reaches the rest of the town's inhabitants, the fear and dismay that already grips them will redouble.

Chapter 4

By the time I reach our house, I'm sure Lucy Rydale imagined what she saw. It is not possible that a dead body found in the first few hours of daylight well outside the walls could have been brought there from inside the town without anyone noticing. And who in this infernal place would have reason to kill a lovely girl who surely did no harm to anyone?

But I cannot cast Lucy's face from my mind, the certainty etched into its sharp lines, the firmness of her voice. She is not . . . For all her bodily infirmity, her mind . . . She is very unforgiving. And as Sir John says, if her words are the truth, then a murderer stalks the very streets I have just walked.

These thoughts circle in my head, round and round. And, since I will know no peace, even as I reach our courtyard, I turn and walk out again. The butcher Wat works for has his shop up on Shaw's Lane, which lies to the north of us, between Soutergate and Walkergate. I stride up there, glad to have something to do that might straddle the dark chasm between the things that seemed to be true and those that might be. As I get closer to the shambles, the corruption in the air rises to overpower me and I plunge retching into a riot of gorse running wild in another forsaken patch where, no doubt, some proud Scottish family once lived in times of peace. I can smell the bile on me still but am glad to be on the street again when Wat comes scuttling along in his usual hurry. He smiles when he sees me, snatching the cap off his head. 'You are looking for me, sir?'

I nod and he grins even more ferociously. I cannot help but smile myself, though I would rather not, for it is a most serious thing I wish to ask of him. He falls into step alongside me, skipping a little to keep in time with the rhythm of his agitation.

'It is your butchery skills I have need of.'

He nods. 'Is it the best bits of meat you be wanting to know about, sir? I would be happy to tell you, if it would please your master and he would be praising you.'

That makes me want to laugh, for I cannot imagine us having the money to purchase anything that looks like meat rather than gristle, let alone tastes like it. 'No, Wat, it isn't that.' I wonder how much I need tell him. 'I am more interested in the killing of an animal, how the . . . how blood flows from the wounds. For on the battlefield. It might be useful.' It sounds quite unbelievable to my ears, but he pulls at his rosy bottom lip, nodding thoughtfully.

We reach the well at the top of Hide Hill, a knot of women talking idly as they wait their turn to draw water.

We walk on. If there is any trace of Alice, if she really was butchered here in Berwick, we should find it soon. Miraculously, there's been no rain these last few days, though there's plenty of shit and offal smeared across the streets. And the town is relatively quiet, no doubt because a girl has just been murdered. I frown. I had almost forgotten about the mad dog. It is uncanny how such a terrible day should begin with a portent of death. I look over my shoulder without meaning to.

Wat is still chattering, but now he too looks behind him. 'What is it, sir?'

I shake my head and force a smile. We are almost past the Rydale house, and I slow down. 'What if' – I say it as lightly as I can – 'I mean, will you show me what would happen if I were stabbed with a knife? What would the blood do if you came at me here?' I point to my chest. 'Would it just drip from the wound or would it, you know, go everywhere?'

'Well' – he strokes his cheek – 'it would be spurting out. That's what is usually happening, to start with anyways. Like when we be killing a pig.'

I tap my hand against my thigh. 'Wat, I want to tell you something you can't tell anyone else.' He stands up straight, taking his cap off again. I wonder whether to threaten him but know I could not. I must put my faith in him. 'I think someone was murdered here.'

His eyes grow round as coins. 'Here?'

'Around here, yes.'

'When?'

'The night before last.'

'Here, you be saying?' He gestures widely with his hands.

'A bit nearer to those houses.'

He steps back and gets down on his haunches to look at the ground. Then he springs up and moves over to the side. 'Look!' I follow his pointing finger towards constellations of vivid red-brown spots on the wall. 'And look.' He moves back a little into the road, pointing down. There, mixed with the dried mud, are spots of a much darker colour. He follows their trail down and around the corner into Hidegate and on further into the labyrinth of the Ness, with its confusion of shops and warehouses. The idlers at the blacksmith's, chattering in the great heat of his furnace, pass their eyes over us, but thankfully Wat does not even notice.

We are among the fish-sellers now, great piles of slippery creatures eyeing us wretchedly, bloodied remnants strewn wantonly around. The smell grows ever more pungent and I pray for a less delicate stomach for fear I will show weakness in front of Wat. I try to think of Alice. 'How old would you say these stains were?'

'Not so old. But I cannot be saying for certain.' He looks around. 'It's hard to be saying with all this trash, but I think they be going over there' – he points further down the road, towards the town wall, where a great expanse of stone blocks the view – 'and then I can't be seeing them any more.'

I try to catch my thoughts. 'Do you know what's down there?' The killer would have needed to put her somewhere safe, somewhere she wouldn't be discovered, for he could

not take her out to the Lamberton road till morning.
And in that somewhere, and on his clothes, there must be
an infernal mess.

Wat shrugs. 'That place where the White Friars live.
And Ralph Holme's warehouse.'

How curious. The man with the mad dog leaps back
into my mind.

'Who was he? Would I know him?' Wat has begun to
jig from leg to leg now he is not actually moving.

'Who? Oh, the dead . . . Wat, you must promise not
to breathe a word of this to a living soul.'

He nods.

'Say it out loud.'

'I swear.'

'It was Alice Rydale.'

He stares off towards the heavens, should he be able
to find anything celestial among the clutter of tumbling
roofs. 'So . . . it was one of us what did it? Not the Scots?'

'I think so.'

'But you're going to be finding him, sir?' He looks
about him most fearfully.

That infernal question again, but I must not lie to
him. 'I doubt it, Wat. I do not think I have the power to
find a murderer. And besides, my master doesn't mean to
stay here very long.' This is not quite a lie, though neither
is it the truth. But that is not what disturbs me now. For
I have no more doubts. Alice died here, perhaps only feet
from where I'm standing.

Sir Edmund stands in the courtyard outside the stables with the farrier. 'Balls of Christ! Where have you been this time?'

'I . . .'

'Don't you dare go away half the day without telling me, do you hear?' He turns back to the farrier. 'You know what needs doing?' The man nods and Sir Edmund stalks off.

I scuttle after him, unsure if he's looking for an explanation. 'Sir, what's happened?'

He stops. 'I want to talk to you. There's no point speaking to Will.'

I blink, surprised still by his good opinion.

'Wysham came to see me. He said he wasn't going to tell any of us yet, but with this business – the Rydale girl – he doesn't want to keep it quiet. It has been decided . . . The king, in his infinite wisdom, has decided that the burgesses of Berwick are to have the keeping of the town.'

'I don't understand.'

He kicks at a stone on the ground. 'I'm damned if I do either. But that's what he said. It won't be the king's men who run the garrison. We're paid little enough as it is, but just you wait till those leeches decide how much we're to get. Though I don't think it can be any less if they want us to live.'

I see a glimmer of hope in all this darkness, but then I remember I have a quest to fulfil and am alarmed. 'So, you think we should leave?'

He blinks. 'Hold your tongue. I was going to say that the king would never have agreed to this if he knew how things really stand. Weston is great friends with this Ralph Hall, isn't he?'

'Holme. Ralph *Holme*. But he didn't have anything to do with . . .'

'Wysham says he's the one pushing for the burgesses to get their damned hands on the town. And if there's thieving to be done, a man like Holme will be in the thick of it, mark my words. So don't tell me he's nothing to do with it when he's such good friends with the chamberlain. If I go to the king and tell him that Weston and Holme are working together to deceive us all, he'll see that the burgesses are not to be trusted with the town.'

'You're going to the king? In London?'

'Were you not listening?'

'But hasn't Sir John already written to . . . ?'

'Tcha.' Sir Edmund spits on the ground so violently, I feel it recoil. 'Wysham hasn't the ballocks for a fight like this. I'll wager my boots he's pushing harder for a post anywhere but Berwick than making sure Weston's summoned back down to England with his big book to get his arse well and truly kicked.'

I close my eyes, but more questions assail me. 'Is Sir John leaving then?'

'He wasn't going to, even once he stopped being warden. But he won't stay now.'

'And when are the burgesses supposed to . . . ?'

He spits again. 'First of July. I must go soon.'

I try to think, to weigh and measure this new

knowledge. One thing is certain. I will need to move quickly if I am to set my investigations at Ralph Holme before he takes charge of the town and becomes even more lofty and unassailable.

I stand above the Cowgate looking out into the heavy darkness, a brisk breeze disturbing my hair and cloak. In the distance the sea crashes on to the rocky shore. I wonder what I would hear if the Scots were scurrying beneath the walls with their infernal ladders, looking for a place of weakness. A little over a year ago Douglas and his men sailed right up the Tweed, intent on getting over where the wall was not yet properly built – between the castle just beyond the town's western wall and where the bridge, which was swept away by a flood long ago, used to be. Only the barking of a dog saved the town.

Sir Edmund left yesterday morning for London and now, as I stand on watch, I am quivering inside with the desire to put my wits to finding Alice's murderer. It would be foolish indeed to ask questions, to look carefully in Ralph Holme's warehouse without Sir John's written permission. But always he is sleeping or out with his closest companions, and I have heard it said he is rarely sober, even at Sext. And so, my mind jangles with unfinished thoughts and suspended questions and I will drive myself to distraction if I do not furnish myself with the means to make some sense of them. For I am sure I will find answers in that warehouse.

And always at my back, I feel Lucy Rydale's gaze boring into me. I dream of a familiar black bird, swooping down to push me awake with her beak, shrieking at me to tell her who killed her sister. And sometimes, on the most unquiet nights, her eyes become one dark grey pool, its waters polluted with a billowing trail of blood. On those nights I wake with a cry, beads of sweat on my brow and Will throwing something at my head.

Heavy footsteps scuff the stone steps and red-haired Peter Spalding returns to stand guard with me on the walls, adjusting his hose. He has a blustering, conceited manner to him that makes him ill-liked, and I have listened to him complain about the weather, the food, the merchants, Sir John, and everything else so often that I know what to say without listening. Yet I feel miserable for him, for he has been a man-at-arms in Berwick many years and has no money to leave. 'Sweet Jesus,' he says, scratching his great red beard. 'Will this damn night never end?' There is no need to answer him. 'I wonder how many of us will be left when Holme and his friends take over? Just the fools and the poor, eh? But which one am I, I wonder?'

I turn to look at him, for this surely does require an answer. 'It is an honourable enough thing to do. We are still the king's garrison.'

He spits. 'And what is the king doing for me? What is he doing for any of us up here in this wet desert? What is this Edward for if he does nothing?'

'You should not say that.'

'I shouldn't have to. But I'm not the only one who thinks it, mark my words.'

I look out into the blackness, which seems to have crept closer. 'Arundel's ships have left for the north. They will not fail this time, surely? If we take back some of the Scottish castles near the sea, we can push out into the countryside.'

'Oh, hark at you! Quite the captain general.' Spalding leans on his spear. 'You mean Arundel, who was sent packing by a few wild dogs at Lintalee, and who isn't even with them? You mean the castles Bruce has cast down in Scotland that will need money poured into them to make them fit for a garrison again? And which, even if we did, would fall one by one to those wily devils.' He shakes his head. 'Don't make me laugh.'

I mislike the way he always thinks the worst. 'So, we might as well go home?'

'Aye, that we might, if you think something good is going to come of us being here. But it's a wage, and that's as certain as anything these days.'

He makes it all sound so simple and so base at the same time. I know I don't want to be here, but I thought there was at least some honour in fighting for England's rights. The monks in Gloucester said Bruce was an excommunicate, damned on Earth, as he will be before God, for the most heinous crime of murder in a holy place. And yet he expels our men from castles and wins battles. It's best I do not think about such weighty matters, for I cannot make sense of them. I turn my mind back to Alice. 'What do you know about Ralph Holme?'

'What would someone like me know about a man like that?'

'More than Ralph would like, I imagine.'

'You're right there. Well, he lives in a large house in Western Lane with a big garden and a pigeon house. He has three children and a pretty wife I wouldn't mind slipping my cock inside, even if her tits are starting to slide towards her belly. The eldest boy takes after his mother, which is just as well since Ralph looks like an overgrown ape. And he won't give you "good morning" unless you pay him for it first.'

'Does he have ships of his own?'

He snorts. 'Of course. Three, I think. And maybe two more shared with some of the other burgesses. His warehouse is down in the Ness, near the Carmelite friary. When you hear your belly rumble, take a walk past it and see all the things *you* won't be eating.'

The bells ring for Lauds and already dawn waits below the surface of the sea, sending her rosy attendants streaming into the air to herald her arrival. The wind has dropped and, though dark clouds press heavily on the land to the north, there is no rain here. I walk along the walls to ease the weariness in my limbs and head, watching the sky lighten. I nod to the other soldiers standing further along. They all seem to think me a magician for what I did to catch Master Weston, which alarms and warms me in equal measure.

At last, I see the next watch arrive and wander back. Peter Spalding lurches down the steps. 'Are you coming to Mistress Fenwick's? I've been standing here for hours thinking about my balls getting a good tickle.'

Mistress Fenwick keeps a whorehouse in one of the streets off Hidegate, in the south-eastern corner of the town, and her girls are popular with the men of the garrison because they will work any hour of the day or night. Will and Stephen never stop talking about what they do there or what they are going to do there, though they rarely have enough money to visit, for their other great passion is playing dice with the fisherboys down in the Ness.

I am curious, I confess it. I have the same urges as everyone else, the same burning desire for release as I lie in bed at night or when I do not have my mind fixed on something else. I have long learned to live with these urges, for I know they are sent to test us. But lately I have been wondering why I alone must resist. I would like to go to Mistress Fenwick's, but not now and not with Peter Spalding.

I walk back across the waste ground towards Holy Trinity, people already stirring in the tents there. One man, big but hollowed out, catches my eye and spits on the ground before turning away. I am too late for Mass, but I am determined to catch Sir John with his wits about him, so I wait for him coming back from church.

Finally, he appears, flanked by his retinue. He is very much the king's man now, looking neither left nor right, keeping his distance from the people in the town he is still supposed to protect. Or perhaps he is just tired of Berwick, tired of the neglect and the boredom. I run to catch him up.

He whirls round, hand on the pommel of his dagger. 'Ah, 'tis you, Benedict. Did you mean to put the fear of God into me?' He looks far older than even before the last full moon, the light dull in his pale eyes.

'I would speak with you privily, sir. I can come back whenever you wish.' I pray he will see me now.

He drops his hand. 'No, let us go and take some wine together.' In his hall, he sits down heavily. 'Have you found him?'

I almost laugh, it is such a preposterous notion. But I steady my face in time. 'No, sir. But I do have more information. As you will remember, Lucy told us that a man came and stabbed Alice within view of their house on Hide Hill before dragging her away. I have been to look and there is blood on the road and some on nearby buildings that then continues round into Hidegate and down into the Ness, where the traces of blood seem to stop' – I pause, eyeing him carefully as he takes a deep draught of the wine Henry, his squire, has just poured – 'near Master Holme's warehouse.'

That gets his attention. 'Ralph Holme?' He scratches at his neck. 'You cannot think . . .'

'It is curious, sir, that it was Master Holme's servant who took out the mad dog before it was light on May Day. I have begun to wonder if it was a mad dog at all.'

He looks at me, mouth half open, before taking another hearty drink. A tiny river of wine trickles down his chin. 'What has the mad dog to do with this?'

I lean forward, palms clammy. 'What if it were Alice in the sack?'

He leans back, a hand thrown up as if to fend me off.

'Her body was taken outside without anyone noticing. And the trail of blood leads to Master Holme's warehouse.'

He nods slowly.

'I need a writing from you to ask questions and search the warehouse.'

He puckers up his lips. 'Ralph would not want that.'

'Would you like me to show you where she fell?'

'No!' He slinks down in his chair, hunched and humped like an old crone. I wait. He frowns. 'There is something I wanted to tell you, but I cannot remember . . .' He takes another long draught of wine, though that is more likely to help him forget. But even before it is fully swallowed, he splutters and waves a finger at me. 'The physician, that was it. He came to tell me what he saw on . . . on Alice's body.'

I try not to think of her bloody carcass, lying there on the road.

Sir John leans towards me, his face urgent. 'She was not violated, praise be to God. That is something, at least.'

It would not have surprised me if someone had found the urge to possess Alice too much to resist. Her beauty had a touch of the divine about it, and I must confess I too wanted to taste it. But though I am glad she was not touched in that way, it makes my task a little more difficult – I am dealing with a murderer whose actions have just become considerably less understandable. But Sir John wishes me to say the right thing. 'I am glad, sir. Most glad.'

He nods vehemently, then presses his hands together. 'But that was not all. The physician said there were three main wounds inflicted upon her. The great hole in her chest was the most plain to see. A knife, without doubt. That was surely what killed her, though the others could easily have threatened her life in their own way.' He begins to tug at his lip.

I think he has forgotten me. 'Please go on, sir.'

He turns to me, as if in sleep. 'Ah, yes. The other things. There were marks on her neck, as if hands, fingers, had pressed most grievously at her throat. And on the back of her head, a bloody mess and a deep gash, like from a stone brought down hard.'

Dear God, it seems poor Alice was the very Devil to kill, her fragility yet another mask she wore to make fools of men. I don't know why I'm so angry with her.

Sir John looks at me and I see that his heart is a bloody mess too. 'I didn't realise I'd miss her so much, Ben. I didn't realise . . . She made me feel a better man, do you see? She could have used her beauty to get whatever she wanted. But she didn't. She was like a candle in the window at the end of a long journey.'

I imagine he is not terribly well acquainted with writing verse. And I think, too, that the thoughts he clings to now are not the ones he had when Alice was alive. But he is probably not the only one to think more kindly of something lost for ever than when it was within reach of an outstretched hand. And all the more so in this forsaken place, where light and even candles are scarce, but not so much as gentle smiles and kind words.

Sir John rouses himself, looks as if he has decided something. He turns to Henry. 'Go and find William.'

I close my eyes. William is Sir John's clerk. I have won my first battle.

Chapter 5

I have a paper sealed by Sir John that shows everyone I have his authority to investigate Alice Rydale's death. Even Ralph Holme cannot gainsay it for the moment, until he and the other burgesses take control of the town. Or, at least, I hope so. Sir John also got his clerk to look in the watch book, which says that one of the men on the Cowgate the morning Alice's body was found was his own knight, Sir Roger Pichard. He has gone to Newcastle to purchase some armour, but the other man with him – Richard Chaunteclerk – lodges in Ravensdowne.

I leave Sir John and head that way, down Hide Hill. I thought I might feel melancholy when I reached the spot where Alice was surely stabbed. But I am too agitated. I wonder if Lucy Rydale is watching me, but don't look up. And then I wonder about Dame Eleanor. For all she seems most mercurial, I have seen how she doted on her elder daughter even as they both tried to cosset the younger one. How does she fare now?

I turn the corner and walk east towards the Ness and Ravensdowne, eyes following me from the stalls and shops, men and women nudging and whispering. I imagine my quest is already spoken of around the town, but I pray hard no one speaks with me about it. I turn another corner and find Chaunteclerk camped out in a tumbledown eyesore, the tiny, dilapidated chamber he sits in missing windows and parts of the roof. He is a cheerful man with straw-coloured hair and a chunk missing from his left ear. He greatly desires to help me, which makes him most unlike any other Londoners I've ever met, but I soon realise he has little to tell. The minute Holme's servant said he was carrying a mad dog, Sir Roger did the talking, though Chaunteclerk was the one who opened the gate to let him out.

'What did he look like, this servant?'

He shakes his head. 'I couldn't tell. His cloak was wrapped up right to his chin and his hat almost covered his face. Whether he was tall or short, I cannot say, but he seemed a little bulky, though not entirely. And strong, to carry such a burden.'

'Did that not strike you as strange, that he should be so covered up?'

He shrugs. 'If I was carrying something as awful as that, I would do the same.'

I suppose he is right. 'Did he give you a name?'

He caresses his beard for a while. 'I know he said Richard, my own name, but I cannot remember his surname . . . Wait a moment . . . It had something to do with birds. Starling. No. Heron, that was his name.'

I smile, for his logic is beguiling and his information useful at last. 'Is that Northumbrian?' I have met a Northumbrian knight with that name on the walls.

'Aye, I think you're right. But he didn't speak like a northerner.'

'What did he speak like?'

He thinks about this, pursing his lips. 'I'm not sure. He didn't say much.'

'And you closed the Cowgate after him?'

'Yes, of course. It wasn't time to open it.'

I nod. 'When did he come back?'

There is another pause, more stroking of the beard. 'Not before I went off the watch, that's for certain.'

'How do you know? He might have uncovered his face once he got rid of the dog?'

'Because the only person to go out and come back in was a girl. She was very pleased with herself because she found a ribbon she'd lost the day before. I don't know her name, but her father's a burgess' – he clicks his fingers – 'John Pontefract!'

I remind myself to speak with the girl who went out on to the Magdalene Fields with Alice and Lucy that last afternoon. It is hard work, this investigating, and I feel my head beginning to ache already. 'Did anyone else go out?'

'Just the old man. Tom Crory. He always goes to gather sticks and things, even on the Sabbath, not long after the gates open. Takes half the day about it.'

I know who he means. 'That was it?'

'Yes.'

'And did you see anyone going past, as if they might have been going towards the Waleysgate?'

'No, not a soul.'

'Do you . . . Would you have expected this Richard to come back? I mean, was there enough time before you finished on watch for him to get rid of the dog and return to town?'

'Now you say it, yes, I'm surprised we didn't see him again. At the time, I was just glad. And now I think of it, too, he carried nothing to dig a hole with. He would be a fool to do anything but bury it.'

I take my leave and pray Sir Roger Pichard can tell me more than Richard Chaunteclerk.

Sir Roger is not at all pleased to be asked questions by a mere squire. He rubs his face and turns his back on me so I can hardly hear him, pouring himself wine but offering me none. He stares at Wysham's paper. 'If you must go poking about in other people's business, you'd be better off looking for traitors. Someone's going to sell us out sooner or later, mark my words.'

'I'm not . . .'

'And what kind of ballocks is it to say the Scots didn't murder the girl? She was found outside the walls! Who the hell else could have done it?'

I stand with my hands behind my back and let him tell

me what I should and shouldn't be doing or thinking
or saying.

'You shouldn't be asking honest men about it. What
about those dogs in the town? I bet they know something.
Rats, all of them. Rats in a sewer. They'll betray us one
day. That'll be all the thanks we get for keeping them
safe.' At last, he takes a breath and a sip of wine.

'Exactly so. I wonder if you could think back to the day
Alice Rydale's body was found. When you were on watch
at the Cowgate and a man came carrying a mad dog.'

'I remember. How could I forget? What of it?'

'Did you know him? Can you describe him to me?'

He rubs his nose with the back of his hand. 'One of
Holme's men, wasn't he?'

'You tell me.'

'That's what he said, that he was a servant of Ralph
Holme. Stoutish fellow. But you needn't bother asking
me anything else about him. He was well wrapped up.'

'Did he tell you his name?'

'No.' He brings his fist down lightly a few times on the
table beside him. 'Perhaps. I can't remember.'

'And how did he speak?'

Sir Roger rolls his eyes. 'I don't know. I wanted him
away as quickly as possible, didn't I?'

'So, what happened?'

'Chaunteclerk opened the gate and that was the last
we saw of him.'

'You didn't look in the sack?' I see a red flush seep
across his face. 'I know that's a stupid question, sir, but
I need to ask it so I know what is and isn't possible.'

His jaw tightens. 'No, I didn't look in the sack. Do you take me for a fool?'

'And you don't think you knew the man, even though you are acquainted with Ralph Holme?'

'Didn't I tell you that already?'

I bow and thank him most courteously, though in truth he has been almost no help whatsoever. But I have my story now, for what little he said was just as Richard Chaunteclerk told it. It will be an easy matter to talk to this Richard Heron. Ralph Holme will know where to find him, though he may not wish to tell me, of course. Yes, Richard Heron must answer for his actions on May Day, and I will have to work out if his master has anything to do with these strange goings-on.

All the same, one question keeps nudging me. If the sack contained not the body of a mad dog but a girl, why did the servant give his own name?

A mist has hung heavy over the town all morning. But now it slinks off and I am hot beneath a fervent sun in my heavy winter tunic and cloak. Daisies and buttercups have lifted their heads to spread a joyful carpet of colour in gardens and especially in the patches of waste ground that otherwise make Berwick a slovenly place. I have never seen so many shades of green, from the dark and glossy to the pale and serene. And beyond is the sea, which, on days like these, sparkles and shines like the waters of Paradise. We are all made new amid such wonders and I confess I have never esteemed the first signs of summer as highly as I do now, after the harsh rigours of only a few weeks in a persistent northern winter that tussled long and hard with spring.

I pass by one of the merchants I met in Master Weston's chamber and he tells me Ralph Holme is down at the wharves on the Tweed, where one of his ships has newly arrived. I confess I am not eager to find him but all too quickly I reach Seagate, where the ground falls away steeply between tiny houses built of turf and straw, a fluttering of nets drying between stakes driven into the ground. The stench of fish still offends me most grievously and I hurry through the Watergate to enter a world of furious activity.

At this end, near the mouth of the Tweed, a great ship lies upon a scaffold, its battered, encrusted hull exposed to all the world. Framed by the bleached wall of the castle tumbling down to the shore in the far distance, the wharves perch like skinny cats hunting for fish on the edge of the river. Two ships are held in place in the low water, men carrying boxes and baskets scurrying up and down the planks that link the ships to the shore. I stand watching for a moment until a man marches down the plank dressed in fine linen and a long, tight-fitting gown of blue. I spring forward. 'Forgive me, sir. I'm looking for Ralph Holme.'

'He's up at the warehouse. Go through Watergate and follow the road round to the right. It's the big one beside the Carmelite friary. He'll be checking through all this.'

He surveys the muddle of boxes scattered across the ground. 'I hope your business is urgent, for he'll be in a fearful mood until everything is accounted for.'

I nod, forcing myself to walk up to the Ness at a commanding speed.

'What do you want?' Ralph Holme growls. 'I have no time for squires or singers. Especially ones who tell fantastical tales about murders within our walls.'

So that knowledge is certainly abroad.

He stands in the middle of a large chamber organising chaos, his clerk – a tiny dormouse of a man – glued to his side and struggling with a pile of papers. With a piteous 'Oh!' he finally drops them all over the floor.

Cuffing the little man, Ralph steps out of the way. 'You've got until he's ready.'

I hand him my paper. He reads it and snorts. 'A singer and a magician, for by Christ you've transformed yourself into something you have no right to be. What do you want with me?'

I feel the heat in my cheeks. 'Forgive me, sir. As you seem to know, there is no doubt that Alice Rydale was killed here in Berwick. She was seen after the curfew.'

He blinks, turns away, fiddles with the lock on a box. 'So, it's true. I'm sorry to hear it.'

I take back the paper and put it carefully in my pouch. 'I beg your pardon, sir, but I need most urgently to speak with your servant, Richard Heron.'

'Heron! What's he to do with this?'

'He was the one who took out the mad dog the morning Alice's body was found.'

He taps his hands against the sides of his tunic. 'I had forgotten about that. I meant to get my steward to speak to him, for I knew nothing about it. But Heron's not here.'

'May I ask where he is?'

'I've no idea. He looks after my flocks.' The clerk is back at his side.

I take a deep breath. 'Forgive me, but I really must speak with him, sir.'

'William!' Ralph Holme's bark startles me. One of the men carrying boxes looks over. 'Go and find Richard Heron and bring him here. Ask his wife. Third house on the left, second street in Ravensdowne.'

I take a few more breaths. He has a gaze that seems to seize a man by the throat. 'And I would be most grateful if I could look around your warehouse, sir.'

Ralph Holme's laugh is vicious. 'I think not.'

I try not to look away from him, for then he will know he has daunted me and I might never have the courage to insist. 'I believe, sir, that Alice Rydale's body may have been put here after she was killed until it could be carried out to the Lamberton road in the morning.'

'Oh, do you indeed!' He turns to the clerk and rolls his eyes at him, as if I were simple. The clerk giggles. 'Get out now and don't bother coming back, to see Heron or anyone else.' His tone is even, quiet, doubling the threat.

I have nothing to lose, and his very vehemence does not speak kindly of his innocence. 'Very well, sir. But if I must leave, then I will return with the warden and some of his men.' I'm almost certain Wysham wouldn't come, but the question is whether Holme believes me. My cheeks are hot, but still I do not drop my gaze.

'Why am I wasting my time?' It is only a mutter to himself, a hand waving at me. 'Look where you like. But by Christ, you'd better not get in my way. If God is good, you'll trip and break your neck.' He turns to the men, who have put their boxes down and are lolling around near the door. 'Get your arses over here.'

I am eager to put myself somewhere else. I smart from the brutality of his treatment of me, but most of all my heart feels sore at the thought that all this fresh merchandise now sits on top of any evidence for Alice's awful end. That is something else that does Master Ralph Holme no favours, though it may indeed conceal his guilt. But I will not give him the satisfaction of seeing me retreat.

I wander about, poking vaguely at boxes, studying the ground. The smells swirling around the warehouse take me over completely. I hurry past boxes of alum, the bitter smell of almonds catching my throat, but pause to drink in the dry pungency of precious spices. I reach out to stroke the dark softness of an otter pelt but think I feel his eyes on me, though when I catch a glimpse of him in my perambulations his gaze is fixed firmly on the comings and goings around him. I wander behind the tidy rows of filled sacks piled up almost to the roof and find a door, scuffed and splintered, that makes me wonder if this is another entrance to the warehouse. If so, it is bound to be locked.

I return to Ralph Holme's elbow. 'What's through that door, sir?'

He does not even glance my way, but fumbles at his waist for a key. The door is unwilling to move, but after a good shove with my shoulder it finally gives way. I find myself not outside but almost at one end of a dingy passageway that extends the long length of the warehouse. A line of tiny windows towards the top of the outer wall provides the only light, which is scarcely enough. Unlike the main chamber, this is a place for dead or dying things and I must pick my way carefully through old ropes curled like snakes, pieces of wood, even an old weighing machine. I stop, feeling a tingling in my nose, then sneeze so many times I fear I will not stop. There is so much dust and so many cobwebs I can't imagine anyone has been here for years.

I walk on slowly, carefully looking right and left for any signs of disturbance, though it is difficult to see. I reach a great wooden door at the far end. For all it seems to be made of oak, the door suffers from neglect like everything else here, its fittings rusty and flaking, the bottom so worn that the wood resembles a jumble of teeth. I try the handle, but, as I expected, the door does not move. This entrance must lie opposite the Carmelite friary that sits right on the walls and would be far less likely to arouse attention for anyone trying to enter with the lifeless remains of a girl over his shoulder. But only if he could walk through a door of solid oak.

I sneeze again, nearly tripping over yet another coil of rope. My foot touches something that falls off the rope and I bend down to pick it up. It is a woman's overshoe. And it is covered in blood. I march back to Ralph Holme.

'What the devil do you want now?'

'A candle, if you please, sir.'

He turns to me, a great snarl on his face.

I hold up the overshoe and he looks at it, looks at me, then looks at it again. 'Is it Alice's?'

I nod, wondering at his bullish innocence.

He reaches out to take it from me. I watch him closely, in case he should seek to get rid of it somehow, but instead he cradles it carefully in his hands, a most gentle look on his face. Suddenly, he hands it back to me. 'What are you waiting for?' he shouts at his clerk. 'Go and fetch a candle.'

The man called William rushes up to us. 'Heron's got a flux. Been sick for days.'

'If we might deal with this first, sir.' I lead the way back into the dark passageway, but when all the men seek to follow us, I stop, afraid they will disturb that which must remain untouched. 'Would you mind asking them to stay back? You and I should go alone, in case we . . .'

He nods quickly and barks the order. Since there is only one candle, we must look together. Even in the meagre light, it is plain to see that everything is matted with cobwebs and dust.

'I've not been in here since I bought the place.' He kicks at a pile of old glass flagons. 'I don't know what half this stuff is.'

I say nothing, for I must keep my mind free of his determined show of innocence. We walk slowly, though nothing looks as if it has been touched or moved in a century of years.

But as we near the outside door, I notice a patch of darker stone, as if the nearby coil of rope has been pushed out of the way, sweeping the dust away too. I bend down and he lowers the candle. Yes, I'm sure of it. 'Look, sir.' Ralph Holme eases himself down beside me with a grunt. He nods. I push his arm to lift the candle higher and there, a foot or so in front of me, are dark splashes. Beyond is a pile of sacks, but I don't need to move them to see the blood seeped into the stone as well as the top layers of canvas.

And there, fallen to one side, is the other overshoe. I pick it up and scratch at the patch on the ground with my fingernail. What was perfectly dark comes away as a muddy red. Alice must have been placed on top of the sacks, which suggests her murderer knew that neither she nor he would be disturbed before he could move her again.

I stand up. 'Does that door open?' I point towards the one that leads out towards the Carmelite friary.

'I imagine so. Like I said, no one's been in here for years.'

'Someone obviously has, sir.' I speak more sharply than I intended.

'Watch your tongue. There'll be a key somewhere.' He turns abruptly and I follow his candle back into the main chamber. He goes to a great box near his desk and opens it with a key on the chain around his waist. Everything comes out, but eventually he brings his hand to caress his chin. 'It isn't here.'

I look at him and he looks away. 'Can we go around?'

He marches off again and we make a ragged procession following on behind, though I wave everyone back when we approach the door. A rusty stain on the ground tells me that Alice's body was dumped there while her murderer opened the door.

'Stop looking at me like that, you hear.' Ralph stomps back inside.

I run after him. 'Please, I must speak with Heron today. Now.'

He stands, hands on hips. 'Well, off you go! I'm not stopping you.'

I nod curtly. 'Thank you, sir. Third house on the left, second street in Ravensdowne?'

'My, my, what a great sleuth-hound you are.'

I turn on my heel, addressing him without looking back. 'And I'm sure you will understand, sir, that I will most certainly have more questions, so please let me know if you intend to leave town.'

'Tell you, my arse.'

I remember I have left the overshoes in the passageway. It is a long walk, there and back, but the exultation flooding through me more than makes up for it.

When I am out of sight of Ralph Holme's warehouse, I stand for a moment, holding the shoes. Somewhere, perhaps only a stone's throw away, is a man prepared to murder a girl in the most brutal way. What possible reason could he have? And if I do not know the reason, is it possible he will kill again? I imagine walking down Hidegate and confronting Alice's attacker, standing between him and her and dealing him a fatal blow. This vision comes to me over and over and I wish with all my heart it might be true, even as I know it would have been me receiving the fatal blow before death came for Alice too. I make a solemn oath to practice my sword-fighting every day, not just once or twice a week, no matter how tired or hungry I am. I pray, too, that our Lord has already drawn Alice to his side.

I rap on the wooden door of Richard Heron's tiny house. A woman appears holding the hand of a child of indeterminate sex. She is flushed and a little slovenly, tunic hanging to one side and her hair tired and unruly as she leans on the door jamb. The child has something encrusted around its mouth that looks like mud.

'What is it you want, sir? It's like Newcastle quayside here this afternoon.'

'I must speak with your husband.'

She steps back. 'You don't want to do that, sir. He's got a most terrible flux.'

Now I am in this disordered place, I am suddenly afraid and wonder if she might ask my questions while I stay at a safe distance.

'Who is it now?' The man's voice is cracked and faltering. The woman peels herself away from the door and I see a small, wiry creature slumped against the wall. He could never be described as stout or sturdy.

'Richard Heron?' I stay near the door.

'Aye,' he says. 'Who wants to know?'

'I am Benedict Russell of the town garrison. I'm here to ask you about the mad dog.'

He starts to cough. 'Why,' he gasps, 'do people keep talking abou' tha'? Ah were not even here on May Day.'

I do not understand him very well, but I understand him enough. My heart falls even further into my belly. 'So, where were you?'

'Ah were down in Lowick. Ma mither was taken ill and then she died. Ahm only just coom back.'

'Aye,' says his wife, 'and bringing the flux wi' you.'

'Quiet, woman,' he barks, before a coughing fit takes him over, violent enough to wrench his guts out.

I wait. 'Ralph Holme didn't know you were gone.'

Richard Heron opens his eyes. 'Ahm his herd. He doesn't deal wi' the likes of me. I spoke wi' Mr Holme's steward, Edwin Braithwaite. He'll tell you. An' he'll be takin' the money off me wages, for sure.'

I walk slowly back along Hidegate. The streets are quiet, with murmurings behind shutters and birds picking at offal on the ground. I could talk to Braithwaite, of course I could. But there's no point.

I have uncovered so much, thought myself so clever, but what do I have to show for it? Ralph Holme, the most powerful man in Berwick, surely hates me with a vengeance now. And I confess I have no idea if the fact he owns the place where her body lay means he was also responsible for Alice's death. I certainly have no way of proving it.

Chapter 6

Though the lengthening of the days tells us we should be enjoying the bliss of early summer, the wind turns savage and full of sharp downpours. One minute the sky is a tousled blue and the next is submerged under voluminous grey, the eaves dripping like fountains to catch the unwary beneath. I know always to wear a hat, preferably tied down. But at least poppies and buttercups are spreading riotously across the Magdalene Fields.

In only a few weeks the truce runs out and we have still not heard if it will be renewed or if the king really is coming with his great army. Before I rode here, I never gave much thought to the Scots, though I knew them to be scoundrels and traitors. If I thought about them at all, I imagined small, swarthy men with sharp teeth and tufted red hair. Like goblins. I am told mothers along the border hush their children by whispering that the Black Douglas will catch them if they cry, and they are right to fear him. But in truth, I cannot tell the difference between

Scots and English in Berwick unless they speak – and even that is not a sure guide unless, like me, they have come from somewhere far away.

But truce or no truce, Douglas and his devils are always on the move, whether as dark shadows in the distance or in tales of those they have assaulted, stolen from or worse. One of the Berwick fisherfolk was out trying to find his nets when they drifted downstream after heavy rain and ran into the path of a party of Scottish riders. He managed to run away and take shelter in a tangle of gorse and thorn, ripping his skin and twisting his ankle. The man hobbled before Sir John, face twisted in pain and fury, asking how he was supposed to earn a living if he wasn't safe a mile from his home. Sir John just shrugged his shoulders and turned away.

I trudge around feeling as if I'm wearing armour that is far too big for me, for I cannot see at all clearly and am in danger of tripping up entirely. But I gave Sir John and Lucy Rydale my word I would look for the murderer and so I must pursue every tiny possibility, speaking and listening until I would gladly embrace a vow of silence.

I know the prattling folk of Berwick will not be long in spreading tales of my visit to Ralph Holme's warehouse, so I drag myself first to Dame Eleanor's house. I enter it and feel I am walking into a tomb. She rises stiffly to greet me, shoulders hunched, back bowed. She is half the woman she was – where once her gown and surcoat strained to contain her ample flesh, now they flow and flap around her. It is as if she is slowly collapsing in on herself, and I feel suddenly stricken on her behalf. I must remember I search for justice not just for Alice, but for all those she left so suddenly and brutally behind. I cannot compare the brief anguish I felt on learning of her death to theirs.

She sends her maid to find Lucy and I search my mind for something to say. But, in the end, I stammer out a most ill-favoured observation. 'Lady, you do not seem well.'

She smiles then, slowly and gently, as if giving up something precious. 'If it is a sin to feel this way, then I confess it but cannot change it. I put my trust in the Holy Mother, for she too lost her child.'

I hold my tongue then, until Lucy finally settles in the window seat. And then I stand before them and recount my discoveries in Ralph Holme's warehouse. I do not know if Dame Eleanor hears my words, but Lucy follows them like a hawk seeking prey, eyes restless and roaming. She stops me to ask how I knew to look in that warehouse and I explain about the blood in the streets. Dame Eleanor breathes heavily then.

'Lady, if you would rather I did not . . .'

She waves a hand at me, rings slipping up and down. 'I want to know it all, however much it pains me. And I am grateful to you, Benedict, please know that. I will find no rest until I see that man hang.'

I nod. 'May I please ask you both what happened on the day Alice went missing.'

Lucy frowns. 'I have told you.'

'Yes, but I would like to know exactly what everyone was doing and when, from the moment Alice left the house right up until we came to you with the terrible news.' I did not know I was going to say any of that, but I see now I need to compile as many versions of this sorrowful tale as I can from as many people as will speak with me. I wish I had brought some writing implements.

'I . . .'

'Wait, Lucy.' Dame Eleanor shifts in her seat, moves cushions out of the way before putting them back. 'I have turned my thoughts often to that afternoon, even though it pains me. We had quarrelled a little, Alice and I. She had been most ill-tempered for some days, and I felt she blamed me for something. But I still have no inkling of its nature.'

That reminds me of a question that perhaps owes more to inquisitiveness than any real belief it will help me to understand what happened to Alice. 'Do you think it might have had something to do with the breaking of her betrothal to Sir John?'

It is surely mere fancy, but I swear I feel the air retreat from the room like a tide, only to come rushing back in almost immediately. And yet Dame Eleanor has not moved, and Lucy is perpetually in motion at any time, shifting back and forth even when sitting.

Dame Eleanor breathes in deeply, stares at the ceiling, which has suddenly become most interesting. 'Alice did not like the thought of leaving here. She had every reason to be pleased with my decision. My business is thriving, and I have no desire to start again elsewhere.'

Why do I imagine she hasn't really answered my question? It does not help that Lucy is leaning forward, staring at me intently. If she is trying to tell me something, I do not know what it is. In any case, I must hasten on.

'I have brought you these. I found them in an old part of the warehouse, which Master Holme tells me is never used.' I place the overshoes in Dame Eleanor's lap.

She lifts them tenderly in both hands, raising them up to the light from the windows. I see her shudder at the blood, feel the weight of her sorrow, which seems to have seeped into every part of her. She puts them down gently on the floor, turning to me with a frown. 'But what were they doing there?'

'I wish I knew. Master Holme protests he doesn't know himself, that he hasn't been in that part of the warehouse for years. But it is right that suspicion should fall on him, though I confess I have nothing to connect him directly to Alice's murder. Is there any enmity between your families?' I would find it tedious to tell her about Richard Heron and the mad dog and the wrong path I have – we all have – been led down.

She leans back on her cushions, knotted fingers worrying at her brow. 'No more than with any other merchant family. Ralph is the richest man in Berwick, and we all have the scars to prove it. But I don't believe . . . I cannot imagine . . .' She places her hand across her eyes. 'But then I didn't ever think she would die before me, in such a cruel way.'

'Pray forgive me, mistress. I should leave you in peace.'

She nods without moving and I nod back, glancing at Lucy, who seems about to speak but instead waves a hand, as if to chase me away. I frown to show her I am displeased and walk quickly out of the door wondering what on God's earth I have done wrong now.

At least Sir Edmund has gone to the king and cannot chastise me for putting my mind – and the rest of me – to what Sir John asked me to do, though Will does his best to remind me I could be enjoying far better pastimes, like whoring or playing cards or dice. He has little time for my endeavours. I think he is finding service in Berwick less than glorious or chivalrous. He still talks about Alice – whom he has taken to calling 'my Lady' – as if she were his betrothed, instead of someone he made moon eyes at but who never knew he lived and breathed. He finds it hard to keep his voice low at table, which earns him many a rebuke, for Sir Anthony prefers silence when he has not invited another knight to dine with him.

I haven't told Will what the physician said about the wounds to Alice's body. I know he would like it if I did, even if he would surely pretend not to. But he hisses at me without end, as if Alice's death was my fault, 'And now she's dead and Book Boy thinks he can save her with lots of dull questions.'

'She was lovely.' Stephen casts a skilled eye over the table for neglected scraps. 'And I don't like the thought of walking past the man who killed her and not knowing it.' Will grunts. 'Don't be calling me a coward, Will – I'm not the only one who thinks that.'

Sir Anthony sends a black look towards us. 'Come here, all of you.' He pushes back the bench most viciously. We scramble towards the floor near the fire as he sits heavily in his chair. 'Well, boys, did you hear that Bruce is back from Ireland?'

'No,' we chorus.

This *is* news and I am suddenly afraid, for our walls are far from stalwart and I am not sure about the hearts of any of the men I stand next to on them. 'You don't think there'll be another truce?'

He breathes deeply. 'I doubt it.'

'And the king?'

'He won't come, Ben. He never does.' For a moment he looks twice his age, the things he has seen and the things he has done written deep on his face and weighing down his body. And then he rises with the vigour of a page and bids us goodnight, Stephen trotting behind him. Once they've gone, Will springs up, sits in the chair. He jiggles his foot until Stephen comes back, and they loudly discuss what should be done to discomfit Douglas or Bruce or both of them together, their propositions becoming ever more fantastical.

I wonder at my disappointment at the thought the king won't come, that we will not be able to ride out of here and teach the Scots a lesson. Perhaps I am tired of talking and thinking about Alice. I put a hand on the arm of the chair. 'I don't suppose you'd come with me to practise the sword?' I have kept my oath to practise often, but there's little point in doing it by myself, for there is no way of knowing if my prowess is any greater at the end than the beginning of the exercise.

Will's nostrils flare. 'It's tedious to spar with you.'

'I would be most grateful.'

'No.'

May he rot in Hell. I don't think to ask Stephen, but a few days later we find ourselves on watch together on the western walls, staring out over the castle and the huddle of houses and churches at Bondington to the broad sweep of country beyond. 'You can see for some thirty miles on a clear day,' he tells me.

I would think it a pity there is so rarely a clear day if the land on both sides of the River Tweed were not so rough and rugged. 'What are those hills?'

'Cheviots, they're called. Good hill country. I grew up on the other side of them.'

'Is that so?' I can see his heart swells with pride at the sight, though I have also seen some of the Northumbrian knights spit and curse at both our king and the Scots for the ruin visited on their native land. 'Are your mother and father still there?'

'My father and my sisters. My mother died a few years ago.'

I throw stones at a rabbit nibbling the grass down below, on the other side of the wall. 'Not too many sisters, I hope?'

He screws up his face. 'Three. They're still young, but that's three dowries to find and our land's worth next to nothing since Bruce brought the war to England.'

I nod. 'Our lands lie a little out of the way of the Scots, but I still worry for my sister.'

'That's what they're for, isn't it?'

'What?'

'Worrying.' We both smile. 'How old is she?'

I think of Elizabeth, the way she strums her top lip with her thumb when she's thinking, which is constantly. 'Eleven. But she chides me as if she were the elder.'

'That's what they're for too.'

The sun falls suddenly below a bank of cloud in a sudden blaze of glory as it sinks towards the western horizon. 'Has Sir Anthony said when he's leaving?'

Stephen shakes his head. 'Holme and the other burgesses want him to stay when they take charge of the town. They *say* they'll get more men to join the garrison. I pray they do, for otherwise I've heard they might get rid of our cook and we'll have to fend for ourselves.' He sighs, his tunic well-ridged from the folds of skin beneath. 'I'll go with you, if you like.'

'Go with me where?'

'To practise your sword. I'm not as good as Will, though.'

I smile to myself, for that strikes me as obvious. He is squat and heavy, whereas Will is lithe as a cat. 'Thank you. I would like that.' And I would, for though he is a coarse fellow and unschooled, he has a kind heart when Will is not leading it astray.

After that, we go to the Magdalene Fields often, for lack of anything else to do. The first time I am quite alarmed, for he is far more sure-footed than he looks. But he proves adept at understanding my failings and coming at me slowly so that I might work out, with his encouragement, the best stroke to use against him. Soon I am managing a few blows myself, moving forward but to one side or the other, which makes me harder for him to reach. I have stopped stabbing wildly to no purpose, which always makes Sir Edmund turn berry red, and feel almost pleased with myself.

But I cannot feel any pride in my investigations, which have led me to the back of the warehouse belonging to Berwick's most powerful man and left me there, as impotent as a ship stranded up on its scaffold. It is as if I have been struck by a sickness that makes me unable to decide anything on Alice's account and I wake anxious and sweating in the night because of it. I must organise my thoughts and decide what to do next.

Walking quickly up Soutergate, I nod a greeting to Sim Taylor, the butcher to whom Wat is apprenticed. Slipping once more into the Franciscan priory, I stop and bow my head out of habit as two friars – one old, one young – turn a corner of the cloister so deep in thought that they do not seem to see me, even though they are only a foot away. Once they have turned the next corner, I scurry towards the door of the church and gently prise it open. The bells for Nones call out. I smile like a child at St Francis, who gently bids me welcome. Motes of dust swirl in the light of the windows and I see only angels dancing for joy, the tiniest, most perfect of God's creations. I walk into the nave, pausing at the screen to cross myself. And, at last, enjoying the pleasure of such familiar tranquillity, I move to my favourite pillar and settle to write down all I have discovered and all I might wish to know.

The friars file in, padding softly across the stone floor in ethereal procession. They pass through the rood screen to another world, silently taking their places in the choir. As the bell's last insistent peals die away, they begin to sing the 'Rerum Deus Tenax Vigor', tentatively at first, but growing in . . .

Though the cough from behind the pillar is gentle, I nearly leap towards the roof.

'Forgive me.' Lucy Rydale crawls round to sit beside me. 'I didn't mean to startle you.'

'What did you think would happen if you made a noise and I didn't know you were there?' I try to whisper, because of the friars, but I sound like a screech-owl.

'I have come almost every day to see you. The fault is yours for not coming to see *me*.'

'I . . . I didn't know you wanted me to.'

Her lips tighten to the size of a small hazelnut, but at last she sighs and pushes her hair out of her eyes. 'I can help you. Don't you think I could?'

She sits there, so small and untidy in her dowdy dress with her untamed hair. It would do no harm to let her believe she is privy to my inner thoughts. 'I suppose so.'

'Tell me what you have found so far. Alice's overshoes in Ralph Holme's warehouse, of course, but you have nothing to show he is responsible for them being there. I have heard it said' – at this, she lowers her brows and gives me a look that tells me she would like to give me a good kick – 'that the mad dog was not a dog at all, and Ralph Holme's servant was not the one who took it out.' She sniffs. 'Is this true?'

'Who told you that?'

'What does it matter who told me? Is it true?'

'Yes, it's true.'

'And what do you think it means?'

I sit back, suddenly tired enough to fall asleep on the cold stone floor. 'I don't know, Lucy. That's the truth of it.'

She clenches her fists, buries them in her skirts. 'You must not give up. You must not, do you hear!'

'But what can I do? I have spoken with everyone.'

'Even Ellie?'

She was the girl who went out with them on to the Magdalene Fields the day Alice went missing. 'Yes. She said the same as you. That Alice was in a strange mood, but Ellie thought it was because of Sir John. That she took you home, then went back to look for Alice. The only interesting thing she said was that she felt scared out there for no reason.'

Lucy sniffs again. 'I imagine she thought so only after Alice was found. She is one for strange fancies, depending on what she has recently heard or seen.'

'You are very free with your opinions, Lucy.' I wonder what she says about me.

Her eyes fly open and she begins to push herself up from the floor.

'What are you doing?'

'Leaving.' She attaches herself to the pillar to begin her strange ascent.

'You don't need to . . . I didn't mean . . . God's bones, Lucy, please stay.'

She stops. 'Why?'

'Because I haven't got anyone else to talk to.' That is certainly the truth.

'Then you will have to grow accustomed to my opinions, for I have many.' She lowers herself awkwardly. 'Don't make me do that again.'

I smile, because she is such a strange huffing, puffing

creature and because I am greatly pleased she has not left me by myself.

She narrows her eyes. 'You do not laugh at me, I hope?'

I raise both hands. 'No, no. I am glad, is all.'

She stares at me for a long moment and then her face does something strange, smoothing out its angles into the glowing softness of a shy smile. She nods. 'Now, tell me everything.'

I explain about Ralph Holme and his herd, Richard Heron, and what the two men on the Cowgate had to say, which is little enough except that the man with the sack did not come back through on their watch. She watches me so closely that, at first, I feel a prickling on the back of my neck, but I soon see it is her way, that she drinks in words. I fall silent and then wonder. 'Lucy, why did you not send for me to come to your house if you wanted to see me?'

She lowers her head. 'My mother is most disturbed by Alice's death. I fear she is not in her right mind. After you came, she stayed in bed for three or four days. I thought it best to meet here, to spare her.'

'I see. Do you know anything more about their quarrel?'

She shakes her head. 'But there was most certainly something vexing Alice. Everyone could see that, even Ellie. We begged her to tell us what was wrong, but she just said . . . In truth, I have been trying to think what she said. Something about her marriage, that it had all been for nothing, the breaking of her betrothal to Sir John, and she wouldn't wed anyone now.'

'But did your mother have someone else in mind?'

She gazes into nothing for a moment. 'I think she wished Alice to marry our steward.'

'Edward? Are you sure?'

'I cannot understand it myself, but it's true that Alice had taken much against him. I heard the three of them talking loudly in the hall a week or so before she died. But they stopped talking when I came in.' She shakes her head, tugs at her tunic. 'As if I were a simpleton who couldn't be trusted with serious discussions.'

'Do you know why Dame Eleanor broke off her betrothal with Sir John? It seemed to be most shocking.'

Lucy leans back against the pillar. 'That is another mystery. My mother always taught us how important it is to keep our word. I suppose it's hard, being a woman and a merchant. She can't afford to be anything less than honest and clear in her dealings. And then she breaks off a solemn agreement, and for no obvious reason.'

There are too many unanswered questions gone with Alice to the grave. But I suppose there must be traces of what she knew or had seen or done that I might uncover. I feel more cheerful, desiring again to put my mind to such knotty matters. And then I frown, for there is something I have almost half-remembered.

'What is it? Are you sick?'

I raise a hand, to stop her from perplexing me with more words. She frowns but is silent. And then the thought springs into my mind. 'You said you saw Edward driving the cart towards Lamberton when you were on the Fields that afternoon.'

'Yes. My mother likes the meat from there.'

'When did he come back?'

She gently pulls a silken lock of hair out from her head and twists it around her finger. 'It was much later.'

'After the gates shut?'

'Long after. We were waiting for Alice, and my mother kept asking where Edward was. He came back some time after Compline, talking like a fool with drink, and she told him to go away. I remember that surprised me, for she does not usually speak sharply to him and he does not usually pay much heed to what she says.'

I blink, unsure what that might mean, remembering that he said he'd been carousing with friends. But I have too much to think about and it will be easy enough to prove him truthful on that. I write down *Edward?* and put my hand out to touch hers. 'Thank you.' She looks at my hand and I get up quickly, a heat rising.

She sits frowning on the floor. 'You will send for me, so we might examine your findings together?'

'Yes. I promise.' And I suppose I must.

Chapter 7

There is something that has perplexed me greatly since talking with Richard Chaunteclerk. How on God's earth did the murderer get back into Berwick without being seen? I wonder too about the old man, Tom Crory, who wanders about across the Fields and the shore, who went through the Cowgate almost as soon as it opened and was out there for much of May Day. Could he have seen the man who took Alice out to the Lamberton road, perhaps on the murderer's way back?

I am busy with these thoughts as I wander up Soutergate. But when I sense someone following me, I move quickly into the middle of the road before turning, feeling for my dagger. A woman stops only a foot or so away, gently stroking one hand, then the other. She is well enough dressed, though not excessively so – a craftsman's wife, perhaps, rather than a merchant's – with a pleasing scent to her. But her skin is well creased and pale with it. She looks down at the ground as if waiting for me to speak.

'Do you wish to talk with me?' I'm sure I do not know this woman.

'Forgive me, sir.' Her voice is very soft, so I step towards her to hear more clearly. 'Are you the gentleman looking for the man who killed poor Alice Rydale?'

'Yes. Yes, I am.'

Now she rubs her arm. 'And do you think you'll find him, sir?'

'I don't know. It's not a simple matter.'

She sighs quietly. 'I have a daughter, about Alice's age. A pretty girl, she is. I don't want to let her out of my sight if there's someone dangerous abroad. But she doesn't like to be kept in. She says it's bad enough she's not allowed very far beyond the walls for fear of the Black Douglas, never mind having to stay so close to home within them.'

'I see.' I remember the freedom of my own childhood, to run and ride where I pleased. But it's different for girls. 'I'm sure she's perfectly safe.'

She tries to smile, but I'm not convinced either, for my words mean nothing until I find the reason why Alice was killed and the wretch who did it. A man is suddenly at her side, then another. And two more women.

'Have you found him, sir?' A youth with a wealth of pustules all over his face pushes himself forward.

'We need to know who it is,' one of the women adds, and they all murmur their agreement, as if I had been keeping it from them. 'We don't feel safe, not knowing. You're supposed to protect us. If it's not the Scots coming to murder us in our beds, it's this fiend.'

'I . . .' What do I have to tell them? That one minute I am intrigued and stirred up by the challenge of solving a mystery, and the next I want to give it up entirely? I see now that would be a terrible thing. 'I still have a number of people to speak to who I believe can help me. Perhaps you know Tom Crory?'

'What do you want with that old devil?' asks the spotty youth.

'He may have seen something the morning after Alice died. When she was taken out on to the road. Do you know where I might find him?'

They all have a view on Tom Crory's habits and hiding places, though little of it agrees. He seems to sleep all over town, tucked under old carts or abandoned stonework, but otherwise wanders where he pleases, as if the comings and goings of the Scots were merely a worn-out story employed to silence children. No one calls him a thief, but I am made to feel he might not be the most trustworthy of witnesses.

Still, it seems to please them to have helped my investigation and they begin to drift away. I feel well and truly plucked and must surely worry now that I will fail them. Carrying on my way past the church and the tents and through the Cowgate, I try not to catch anyone's eye. The wind ripples across the shaggy coats of the cattle grazing outside on the Fields, but they pay it no heed. I imagine they do not feel the cold, but I long for the fragrant bliss of unmeasured days of sun flinging warm kisses on to flesh. The cowherds are huddled together, blowing through blades of grass and hooting at each other.

They grin at me and I wave back. The smallest one is Wat's younger brother, Ed.

I have not gone far when I hear my name called behind me and I turn reluctantly. And yet my heart does sing a little when I see Will and Stephen coming out of the gate and Stephen running towards me, still shouting my name. 'Where are you going?'

Will ambles up to join us, pretending he is not much interested in whatever I might be doing. In truth, I have already decided that one is more than enough to stalk a vagabond like Tom Crory. Which means I must get rid of them. 'I . . . em . . .' I cough for greater effect, looking modestly towards the sea, as if to save my blushes.

'Oh!' Will understands immediately.

'What?' Stephen pokes him.

'God's ballocks!' Will puts an arm across my shoulders. 'Now that I never thought I'd hear. You be careful, my lad. Girls are like crocodiles and they'll bite you hard if you let them. Make sure her mouth's too full for talking. And no promises! Knowing you, you'll fall in love and tell her you'll give her the moon, and before you know it you're in shackles.'

'Ah!' Stephen beams across the Fields and I feel a little sick at the deception. But it's done now.

I walk carefully, trying to imagine the weight of a heavy sack, to the far end of the Magdalene Fields where few now venture, even at the height of the day. Just because the barbarous Scots didn't murder anyone this time means nothing. We wander at our peril.

All except Tom Crory. From this side of the Magdalene

Fields, I can see right across the flat plain towards the Lamberton road and beyond, patches of brilliant gorse still flowering. A man might find ancient, dried-out sticks in there among the yellowhammers and stonechats to feed at least a small fire. I have had to get used to the wintry chill that might stalk these northern summer nights and which might yet harm those living without stout walls.

But he is not there. As I turn back towards the sea, the sun is behind me, but still has much further to go across the firmament. That is something else I have found strange: the tenacity of light at this time of year, which makes up in duration what it lacks in strength. I head towards the rocks.

I've never been right down on to the shore, which is mostly the haunt of poor wretches looking for something they can eat or sell, as well as a few of the more adventurous lovers seeking shelter from prying eyes. The wind races through the grasses and sends the waves crashing most ominously towards my feet. But winter's sting is gone from it and I soon wish I'd left my cloak behind.

Down here, where the sea constantly harries the land, Berwick disappears from view altogether. I try to clear my mind of the stink and worry of it, to send my mind out like a seabird skimming my way through another man's thoughts. If it is possible to negotiate a path between the sea and the land towards the great mouth of the Tweed, then it would surely make sense for the killer to have done so, for the wharves next to the Watergate bustle with people and loud business as soon as the gates have been pushed open. A man could easily pass unremarked, though I should perhaps question those on duty down there to see if any of them remember a man with a large-brimmed hat and dark clothing.

I clamber unsteadily across a slanting rock pavement and stand for a moment, watching the waves and trying to stop myself from feeling as if I'm being tossed like a mouse in a cat's mouth. It has suddenly jumped into my mind that I should look to see if the tide is going in or out. I decide it is going out, which brings me great relief, for it fills me with utter dread to think I might be caught in such a pitiless place with no way of escape. I think of my poor brother, Peter, who entered the calmest of rivers to cool off on a summer's day but was quickly lost in an ungovernable eddy.

I carry on and soon find myself on wet sand, sinking with each step. There is only a narrow strip as yet, so that I must walk very near to the rocks, where my eye is caught by a dark circle in a marooned patch of sand. I scramble towards it, getting down on my haunches and prodding at the blackened material. Since it's above the line of the tide, it's not as moist and muddy as further down and I can see clearly it is the remains of a fire. In the very middle of it are the threadbare remains of the brim of a black hat, which I pick up with my dagger.

I feel sick. Such an ancient woebegone pile of rags can give me nothing with which to find the murderer. But I suddenly see the solid outline of him beneath the hat, the firmness of his flesh and the beating of his black heart, where before he was an evil spectre who existed mostly in my mind rather than on our streets. I shudder to think that his was the last face poor Alice gazed upon on this Earth, offering her no pity for her youth and beauty.

I look up and see Tom Crory ahead of me, peering into a pool, digging at it with a stick. He pulls something out and pops it into his mouth, white hair lying flat across his head. I wonder whether to call to him or wait till I'm nearer. But then he looks up at me, eyes like narrow slits set within rough stonework. He moves faster than I thought he would, straightening up and dashing from rock to rock and over the shifting sand far more nimbly than I. He would have left me far behind but slips on loose stones and comes down heavily on his side.

'I just want to talk to you.' I try to help him up, but he will not stretch out his hand to mine.

'I don' be wanting to talk to *you*,' he wheezes, struggling for air.

'You might be able to help me.'

He sits up slowly and starts to peel away his fetid layers, finally revealing gristly flesh on which small rivers of blood ooze their way. 'Look at tha'.'

'Forgive me. But you had no need to run.' He looks at me as if I were speaking some obscure language, though my English is good enough. 'Did you hear of the mad dog that was put out of the town on May Day?'

He frowns, turning away.

'Did you?' I ask again, for if he didn't, our talk will be of short duration.

He looks back at me and licks his lips. 'Maybe I was hearing.' He speaks like the country folk who sometimes sell their goods at the market, their words sounding gentle whatever their import. But their English is most difficult to understand.

'Good, then . . .'

'I is too hungry to be remembering.'

I look at him. He stretches his toothless mouth out into a blissful smile, and I finally realise what he means. 'Come then, we shall get you fed.'

We walk back. I do not wish to offend him – not until he has told me what he knows – but he does send forth a most awful stink from his person. I try to breathe as little as possible, while he hums a dreary little tune. We pass through the Cowgate, the eyes of the soldiers guarding it fixed upon us, for we make a most unlikely pair.

We walk down to the baker's shop on Soutergate, passers-by staring but moving well out of the way. Tom seems most agitated as we approach, ceasing his humming and casting glances on all sides, as if he is afraid someone will stop him going any further. I buy him two pastries, imagining he will feast quickly and roughly, even as my own belly rumbles at the smell of them. But he nibbles most delicately, pulling the pastry apart, raising it up to look at, sniffing it and finally bringing it to his mouth. I find all this most irritating and wonder if he is doing it deliberately, but at last he smiles again and wipes the crumbs away with the back of his filthy hand.

'What is it you was asking?' He pulls out a piece of bark from inside his clothes and begins to chew on it, sinking down to sit by the side of the road. I have little choice but to squat beside him.

'It was a while ago. On May Day. A man took a mad dog out of the Cowgate before light. You came out a little later, once the gate was open. I thought you might have seen him making his way back into town. The' – I wonder whether to tell him it was really a dead girl the man carried but decide not to confuse matters – 'dog was in a sack.'

His eyes are a faded blue and they cling most intently to my face. He says nothing for a while, chewing vigorously. 'Is that the day the Rydale girl is dying?'

I feel a relief that almost makes me weep. 'Yes. Yes, exactly so. I think it was really her body he was carrying.'

He nods and chews again, while I wrestle with the urge to shake him. 'That were a good day for me,' he says at last. 'I am getting a whole heap o' birds' eggs and making me a grand fire.'

'Yes?'

'I were out all day.'

I nod. That at least is helpful. At least, I hope it is.

'It were warm, I'm thinking.' He nods to himself. 'I am making meself a little nest. After I was eating o' the eggs. You get a big stone, do you see? And crack 'em on it in the fire. Down by the Skerrs. That's where I made the nest. There's a place there, a little circle o' rocks wi' sand inside, at the back. A nice place for a little bit o' rest. An' if folks comes down there, they won't see me.'

I feel my smile begin to ache with the effort of keeping it in place.

He chews some more. 'Young folks was coming down. I be hearing 'em, though they was quiet. But that were a bit later. You would be thinking of before, when I were walking along looking for more eggs, do you see? You always think there'll be more, when you're finding something.'

He starts to cough, drawing himself out before collapsing again with a great rattling and wrenching. I see the blood smeared now across his lips and on the back of his hand, but it does not seem to daunt him. 'I am behind him, do you see? He came from up on the Fields.' He rubs his hands on his knees and begins to rock to and fro. 'I am not wanting him to see me. Even if he is stopping and looking round sometimes and starting to undo the fastenings on his clothes with his devil's hand.'

'Did you know him?'

But Tom Crory waves a hand at me and keeps talking and rocking. 'I am like a cat, do you see? I can be still and creep along, if I am wanting to. He is looking to where I am, but he sees nothing. He is walking fast, but I is creeping fast behind him. And then he is stopping and I am hiding.' He grins most broadly, as if he has told me a most important secret.

'What do you mean?'

He taps his nose. 'He is making a spell, to be changing hisself. In a fire, right there where you was standing, near my nice sleeping place.' He scowls then, but as quickly as the passing of a summer squall he is smiling again. 'I am thinking he is a devil, with his black coat and hat. So, I am sitting where I am and waiting.'

'What do you mean, a spell?'

He frowns. 'Shhh. I is telling it. He is staying there a

while and I cannot see him for all the smoke. And when he leaves, he is not the same man.'

I stare at him. 'That cannot be right.'

He taps his nose again. 'I am telling you what I am seeing. When he is starting the fire, he is looking like a fat crow with a big hat, and the other man is much thinner and wearing all colours like you and no hat.'

I try not to laugh, but at least I know the murderer was wearing more clothes underneath the black ones, though he still did not pass back through the Cowgate. 'And did you see his face? Did you know who he was?'

The chewing gets faster. 'He be too far away. But I is thinking I have seen him before.'

'Do you think . . . Did he look anything like Master Holme, the merchant?'

His eyes narrow. 'Nooooo. Master Holme is much bigger all round.'

I sigh to myself. 'Well, do you think you would know him again if you saw him?'

He moves his head from side to side, as if pondering the question. Then he licks his lips. 'It is hard to be saying.'

'Would you tell me if you do see someone that reminds you of him? I will buy you more pastry if you do. Come to the house with the archway on Marygate and ask for me. I will tell them to let you in.' I wonder how much this will cost me.

He wrinkles his nose, as if this is a most unpleasant prospect, but at last he says firmly: 'I will be looking at everyone and I will be finding him.'

I get up, wondering if I should give him a helping hand. But he rises nimbly enough and ambles away.

My sister Elizabeth writes to me at last. My last missive home berated her for her negligence, but it seems her own must have gone astray, for she chides me in turn for my lack of faith in her. She is cheerful in relating her tidings, such as they are, in her large, determined script, but in truth she has nothing joyful to tell. Our stepfather has chills and a fever, but that is scarcely news. One of the hunting dogs had to be killed for biting the others. I wish she had told me which one, for I grew fond of most of them when I was at home last summer. She is trying her best to be good at needlework but would rather be reading Pliny. Though it was nearing Midsummer when she wrote, they had not heard if there was to be another truce or if the Scots were already preparing to cross the border. We are now passed the longest day but so far there are no rumours here about the Scots. Please God it stays that way.

Sir John sends for me. Ralph Holme and the burgesses now have the keeping of Berwick, but Wysham still has charge of the garrison and old habits seem to serve as threadbare reassurance for lack of anything else here. Even Master Weston feels the winds of change. Sir John tells me our chamberlain recently paid him a visit and was

most displeased. It seems he has been sent for by the
Chamberlain of England, a much more important man,
to answer certain accusations, which surely means that
Sir Edmund has succeeded in making his case. I have
become adept at keeping out of Master Weston's way,
turning quickly if I should see him in the street. But now
I am pleased I will soon not have to worry, though
Wysham seems wearied by it. 'You have good reason to
feel clever,' he says without meeting my eye. 'But I fear
it will do more to upset the garrison than bring us
anything better.'

A fiery arrow pierces my heart at the wrong he does
me, for I only revealed another's evil conduct and he was
pleased with me at the time. 'Perhaps when the king
comes . . .'

He looks at me then and barks out a short laugh. 'You
haven't heard? The muster's been moved till the morrow
of St Laurence. And before July is out, it will be moved
again, as sure as the nose on my face.'

I go home smarting from his words, left bereft that
prophecies of the king's negligence have come true. But
I will not let any of it distract me from the important
work I do. Sitting with pen and inks at the great table in
the hall, I add to my paltry tally of deeds connected to
Alice's murder. I do know so much more than we did on
the day she was found, when it seemed she would be just
another unavenged death in this interminable war.
At least now I have some hope that justice will be done,
even if I alone must carry the burden of bringing it about.

Pretty Edith comes out of the kitchen carrying a bowl

and a cloth. 'Would you mind, sir, if I worked here?'
She keeps her distance, eyes lowered.

'I am happy to move, if you need me to.'

She looks up, startled. 'Oh, no, please don't stir
yourself.'

'I would not want to get in your way.'

She smiles ever so slightly and sets her bowl down at
the other end of the table. Pushing up the sleeves of her
gown, she picks up a handful of fat and starts rubbing it
vigorously into the wood with the cloth. From time to
time she stops to stand fully upright, kneading her hands
into her back. Her face is flushed, lips full and bright. She
catches me looking at her and frowns, returning to her
scrubbing with even greater vigour.

I go back to my own labours but am soon disturbed by
the clatter of the bowl as it is set spinning. Looking up,
I see her running back towards the kitchen, face pale. I
wonder what ails her, but she does not return, so I keep
writing.

It is Mark, the cook, who comes out, wiping his hands
down his apron. He carries a cup of something and stands
before the fire in the middle of the hall, sipping delicately
and contemplating the flames. I'm not sure he's seen me
and wonder if I should cough or make some other noise.
But we are doing each other no harm.

When he turns, he does see me, stopping in surprise.

I smile and nod. 'Is Edith sick?'

He contemplates me for a long moment. 'Aye, you
could say that, sir. But on the other hand, no she isn't.'

'What on earth do you mean?'

'You don't know much about women, do you, sir?'

'Stop speaking in riddles and tell me what's wrong with her.'

He rubs his nose. 'Do you know how many girls in Berwick have been in the same condition as Edith, thanks to you *gentlemen*? How many even in my own kitchen I've had spewing up their guts every five minutes, because you can't keep your cocks to yourselves?'

And, finally, I understand and remember. 'You must not blame me for that!'

He snorts. 'Oh no! I can't blame anyone. But I don't see anyone giving me back the time that's wasted.'

'Perhaps he will . . . they will . . .'

'Oh, yes. And wouldn't that be a happy ending! She'd be more than glad never to see his face again, not bind herself to him for the rest of her life.' He jerks a head up towards the ceiling and our room. 'He wouldn't have her anyway.'

I don't know what to say. I want to ask his forgiveness, but that would sound inadequate. And he's right, of course. Will was quite happy to take his pleasure with her but there could be no question of marriage, even if he wished it. Which I very much doubt he does. By the time I've thought all this and considered the fate of the innocent child and wondered what would become of it and Edith, the cook has disappeared. But such thoughts will not make a jot of difference to either of them, for what's done is done.

Chapter 8

I join the watch after Vespers with a skip in my step, though the longer I think about it, the more frustrated I become. Unless Tom can point his crooked old finger at the man he saw, all I have is the shape of this tale and nothing to draw it out in any detail. I can't help fearing he will not even remember we have spoken, but, then again, he did recall very clearly what happened on May Day after all this time. And he does like pastry very much.

Percival comes bounding up to me, pushing his head into my hand as his master returns from a perambulation of the walls. Sir Anthony leans on his lance. 'I doubt all that thinking is good for you.'

'You may be right, sir. But I can't stop now.'

He grunts. 'I suppose it keeps you out of mischief.' He turns and stares out to sea, the sky softening in the evening light.

I go to stand next to him. 'Are you sure you're not doing some thinking yourself, sir?'

He smiles gently, still staring ahead. 'There's not much else to do, now, is there?'

We stand together for a while until I begin to wonder if he, being a northerner, has heard news from outside. 'Is there any word from the king?'

His chin rises slightly as his lips tighten. 'Only that he desires no one in the north to gather together for any reason. An "unlawful assembly", he calls it. It's not what I'd call it. It's a terrible thing, when a king begins to fear his own people.'

Only a few months ago, I would not have understood his meaning. And while I imagine King Edward has every right to stop armed men from gathering if he thinks they mean harm, I see too that the people of the north need someone to protect them. I used to find it comforting to think of our king. Ever since I was a child, I listened to the monks praying for his well-being and we schoolboys thought of him with awe, just as we thought of Jesus and the saints. Now he is more often spoken of with irritation or reproach, as if something is broken, though we surely all hope it can be fixed, that he will listen to wise counsellors instead of greedy, foolish ones.

Sir Anthony spits over the wall.

'But the muster was only moved until August.'

He turns to me then. 'I tell you what, Ben, if the king comes north, I'll lay on a feast that'll fill you fuller than an abbot.'

Sir Anthony hasn't much money, so he must be very sure. We stare out to sea again.

'Should I take a turn along the walls, sir?'

He nods and I set off. But I have only reached the first brattice when I hear him shout. I run back. He grabs me by the shoulder and points towards the east. 'What do you see?'

The sun is far away behind us on the western horizon, so that the five ships creeping south are etched in gold. 'Who is it?' I whisper, sure it is an invasion.

Sir Anthony stares intently. 'I think those are Arundel's ships,' he says at last. 'Do you see the red banners flying from the masts?'

The fear running from my jaw to my toes abates.

'Go and tell Ralph Holme.'

I run as fast as I can, wishing I was going in any other direction. I have not spoken with Master Holme since I found Alice's overshoes in his warehouse. I have *seen* him, of course, for he is always coming and going in a grand state now that he has charge of the town – and I cannot spend my time hiding from all those I seem to have offended. Not that he has any inclination to speak to me, in any case.

It is late but still light, so I go to look for him at his home in the Western Lane. He sits at table with his wife and children. For a moment, as I'm ushered in, I see him sitting with the littlest one, a curly-headed boy, upon his knee. But he immediately sends them all away until it is just the two of us. I stand opposite him, the table between us.

'I hope you have not come with more ill-founded accusations.' He scrapes at his fingernails and twists his rings, as if sitting still was a punishment and not an indulgence.

'What I have been sent to tell you I have seen with my own eyes. Arundel's ships are returned.'

He springs to his feet then, shouting for all and sundry so that the hall is suddenly as full of activity as the quayside. One of his servants is despatched to bring the masters and constables of any ships coming into the harbour to him, whether they will it or no. I am loath to go back on watch without hearing what news is brought, for I have heard that, between the five ships, they carried over 1,500 men. Though Arundel was not with them, they must surely have been able to inflict some damage on the Scots in all this time. But I must return to the walls, my leaving entirely unremarked by Master Holme.

We must wait until the relief watch arrives a little after Compline, but the news they bring is enough to depress the spirits entirely. The ships put into land in a place they call Fife, which stands on a great river. They spread out across the country, plundering wherever they could, and the Earl and the Sheriff of Fife could do nothing to stop them, retreating even though they had a large force. But then a barbarous bishop with no more than a hundred horsemen rode against them, giving heart to the rest. They chased our men back to their ships, coming at them with sharp spears and killing many, while others drowned. Only one Englishman showed the courage expected of him, seizing a Scotsman who was chasing him and throwing him onto his back before dragging him to one of the little boats they used to get ashore. But that was the only show of strength and, in truth, they were easily driven off.

Sir Anthony strides away without a word, Percival ahead of him, while I walk slowly back to Marygate. I tell myself we should not have expected much from five ships full of sailors who, though armed, were unlikely to show the skill and courage needed to face a determined enemy. All the same, I do wonder if the Earl of Arundel will ever inflict enough damage on the Scots so that those of us behind Berwick's walls can sleep more soundly and the people of the countryside beyond might not fear the coming of those brutes.

But in truth it is already too late. Bruce's men have nothing to fear from us, pouring into the western counties of northern England as if they were in their own country. Even when they return, laden with money or beasts, we cannot seem to stop them.

The next day, the townsfolk have again taken to murmuring together in low voices, clumped at the well or the market cross or even in doorways. The soldiers of the garrison do the same, with much to say now they can condemn the cowardice and incompetence of the sailors, who quickly retreated to their ships last night. They sail on towards England soon after Sext and few regret their going, for they have done nothing to help us. Unless our prayers are answered and King Edward really does march north with a proper army, all we can do now is watch for the plumes of smoke that mark the progress of a Scottish raiding party galloping unchallenged down the valleys of Northumberland.

Tom Crory leaps out of the shadows in the yard at Marygate and stands shifting his weight endlessly from one foot to the other. Stephen is about to chase him away, but I put a hand on Tom's shoulder and walk with him towards the stables. I find I am pleased to see him, if not to smell him.

'I is not forgetting.' He taps the side of his nose.

My agitation withers, for I thought for a moment he had seen the man who killed Alice. But at least he is looking. I nod and smile, wondering if it would offend him if I turned away. But, having delivered his fruitless message, he trots back out of the yard and is gone.

Sir Anthony comes out of the stables. He casts an eye over the departing Tom. 'Who on God's earth was that?'

'My best witness. He saw the man who killed Alice, but only from a distance.'

'And you trust him? I mean, you trust what he tells you is true, that he wasn't imagining it?'

I do not hesitate. 'Not everything he says makes sense, at least not to me. But I do believe he saw the murderer change his clothes and burn the bloodied ones down on the beach.'

'And what will you do now?'

'I'm hoping Tom will find me the murderer – he has promised to look.'

'I admire your faith in a man like that. I would be whipping him outside the walls and locking the gates. Though I must say, your way seems to be the better one, if it's answers you're looking for.' He pauses for a moment, looking out somewhere beyond the walls of the yard. 'Have you heard from Edmund?'

'He said before he left he was damned if he was going to pay another clerk to write a message when he was already paying two of his own. So, I'm not expecting anything. I suppose he should be on his way back by now.'

He smiles and nods. 'He did manage to write to Sir John, for which we give grateful thanks. And Sir John gave it to me, since he is leaving the day after tomorrow. The message came yesterday.'

I feel hot all over. 'What did it say?'

'That he has agreed to stay till Christmas and should be back here soon enough.'

The relief floods through me like a warm wind. If he had decided to leave, I don't know what I would have done. I cannot imagine telling Lucy I was going without finishing what she asked me to do – *me* out of everyone here. And in truth I cannot imagine not knowing. It is the why of it that most perplexes me. Such a terrible, fiendish thing.

'I suppose we must all make the best of it.' Sir Anthony is in a sombre mood, his hand constantly searching for his dog's head.

It occurs to me he is none too happy about staying, which surprises me. But then, it is foolish to imagine knights have no opinion about the tasks allotted to them. Indeed, I have learned they can criticise and complain as long and loudly as any foot soldier. But I thought Sir Anthony indifferent to where he was and what he did.

Perhaps he is just better than most at keeping his thoughts to himself. One thing we can be sure of is that Sir Edmund will not be so discreet. But he knows the burgesses have taken over responsibility for the garrison, despite his best efforts to stop that happening. Yet he has agreed to stay.

And I think, too, that Berwick is no longer as fearful and desolate a place as it was when we first came. I know many of the inhabitants, both in the garrison and the town. One or two even smile at me. And I have something important to finish. I remember I still have Dame Eleanor's steward to question. He is a difficult man to find with a moment to spare. But his account might also bring light into this obscure, sorry business, for if he was out and about inside the walls during that dreadful night, who knows what he saw? Though I suppose the drink might have addled his brain such that he remembers little and imagines much.

Edward moves around the town so restlessly I soon feel giddy pursuing him. Dame Eleanor sends me to the wharves; a sailor there says if I want to find him I must go to the Rydale warehouse in Hidegate; and there a curly-haired boy tells me he's in the tavern on the corner of Fishergate.

I open the tavern door and stare into the gloom, the

sooty beams sitting only just above my head. A great babbling hits me, along with a fetid heat, and I feel my eyes watering. I slip inside and along the wall, a little light seeping through a tiny window. And then I see him, sitting with a man I saw first at Master Weston's house, when I sang an eternity ago. I think his name is either Walter or William Roxburgh and he is a well-respected burgess in the town, even though he's a Scot. Young enough to have only a splash of grey at his temples, he is in the habit of wearing bright colours that do not always sit easily together. But that does serve to pull the eye away from his plain, fleshy features.

They sit on stools in a dark corner, heads bent close together, but Edward soon glances around, finds me looking at him and blinks quickly a few times. Then he smiles.

I push my way towards them as he leaps to his feet, a frown replacing the smile. 'Has something happened? Eleanor. Is she . . . ?

I wave a hand. 'Nothing's happened, so far as I know. I just want to speak with you. About Alice. In case you have something to add. I can meet you another time, if it's more convenient.' I smile at his companion.

But Edward has already found another stool and brought it next to theirs. 'No, no. If you wish to speak about that terrible night, you have chosen well. I was with William here for much of it. Do you wish some ale? It would be my pleasure.'

The other man rises too, brows furrowed. 'I will leave you in peace.'

But Edward lays a hand on his shoulder. 'Not at all. We don't want Benedict having to go searching for you to verify my story, now, do we? He has better things to do.'

I feel a little overwhelmed by the generosity of his speech, the warmth of his welcome, for we have scarcely exchanged more than a few words until now. 'I do not wish to trouble you for long.'

'If we are to talk about such weighty matters, you will need some sustenance.' With that, he disentangles long legs from around his stool and slips through the throng. Moments later he pushes a jug into my hand. 'I must warn you now – and I am most heartily ashamed of it – I have little memory of that night.'

I nod, having expected as much. 'But you went to Lamberton in the afternoon, didn't you?'

'Yes, at Dame Eleanor's insistence.'

'You were not afraid?'

He breathes a little more deeply. 'I would not wish to be caught. But I do my best.'

'Can you remember when you returned?'

He kneads a hand into his shoulder. 'That's not difficult. It was a most vexing afternoon, even before . . .' He looks straight into my eyes. 'Forgive me, I did not mean to compare my own troubles . . .'

'I'm sure you meant no harm. Pray, continue.'

'As soon as I started back from Lamberton, I could tell the pin on one of the cartwheels was loose. I had a look and thought it would probably hold if I went slowly, though not so slowly the town gates would close before

I reached them. But it got worse and worse and I made a most dreadful noise coming in. My bones got a good rattling too.'

I doubt those on duty on the Waleysgate that afternoon will have forgotten him, even after all this time. 'So, you came back just before the gates closed. And you saw nothing of Alice or anyone else?'

'Not a soul.'

'And what did you do then?'

'I drove the cart down to the wright's yard in Ravensdowne. He was just finishing for the day, so he told me to leave it there and he'd look at it in the morning. I took the meat up to our kitchen and went out again.'

'Did anyone see you?'

He smiles. 'No, but how else could the meat have got there?'

True enough. 'And then you went to Master Roxburgh's?'

'That's right. And stayed there far too long.' He lifts his mug and drinks deep.

'Was it just the two of you?' I look at William Roxburgh, whose eyes flutter towards Edward and back to me.

William wipes his mouth with the back of his hand. 'No. There were a few of us, for a while at least.'

'Can you give me their names?'

'Em, John Pontefract and Roger Bishop.'

Two more burgesses. It is good company Edward keeps, even if they don't know how to restrain themselves. I take a sip of my own beer.

William leans forward then, puts a hand on my sleeve. 'We had business to discuss. Ralph is eager to ensure there's no fault on our part with supplies.' He sits back again. 'And then, with it being May Day . . .' He shrugs. 'John and Roger left at' – he turns to Edward – 'when would you say?'

Edward raises his eyes heavenwards. 'You ask an impossible question, William.' He looks at me, always with a half-smile suggesting his remorse. 'But I'm sure they will be able to tell you, even if we cannot.'

'And you two stayed together. I realise you probably won't know how long.'

Edward nods. 'We may have fallen asleep. I'm sure I did.'

'I did too.' William says it quickly.

'And then I went home.' Edward lowers his head, puts a hand to his brow. 'And to think, all that time . . . Poor Alice. Only a few streets away.'

I know there's little point in asking, but I do it anyway. 'You saw nothing at all? Not even when you were walking home?'

He sighs deeply, stares at the feet of those standing a little in front of us and shakes his head finally. 'Not that I can recollect. I dearly wish I could. I have asked myself that question a thousand times, but it is always the same.' He looks at me, face taut. 'I am not in the habit of drinking wine.' William Roxburgh nods vigorously. 'I can only think the Devil was abroad that night.'

I feel the pain in his words even as I want to throw my beer over him for being of so little use to me. But there is nothing to be done now. I take one last sip and thank them both, leaving the tavern none the wiser than when I went in.

Stephen puts his head round the door of our chamber and looks at me. 'There's a girl downstairs asking for you.'

Will gives a loud whistle. 'Are you sure "she" is not a "he"? We all know cathedral boys prefer a nice fat cock to a bit of juicy cunt.' He's still most annoyed at me for not telling him anything about the girl I supposedly met on the beach. I have not the strength to put together some fabulous tale and then remember it myself – and anyway, he would be sure to ask me constantly to point her out or take him to spy on her.

I move quickly towards Stephen. 'Do you know who she is?'

'No idea. But she looks as if she'll run away if you don't hurry.'

I find her just inside the hall, picking her teeth with her fingers. She is a pasty little thing with a crooked mouth, but I have seen her before. Lucy's maid, Mary. I feel my heart quicken at the thought of Lucy wanting to see me, though my findings are meagre, unless you count Tom Crory, which I certainly do, up to a point. Before I can say anything, Mary asks my name. When I give it, she bobs her head, tells me to meet her 'little lady' in the friary this afternoon and disappears through the kitchen and away.

When I get there, Lucy is very agitated, hobbling about from one pillar to another and I feel queasy watching her. 'Pray, sit,' I beg her at last.

'My back pains me today.'

'Forgive me, I didn't think.'

'Why should you?' But she lowers herself slowly to the ground beside me, a faint beading of sweat glistening on her brow. I do not speak while she adjusts her breath, opens her eyes. 'I thought you might have something to distract me. What news?'

I had not expected her to approve of Tom Crory, and I was right to do so.

'What does a man like that know of my sister?'

'We must give him time and we might have a name. I am certain he saw the murderer going back towards Berwick along the shore.'

'That sounds most unlikely.'

'It's all we've got. I did speak with Edward.'

'Did you? What did he have to say for himself?' She sniffs. 'I know he was quite incapable of standing or talking when he came home. I've never seen him in such a condition and no help to us at all.'

'Yes, he told me. He'd been with William Roxburgh.' She nods, as if that was not at all unexpected. 'And the cart needed to be fixed, which was why he was late coming back from Lamberton.'

She nods at that too, chewing the end of her hair. 'We certainly didn't see him when we returned from the

Fields. And he didn't see Alice?'

'No, not when he drove in and not later, when he came back to your house. But in truth I doubt he would've noticed the Second Coming that night.'

'Fool.' She whispers it, seemingly lost in thought. 'I think . . .' She glances at me, twists her mouth.

'What?'

She puts her hand out, lightly touching my thigh. 'Did I tell you before that I'm certain Mother wanted Alice to marry him, but I cannot understand why.'

I feel strangely afflicted, a great weakening taking hold so that I dare not speak, for fear she will see what just passed through me. 'Yes.' It comes out high-pitched, like a child.

She looks up at me, eyes darting, takes her hand away.

I feel my voice return. 'What a strange thing it would have been for him to marry Alice if he and your mother are . . .' I try to swallow my words but it's too late. I had never intended to mention what might only be idle talk, about Dame Eleanor and her steward, though plenty take it as gospel.

Her eyebrows are thrown up almost into her hair.

'Pray, forgive me. I did not mean . . .'

'I have often wondered if she was taking comfort there – my father has been dead these past nine years and I would not begrudge her what is only natural.'

'But sinful, surely?'

She gives me a long look through shuttered eyelashes. 'If you must. There is no denying she defers to him.'

'He certainly seems most attentive. That is surely

worthy of praise, even if . . . I would not wish to excuse
. . .'

We both find the flagstones of considerable interest for
several moments, but I soon look up to steal a glance at
her. I never imagined speaking of such matters with a girl.
And yet she seems the more worldly wise. A shaft of light
from an upper window suddenly slices across her face, and
I think of how much I don't know about what she thinks
and feels. 'It's curious, isn't it, that you and Alice should
look so different? You so dark and she so fair.'

'I am like my father and she like our mother. As for
her father, I never heard a word about what he looked like.'

I hear a door gently open somewhere far away in my
mind, though I cannot imagine this revelation amounts
to much more than the kind of tattle Will enjoys so
much. 'Alice was your half-sister?'

She nods. 'Are you surprised?'

'I suppose not, now you say it. So was your mother
married to another merchant in Berwick?'

'Oh no. It was somewhere far away in Scotland.
Stirling, it's called, where our king lost the great battle.
She fled here a long time ago when they killed her first
husband. She was already carrying Alice.'

'Edward's Scottish too, isn't he?'

She nods. 'He stood against Bruce like all the other
Scots here and had to leave his home. I think he was
in prison.'

'They are brutes, the Scots.'

'That they are. Though it seems they're not brutes
enough to murder my sister.' This time her smile is small

and taut. 'That will most likely be someone we know.'
She starts to pull herself up on the pillar. I watch her, the
harsh set of her jaw and the little piece of skin on her neck
that sometimes jumps to its own beat. She starts across
the stone floor, and I think she will not say goodbye. But
then she turns a little, smiling softly to herself, and holds
up her hand, curling her fingers towards me.

I ache from my neck to my toes, for Sir Anthony insists
we all ride together every morning to be sure we can turn
safely on our horses and use our weapons. We must also
practise with sword and lance on the ground beside the
foot soldiers, even those who have just been on watch –
for, as he says, the Scots will not care if we've been up all
the night. And meanwhile, rumours come and go: that
Bruce and his band of thieves are coming; that they have
already entered England; that they are only pretending to
invade but are really intent on approaching our walls by
stealth. And that the king will not come north this year.

The Earl of Arundel is still somewhere on the border,
but few believe he has managed to protect it well. I doubt
it is truly his fault, for it seems largely a question of
money. Once, so I've heard, the nobles of the north
eagerly played their part in the wars with Scotland, both
in our king's time and that of his father. They served in
armies and garrisons, paid their taxes and did so willingly,

believing these wars were just – and that there was land and money to be made in them for gallant Englishmen. But now they must give what little they have to Bruce and the brutes that ride in his name, even as harvest after harvest fails. In truth, I now understand why they wonder what our king is for, other than taking what little is left.

Sir John is long gone and the burgesses asked Sir Anthony to be our captain. That, at least, is one decision no one condemns. He is a good man to lead us, for he knows exactly what he wants and makes it clear to us when and how he wants it. But he takes a risk gathering us together so regularly, for it gives ample opportunity for comparing grievances and bringing them out into the open like a beggar's dirty washing. The foot soldiers complain they are treated no better than dogs and must work harder for even less money. The men-at-arms tell them to hold their tongues, but flock together to tell the same story.

It does not help that a new official has arrived. He is called the Chancellor of Scotland – which is a very important title for a man whose writ runs no further than our walls – and his name is James Broughton. His main task is to oversee how the 3,000 marks the king is paying the burgesses to look after the town are spent. That, in itself, is not likely to endear him to those of us who toil on Berwick's walls, but it certainly does not help that he is an unkind man lacking in fellow feeling who has already decided we are all thieves intent on robbing the king. Even Ralph Holme finds him overly zealous, though he too is eager to make every penny stretch as far as it can. I wonder what it will be like over the winter, when everything costs more and fuel eats up a man's pay quicker than a crow on a newly seeded field.

And I cannot help wondering, too, what has happened to the chamberlain, now that this James Broughton has taken over his duties as paymaster. I imagine this means Master Weston isn't coming back. I wish Sir Edmund would return so I could know how that curious affair ended. Though much has happened since I extracted the documents from the pile on the chamberlain's desk, I feel accountable. It weighs on my conscience, even though it was the right thing to do. In truth, I am most curious.

I walk swiftly down Soutergate in the teeth of a sharp easterly breeze, the smoke from every house spinning and dancing as if hastening on some lively adventure. I hope to find Stephen at home so we might practise the sword, for I am become much more skilled and don't wish to lose that which has been purchased with so much sweat and anxiety. I reach the corner with Marygate and am just turning into it when I almost bump into a man coming the other way, lost in his own thoughts. I put an arm out to steady us both and see it is William Roxburgh.

His head jerks up, eyes wide. 'Forgive me! Ah, it's you.'

I cannot tell if he's pleased or not.

But then he smiles, and his eyes lighten. 'We are well met, Benedict. I have wanted to speak with you, for fear I was somewhat uncivil that last time. I had much on my mind.'

'I'm sorry to hear it, but you need not worry on my account.'

'Good. These are difficult times we live in, but we can still be pleasant to each other.'

He puts a clammy hand on mine and I struggle with the urge to draw away.

'Ah, William, there you are!' Edward lopes towards us from Hide Hill. I am struck by how taut and muscular his body is beneath the clinging folds of his handsome blue tunic and how gracefully he moves. He is quite unlike William and so many of the other burgesses, whose flesh seems to throw off youth's firm restraint almost as soon as their first shipload sails. I almost neglected to ask those on the Cowgate about his story of a broken cart, since it was not obvious what difference it would make. But on second thoughts I decided I should not trust anyone's story and it was easily enough confirmed.

William turns quickly towards him, an anxious smile pushed on to his face. 'I was just coming. I wanted to ask Benedict here . . .' He turns back to me, wipes his brow. 'My older boy is . . . My youngest is still with me and is not so very old . . . We had a difficulty before. Do you think he's safe? From this . . . this monster?'

I wonder what I can tell him.

Edward nods vigorously. 'Good question. Have you nothing from the poor man who . . . I forget his name?'

'Tom Crory. No, but I do expect him to come to me any day now.'

Edward nods slowly. 'There is hope he will remember the man he saw?'

I don't want that hope to be false, but there's no doubt I have faith it will happen. 'It is not certain. But he's sure he's seen the man, though he cannot yet put a name to him.'

Edward breathes deeply. 'You do not know how marvellous your news is. My mistress cannot sleep. I fear she will lose her mind. Who can say how the murder of a child will play out in the woman who gave her life?'

I suddenly think of Edith in our kitchens. As the child quickens inside her, will she welcome that life, or will she abhor it because it was conceived in violence? 'I had hoped that with time your mistress would recover.'

He sighs, runs a hand through his hair. 'We all hope for that, but I do doubt it.'

William nods. 'We are grateful, Benedict, very grateful.' He gives me a quick smile and trots away.

Edward sighs again. 'I will pray you hear soon.' He turns too.

'Is it true you were going to marry Alice?' It is a stab in the dark, but worth asking.

He turns his face slowly back to me then, eyes leaden grey. 'If you know that, then you will understand the burden I have carried. But it is as nothing compared to her mother, and I do not speak of it.'

It's true, then, what Lucy thought. 'Did' – I feel I must pick my way through a morass – 'Did Alice wish to marry you?'

He gently strokes his chin. 'No, I don't think she did. Indeed, if I were honest, I would say she was most displeased with the notion. But her mother has come to trust me, and she thought it would serve the family well to keep matters as they are. Perhaps it was a mistake. We will never know.'

There is much sense in what he says, in what ailed Alice. She had gotten used to the notion she was to marry Sir John, then suddenly she was not. Perhaps she wouldn't even be mistress of her own house when she was expecting to become lady of the manor far away from here, surely a pleasant prospect in itself. It was probably foolish of her to seek to discuss the matter with Sir John that last afternoon, but if he was willing to attempt to change Dame Eleanor's mind, no doubt it was worth the trial. 'Pray forgive me for speaking of such sad things. May I ask how long you have served the Rydales?'

He looks up at the dark folds in the sky. 'A year and a half, is all. I have been in Berwick some two years, but I worked for Master Holme first. Dame Eleanor was kind enough to take me away from that.' He gives a little smile and I smile back.

'And you were in Scotland before then?'

The smile disappears. 'Yes.'

'Do you not miss your home?'

'My home is here. I want nothing to do with them. It is a very great pity our king did not kill that murderer at Bannockburn. Then I would still have everything.' He lifts his shoulders, eyes black as coals, his mouth a thin, hard line.

'Did you know Dame Eleanor in Scotland?'

His rubs a knuckle with the palm of the other hand. 'Why do you say that?'

'You speak in a similar way.'

He smiles, once more amused with all he sees and hears. 'Because we are Scots?'

I shrug.

'No, I didn't know her before I came here. But I have good reason to be grateful to her. And if you are successful in your quest, I will be grateful to you too.'

I nod and we part with more smiles. It has been pleasant, speaking with him, and I feel somewhat reassured there was an honest reason for Alice's ill humour. And that Edward does not imagine his reputation is worth so much to conceal it.

Chapter 9

I come out of our courtyard into Marygate and take a few great gulps of air before walking along the road towards Soutergate. Sir Anthony has arranged for some wrestling games to keep us occupied after Sext. I am a little early and sit looking over the Magdalene Fields, trying to find the skylarks trilling high above me. I am gladdened to see the flowers nestling in marshy corners or dry banks. They are mostly yellow and useful – flesh-and-blood, sticklewort, nasturtium – as if reflecting the sun and its gentle healing. Its rays are quite warm this afternoon, though the wind blows strong and unfriendly.

I do not mind such games as much as I used to, for I am become strong with all the practice. At the same time, I am much thinner than when I first came to Berwick, my ribs lying taut against my skin. But, for all that I am always hungry, I am much more agile, my mind slipping quickly from one possibility to another and my body eager to follow. Will and Stephen stand by my side without thinking now.

I see a few men trickling out of the Cowgate. They seem to be conversing vehemently about something, hands moving and heads nodding hard.

Will comes running up. 'You're on first.'

'Who am I fighting?'

'Alwin.' He winks, for he does not think much of the Northumbrians. When I lose my first bout, he slaps me on the back and tells me Alwin tricked me with a forbidden move that no one else saw, though I know he did not. But I should not fail again. In our second bout, Alwin and I have scarcely stepped back into the ring before I fell him by pretending to come at him from the left, only to leap at him from the right.

I hear the cheering and clapping and turn to smile at Will. And there, striding towards us, is Sir Edmund. 'By Satan's anus, what have you done with my squire?' He has a broad grin slung across his face.

It is good to see him, though I wonder what news he brings from the south. Everyone stops what they're doing to crowd round, for all know he went to the king on our behalf and there is much he might tell us.

Sir Anthony steps forward to give Sir Edmund a kiss on both cheeks. 'Welcome back. How was your journey?'

'Long and tedious.'

'And London, sir?' Will has slipped to Sir Edmund's side.

'Full of arseholes. But the king's council liked my words and Ben's writings.' He looks at me and smiles before turning his gaze on everyone in turn, holding us captive. 'So, they have sent for the chamberlain's big book and the chamberlain.'

I imagine he thinks we are astonished and pleased, but that we already knew. I am now consumed by a vast curiosity I thought I had put aside. 'Do you think . . . will the king . . .'

'Speak up, man!' Sir Edmund's hand twitches as if he might strike me, but for once he resists.

'Do you think the king will punish Master Weston?' I am remembering Sir John Wysham's words, the ones I did not thank him for at the time and do not wish to believe now, that it will make not a jot of difference to us in the end. But I fear Sir John was right. Rumours are spreading like flies through the garrison about what the burgesses are planning. They have already cut our pay but it's said they will not replace all of those who leave, even though there are few of us as it is. I hear the swords rattling, though everyone knows all we can do is leave too. But few can afford to.

Sir Edmund glowers at me and I think he does not know all this. I tell myself to put all thoughts of Master Weston away, for it will only depress the spirits, that we still suffer even as his sins are revealed. We all sink down into the grass, enjoying the sunshine out of the wind. Sir Edmund is far from finished recounting his adventures in London, though, so far as I can tell, he is spinning a glittering web out of them rather than telling us anything of much import. And yet, there is no doubt the king's council took him seriously and perhaps there is hope yet that we will not be so neglected now that they understand what we must contend with.

At last, we start back through the gates. Sir Edmund

puts a hand on my shoulder. 'Thomas is dead, the wretch. You can be my clerk for now, as well as my squire. I'll give you an extra two pence a day.'

'Thank you, sir.' It's hardly a chore. 'I'm still looking into Alice Rydale's murder. I'm hoping to find the man who did it very soon.'

'You won't have time for that. The maid's dead and buried, isn't she? You don't need to go picking over her bones.'

'But the . . .'

'So, is your sword as good as your wrestling these days? And what about the Scots? Is there any news? They want Berwick, that's the long and the short of it, so we'll need to be ready.' He stretches, shoulders clicking. 'I brought us some lamb for a feast.'

I try to smile, but my heart aches at the thought of giving up on my investigations. What will I tell Lucy? I find I can scarcely breathe for thinking about it.

'What the devil's the matter with you?' Sir Edmund's pleasant mood is fast disappearing.

'Nothing, sir.' I force a smile. 'It's the lamb. I am quite overcome by the thought of it.'

He grins then, punching me on the shoulder with a blow that is meant to be gentle but leaves my eyes watering.

I pray Tom Crory will come right away with the name – or at least a description – of the man who killed Alice. And then, if it must be over, I will have done what I set out to do. But if he doesn't, the town will be left uneasy, knowing that danger still lurks within our walls. And I will be blamed for not fulfilling my promise.

I am set to cleaning and mending Sir Edmund's armour once more, which does not disturb me in the least, for it makes me easy to find. But still Tom Crory does not come and the bells ring for Nones soon enough; even the thought of lamb makes me feel sick, for the weight of my quest presses down upon me. With a heavy heart, I put everything back in the chest and go to the hall. I am to serve Sir Edmund, which sets Will to scowling, but I confess I do it with little grace. Thankfully, he is too busy talking with Sir Anthony to notice.

We sit quietly by the fire, Percival spread out closest to the flames. Our masters are talking about the Scots, Sir Edmund demanding to know what is being done and Sir Anthony eager to find out if the king really might bring an army north. There is talk of spies being looked for in some of the neighbouring villages to provide information, but I cannot divine anything of substance that might relieve the feeling that Berwick is a wounded stag cornered in a high gully.

The sound of knocking alerts us to the arrival of unexpected guests after curfew. The loud voices coming up the stairs suggest, too, that they either have something urgent to impart to us or are too important to wait, and we all stand, our hands tending to rest on the hilts of our daggers. When the door is thrust open, I see that both my surmisings are true, for Ralph Holme leads a trio of burgesses. They march across the room and stand before us, resplendent in their bright gowns. But I can see Ralph is most unhappy, his flat, full-lipped features pinched and forlorn.

'Greetings, sirs.' He takes command as usual. 'Please forgive this intrusion, but I must inform you of a most serious matter.'

Sir Anthony invites them to sit and sends Stephen for wine. I have the feeling Ralph is sending out more than one glance in my direction but cannot imagine why. He flicks his gown beneath him and sinks gracefully into the chair, a bejewelled hand resting on its arm. 'A body has been found. It was caught in one of the fishermen's nets late this afternoon.'

Sir Edmund's leg begins to jig. 'So, a man drowned. What has this to do with us?'

Ralph's fingers caress the arm of his chair. 'He did not drown, or at least I doubt it. The back of his head' – he sighs softly – 'The back of his head was smashed to pieces. Someone must have hit him hard with a rock and thrown him into the sea.'

'Do you know who it was?'

Ralph turns and looks me straight in the eye. I know the answer even before he says it. 'Tom Crory. It was the old man, Tom Crory.'

I don't care if Sir Edmund must search all morning for me, but I rise in the night and go to the friary for Matins.

I stay there for an eternity, singing and saying the liturgy of the hours while kneeling on this side of the rood screen. I wonder what would happen if I went beyond it, to sit in the choir so I would be that much closer to God. But though I can imagine being there, my limbs will not move.

At last, I feel weary and ask the warden, whose name is Adam Newton, to take what little I have managed to save of my pay to say prayers for Tom's soul. He does not want to take it, for the Franciscans make their money by begging. But I see he is moved by my story and it is perhaps Tom's very poverty that persuades him. I know Sir Edmund and the others cannot understand why I should feel such anguish over the death of a man who, for whatever reason, cast himself out of the company of others and, if he were noticed at all, was spat at and called disgusting names.

But I liked him. For all the strangeness he wore inside and out, there was a wisdom to him too. And a kindness. I should have protected him, not been the cause of his terrible death. I can only pray life really had left him before he was cast into the smothering turmoil of the German Ocean.

I stumble back down Soutergate, tears swelling. But they are as much from anger as grief, and I will tear down every stone in this miserable town to find the man who did it. The only good thing to come from Tom's death is that Ralph Holme asked me to redouble my efforts. I confess I wished the words would choke him after the way he treated me in his warehouse. But, at least, since he desires it and Sir Anthony nodded his agreement,

Sir Edmund has little choice but to give me back my freedom to go where I like and ask questions, so long as I fulfil my duties as clerk and squire as well.

But how can I find the murderer without Tom?

I try to put that thought away. I need to speak with the fishermen who found his body. It's true I was speaking to Edward and William Roxburgh about my hope Tom would soon give me the name of the murderer only yesterday. But the truth is, everyone in Berwick knew I had been speaking with him and everyone in Berwick knew he liked to spend his days poking about on the shore or other out-of-the-way places. So, the murderer could easily choose a time and place to despatch him when he was unlikely to be discovered.

Ralph Holme told the fishermen to come to his warehouse at Vespers, so as not to stop them going out in their boats. They are standing awkwardly outside when I arrive, three spindly men with scoured faces and a habit of leaning slightly to one side or other. The bells ring out across town and one of Ralph Holme's servants soon appears to beckon us inside. This the fishermen dislike even more, but, after a brief discussion, they follow him, eyeing me uncertainly as someone they do not know and have little desire to speak with. I smile as reassuringly as I can, but they seem as likely to hasten away as deer. Or fish.

Ralph Holme will not suffer his time to be wasted, though he does make sure they are all provided with ale. He certainly pretends a great disquiet at Tom's untimely death, but I know it is the town's safety that concerns him.

I confess I no longer give much credence to the notion he might have killed Alice. He is so well known in the town that no disguise could truly hide him, and Tom himself did not think he was the man in the black cloak and hat.

The fishermen sit in a circle on the floor and I get down beside them. Ralph tuts and sits in a chair nearby.

'How long do you think he'd been in the water?' I have a list of questions and this is at the top of it, for, now I think of it, I haven't seen Tom for nearly a week.

They rub their noses, take off their caps and put them back on again, but in the end the answer is a simple one. 'Not too long,' they agree, speaking almost together.

'The same day?'

They nod vehemently. 'He was hardly wrinkly at all,' says the smallest one. His teeth gleam white against his reddened skin. 'Nothing is . . . there is nothing being bitten on him.'

I hold my gaze even as my stomach turns.

'The tide, it was coming in strong yesterday,' says the tallest of them.

'We was driven home as if the good Lord Himself is pushing us,' says the smallest, and they all cross themselves.

I wonder why they are telling me this and try to gather my thoughts for a moment. And then I understand. 'So, would it not be foolish of any man trying to get rid of a body to throw it in when the tide was like that, for surely it would just come straight back to shore?'

They all nod gravely. 'But the land people is foolish that way,' says the little one.

'Aye,' says the youngest, 'but even a fool would be quickly knowing his foolishness if he did that. The wind was strong all day, do you remember, for we was working hard to get out even with the tide. A north-easterly, it was, bringing the cold with it. But it was blowing even stronger when the tide was a-turning.' They think about that and finally agree with more nodding.

'When was that?' I had not imagined these simple souls could give me much help, but this will, at least, tell me when the murder did *not* take place, for I think the boy is right that it would be quickly obvious to the murderer that the body was bound to come back to shore on the incoming tide. And this man is not a fool, I'm sure of that.

They take their hats off again, turning them in their hands as they speak together so quickly and strangely that I cannot understand them. Finally, the small one, who seems to be their leader, delivers the result of their deliberations. 'Not long after the sun was at its highest.'

So, between Sext and Nones, but nearer to Nones perhaps.

'And we was far out to sea yesterday.' The boy is eager to be helpful.

'What do you mean?'

The small man answers. 'We're not going so far now, because of the Scots, but we could be seeing a long way and there be no ships, so yesterday we was going further.'

This, too, is useful, but I will need to think through what it might mean. I hear Ralph Holme shift in his chair behind me, but I do not care if he must wait longer. I like the way the fishermen sit quietly with their own thoughts, or none at all, but quite content. And then I think of the question I must ask. 'When did you find him?'

This question does not require any consultation. 'We was nearing the Calot Shad on our way home. Gave us a great fright, so it did.' The little one puts his hat firmly on his head.

'We thought we was catching a tuna or something big,' says the taller one, a mournful look on his face.

I nod. So, they were nearly back into the Tweed, for the Calot Shad is a great sweep of sand at the river's northern entrance. 'And when do you think that was?'

They deliberate again.

And now Ralph Holme intervenes. 'I was brought word of what they'd found just before Vespers. I don't imagine that was long after they tied up. With the wind strong and from the north-east, I would think Tom's body might have drifted some way south.'

They nod and so do I. I think the most I can say is that Tom was killed before noon when the tide turned. Given the amount of time till he was found, he must have been in the water for a good six hours, so he could have been despatched into his watery grave from anywhere along the shore, presuming the murderer did not delay between killing him and getting rid of him. Even so, the time of death would still be the same. I can ask those on duty at the Cowgate yesterday morning for the names of those who might have gone out that way after him. But I already know the murderer was able to pick his way from the shore below the Fields down to the Tweed, so he could just as easily have gone the other way. Grasping the small fisherman by the arm, I thank them all very much. They smile, looking down at their feet, caps in hand once more, before quickly shuffling out of the door.

I walk back to Marygate pondering all the tangled and bloody threads that stretch from Alice to Tom to me, and on into the darkness where a man waits, dagger in hand.

Chapter 10

Miles Tavisham, Sir Anthony's clerk, keeps the watch book now, so it's an easy matter for me to find out who stood guard at any of the gates yesterday morning. But it is too late to speak with them tonight and I'm on watch myself from midnight. I run to the Waleysgate in a light rain that the country people call a smirr in the English tongue, the town hushed and obscure, and the smell of woodsmoke dampening down to a faint perfume. A door opens nearby, and I hear voices, shrill and unhappy, then it bangs shut again. An army of cats moves stealthily through the night, reclaiming the town with fearsome cries and leaving a trail of mangled creatures in their wake.

I am pleased to find Richard Chaunteclerk waiting for me on the walls. He is a most pleasant fellow who does not curse or chatter idly but has a tranquillity about him that always brings me ease. He tells me about his life in London, where he was a baker before he decided to become a soldier. His wife and two children all died of a fever and he did not want to walk the streets where they had lived happily enough. I wonder that he has endured such sadness and does not rail against the world as I have heard many here do. I wonder also if I would be so cheerful if I lost what I loved most. I think of my sister and our mother and pray they are safe, and that Elizabeth will write soon.

I find, for all the lightness of the rain, I am soon soaked from my boots to my hair beneath my hat, but at least it's not particularly cold, even if the wind does pull and stab at us without mercy. We wander back and forth, meeting from time to time and sharing a little bread and ale. It is curious to feel so forcefully the boredom that comes with the fact nothing ever changes here, even as we spend all our time worrying that it will.

The cats continue their nocturnal roamings, but otherwise the night smothers everything. I walk east towards the Cowgate, leaving Richard talking to his great friend Robert Welles, who has come from the inner Marygate in the other direction. Robert has just received word of his father's sudden death and Richard was most eager to lament with him, to share the burden of his grief even a little. The wind, being a westerly, is a little less turbulent on this part of the wall and I am in no hurry to turn back into it.

I am adjusting my hose after taking a piss over the wall when I hear a cantering of footsteps. It is Robert Welles, his face emerging like a ghost out of the darkness. 'You must come.'

'Why? What's happened?'

And he utters the one word we fear more than any other. 'Treachery.'

We run back to the Waleysgate and down the steps. Richard Chaunteclerk is standing with his back to the gate, arms folded and a grim look on his face. He greets me with an equally grim nod. 'Someone took out the bar.'

Some of our great gates have keys for their doors, but the Waleysgate is not one of those, which is why there is always at least two men standing above it. Since its wooden bar can only be removed from the inside, this was treachery without a doubt. 'It was bolted when we came?' I am sure of the answer myself, but we will certainly be asked this very question by our masters.

Richard nods. 'We must tell Sir Anthony and Master Holme immediately.'

They both look at me and I sigh a little. 'Very well. Can you tell me why you thought to look? Was there a noise?'

They look at each other, scratch a chin, the side of a nose. Richard answers at last. 'There was something strange. In the wind. Not a banging, exactly. More a great creaking that shouldn't have been there. I put it out of my mind to begin with, but it kept crawling back in.'

'Do you think they're out there?' We all turn our heads as if to look through the walls to a gathering storm of Scots beyond.

'Not a lot of point risking being caught as a traitor if they're not.'

I nod, swallowing a shiver. 'I haven't seen anything.'

Richard sniffs. 'Me neither.'

'You'd best get back on the walls. Or perhaps one of you should walk all the way round and tell whoever's at each gate. I doubt they'd try to attack more than one, but we'd best be sure.'

I leave them and run without stopping all the way back to Marygate. Sir Anthony is lost to sleep and I must bang on his door sufficient to wake the entire household. They all come stumbling to the hall where I tell my brief tale.

Sir Anthony listens most attentively, never once stopping me. Sir Edmund would clearly like to interrupt, looks as if he might boil over at any moment – but he keeps his counsel and I finish very quickly. Sir Anthony stands up. 'We must double the guards on the walls,' he tells Sir Edmund before turning to me. 'And you must come to Master Holme's. Give me a moment to dress.'

We walk swiftly round the corner and on and down Western Lane. Ralph Holme, too, is quiet and decisive, leaning forward with one hand – strangely unjewelled – on his knee. 'If the gates are secure now, we need do nothing till morning. Then we must meet here and decide what to do. Tell Horsley to come from the castle.'

We leave as the houses and gardens draw near again in the grey light before dawn. None of us can imagine sleep carrying us off, so we sit in the hall and talk while Mark, the cook, and the other servants bang pots and yell at one another as they start to make bread and whatever else they can conjure up out of our supplies. Sir Edmund is full of rage, and Will follows his lead, thumping his fist on the table every time Sir Edmund complains we never do anything, just sit here like fowls ready for plucking. I would ask him what it is he thinks we can do, but I am not such a fool as to risk a beating just to show how clever I am. Sir Anthony has gone to fetch Sir Roger Horsley from the castle, so there is no one to bring sense to this unholy gathering.

As the one who brought the news, I am permitted to attend the meeting in Ralph Holme's house. To begin with, the burgesses already sitting in the best chairs murmur to one another and we men-at-arms hang on to the wall, heads close, mingling among the figures on the tapestries. But we all flutter and fidget like sparrows when Sir Roger Horsley strides into the room.

I have only seen him once or twice before, but his reputation casts a long shadow across the town. I have heard he came to Berwick in disgrace, for he was once in charge of the great castle of Bamburgh in Northumberland, whose noble outline we can see from our walls on a clear day. For a while, I was never sure what terrible thing he was supposed to have done, for he is a native of those parts and the other Northumbrian knights do not like to tell tales on one of their own. But Peter Spalding told me later it was because, when the Scots came towards Bamburgh and the local people fled to the castle, he wouldn't let them in without payment. Peter said that was a step too far even for a careless king sitting in comfort hundreds of miles away. Sir Roger was removed and sent to Berwick castle.

You would not think to look at him that he has a cruel heart, for his face is broad and open, well scattered with freckles, and his eyes dance as if he is perpetually pleased with life. Even so, men speak of him in low, uneasy tones, even the Northumbrians, so I have every reason to believe Peter told the truth. Sir Roger leans over the table now. 'Where are we supposed to sit, Holme? On your laps?'

But Ralph Holme will not yield easily to even such a man. He wafts a hand towards a bench lying along a wall, even as he is sending a servant to bring fresh strawberries and fine wine and telling us we have urgent work to do. Before we know it, we have pulled the bench to the table and the knights are all sitting together, eyes flitting from Ralph to the door as we wait for the servant to return. All except Sir Roger, who jumps like a panther on to a chair in the corner, pulling it a little way towards us and sitting down with his legs stretched out in front of him.

There is an epidemy of talking that leads quickly to shouting as every man who believes his opinion is the only one worth hearing puts forward his case. The only person I can make sense of is Sir Edmund, because I am standing behind him. He urges the immediate arrest of all Scots in the town, just as Sir John used to do at any hint of trouble.

I watch Ralph listen carefully, hand splayed across a cheek and eyes lowered. At last, he holds up his hand, nodding seriously. 'We must of course keep our enemies where we can see them. But I am minded to try something a little different. If we allow everyone to go about their business, there will be ample opportunity for the traitor to try again. At the same time, we might encourage all our loyal citizens to look out for anything unusual. I am also willing to offer a reward for information leading to his capture.'

Horsley bangs his fist on the table. 'Well spoken, Master Holme. I like a man who's not afraid of putting up his own money. I'm still owed for the last time I had to keep Scots' filth in the castle.' He stands up abruptly. 'You don't need me here.' With that, he is gone.

Ralph Holme turns to Sir Anthony. 'The crier can go around the town. We should make as little of our traitor as we can, to encourage him. Is that possible, do you think?'

Sir Anthony raises his eyebrows. 'We can try.'

'And they must come to you.'

'Who?'

'Those who desire to be helpful and earn themselves a reward.'

'As you wish.' Sir Anthony too rises quickly and departs, perhaps because he had words boiling up inside of him that he did not wish to reach his lips. Sir Edmund strides out and I quickly follow. But as I pass him, Ralph Holme catches my sleeve. 'I don't know which is more urgent, the murderer or the traitor, so keep your wits about you. Come straight to me, do you hear.'

As always, there is nothing else to do but nod.

I seek out those who were on watch up until Nones on the day Tom Crory was killed, but they are far more eager to tell me their woes than to remember what has already become obscure and confused. Those at the southern entrances look at me as if I have a horn sticking out of my head, raising their shoulders helplessly. I did not expect more of them, for so many people work or trade on our wharves. But I did hope.

Peter Spalding comes to me, for he was on watch at the Cowgate on the day Tom died and I left a message at his lodgings saying I needed to speak with him most urgently. He finds me in the stables, for I like to brush Morial when I'm feeling low in spirits. I have not seen Peter for a week or so, but he is even more irritated and morose than ever, his face twisted into a permanent scowl. 'I don't know why you're bothering about that old goat,' he says, spitting on the floor. 'No one'll miss him.'

I look at him and think *I* will, but there's little point in saying so. 'Did you see him leave?'

'No. I didn't go on the walls till Terce. He always comes out not long after the gates open.' He spits again and gives me a sharp look. 'I thought you knew that.'

'So, you didn't see Tom Crory on the day he died?'

His lip curls into a sneering smile. 'I didn't say that, did I? You asked me if I saw him go out of the gate – and I didn't. But I watched him poking about in the gorse bushes later on. He had a right pile of twigs and branches by the time he trotted off towards the shore.'

'What time do you think that was?'

'How the devil would I know?'

'Well, was it nearer the beginning, the middle or the end of your time on watch? Was the sun on the side of your face, or more on the back of your neck?'

He folds his arms and shakes his head.

'This is really important, Peter.'

He sighs and goes over to Caspar, Sir Anthony's bay courser, stroking his graceful head. He turns back to me. 'I would say it was not long before Sext, when we finished. I remember being desperate for a shite but thought I could wait till we were done with the watch. That wasn't long after I saw Crory.'

So, Tom only went away from the walls and down to the shore late in the morning. That makes it easier to establish who was out there with him. 'Thank you. That is exactly what I need to know. Was there anyone else?'

'Those two old foxes . . . what are their names now? The silly one with the nodding head.'

'Rebecca Scot?'

'Yes, that's the one.'

'I suppose she was with Elizabeth Belford?'

'That she was. Every bloody Tuesday, the two of them, regular as maggots in Joe Knapton's pies.'

I don't bother to tell him it's always Wednesdays, after they've been to visit their husbands' graves at Holy Trinity.

'And the usual rabble from the tents, trying to pick the place clean. They mostly start down on the beach and work their way back in. All except the tall, surly one – Henry Cranston, or some such. He does it the other way around. I can't decide if he doesn't like everybody else or they don't like him. He's usually on his own, anyway. Can't say I blame him.' With a nod and a grunt, Peter takes his leave.

It does not fill me with joy that I should go and speak with more of Berwick's wretches and outcasts. For a start, I have very little money left for pies. Maybe I can ask Ralph Holme for a special allowance. That makes me smile a little as I lay my head against Morial's dark flanks. He stands quietly and I take comfort from his warm strength. But, after countless moments, I tear myself away and go to stand at the door. Edith crosses the yard. She is not yet so very great with child, though I confess I have no notion how quickly one grows inside a woman. But there are definite signs now. She holds her arms protectively across her belly, which has become firm and round, her breasts arching strenuously against her gown. I am struck by the desire to lie beside her, to feel the soft warmth of her skin against mine, to nestle between her breasts and tie myself in knots with her hair.

But she is already gone.

The crier has obviously done his job well, for I am not long returned to Marygate when our steward comes to ask if we know where Sir Anthony might be. He looks most downcast when we tell him we do not, explaining there is a man and woman outside who say they have something important to tell him. I look at Sir Edmund, who is playing *jeu de dames* with Will, and he jerks his head, though I don't see why I must go.

The woman is of middling years, tall and straight in her person and neat in every particular. Her husband is a few inches smaller, and fatter and more untidy, his cloak thrown on so that it leans to one side, his hose wrinkled and unruly. He opens his mouth to speak but his wife has already stepped forward. 'Our neighbour will not remove his dungheap from the street.'

The man bustles forward, thrusting her out of the way. 'He has been told to do it too many times to count.'

I blink. 'Pray, forgive me, I don't understand. We are looking for information about unusual comings and goings, things of that nature. This sounds' – I try not to smile – 'entirely unremarkable.'

'So, you will do nothing.' She folds her arms. 'As usual.'

I take her by the elbow. 'Thank you so much. Do let us know if you see anything unexpected.'

And so they come, telling tales and secrets against neighbours, friends, fathers, mothers, children. Sir Anthony returns from the walls, and barely has time to take some bread and ale before there are more. One woman whispers that her husband went out in the night. This excites great interest and Sir Edmund and Will are sent off to speak with the man. But after Will puts his sword to his throat, he admits he has a leman in Shaw's Lane and begs them not to tell his wife. The leman says the same and please not to say anything to her husband, who is a sailor on board a ship bound for Gascony.

Another man heard two witches flying down Walkergate shouting that the Scots were coming, one of whom was most definitely his daughter-in-law.

I had thought to write down the things that might bring fruit, but all I have is parchment with lines through the writing. As the days pass, Sir Anthony grows more and more weary. Sir Edmund urges him to go to Ralph Holme and say this is utter foolishness, that we should arrest all the Scots as he said in the beginning. But Sir Anthony just lays a hand on his arm and bids him wait.

She comes as the light is stolen by a dense grey mist on the third day, a dishevelled sparrow of a woman with mottled lumps on her neck and hands. She will not enter the house but waits, hugging herself tight, near our dungheap on the other side of the courtyard. Sir Anthony raises his eyes at me as we approach, trying to tempt her away from the smell and the flies, but with little success. I bring up my cloak as near to my nose as possible and breathe through my mouth.

'I is just hearing about this reward.' She stares over towards the stables rather than at us, which causes me to look round more than once. 'But I be thinking it strange long before.'

This will doubtless go the way of all the rest. Sir

Anthony sighs. 'Is it the reward that is strange or something else?'

She shoots him a fierce look. 'Not the reward. The purse.'

I hear Sir Anthony draw a long, slow breath, which is brave of him in the circumstances. 'What purse?'

'In his tent, o' course.'

He runs a hand across his brow. 'Woman, I am tired and of little patience today. I suggest you begin again and tell us what brought you here.'

'I be seeing the purse in his tent. Been there since a few moons back. It be not his, tha's for sure. A pretty purse with threading on it, for a lady no doubt. Full o' Scottish gold, no doubt.'

We look at each other. Sir Anthony takes another deep breath. 'Whose tent?'

She looks at him as if he is foolish beyond measure. 'Henry Cranston's, o' course.'

I feel a little door opening somewhere in my mind. 'Forgive me, sir. I will come back anon. I must . . .' Running back into the house and up the stairs, I open the door to our room most hastily and nearly hit Will.

He leaps back. 'Do you want my fist in your teeth?'

I am already picking up my papers, pulling out one from the other. 'No.' He says nothing and I look up. 'Does something ail you?'

'No!'

'You're sure?'

He steps across the room, turns sharply at the wall and marches back again. 'It's so tedious here. I think I'll go mad with it. You don't understand. You've got' – he gestures wildly with his arm – 'whatever it is you're skulking about at.'

'Alice Rydale. Remember?'

He shakes his head. 'I should knock you down, just for the pleasure of it.'

I move towards him. 'Not now. I'm . . .'

He comes for me, head down, but Sir Anthony appears at the door. 'Will!' I have never heard him shout before. 'If you have nothing to do, I can always send you back on to the walls.'

'Begging your pardon, sir.' He slinks off to the other side of the room, sitting down heavily on the floor and picking up a pair of dice.

Sir Anthony turns to me. 'Why did you leave so suddenly?'

I have found what I was looking for. 'I know the name she spoke of. Henry Cranston. He was one of those who went out the Cowgate the morning Tom Crory died.'

'So, you think he . . . ?'

I shrug. 'I don't think anything, sir. I just remembered the name, that's all.'

'Come, then. Will, go and fetch Edmund.'

We march quickly up Soutergate, Sir Anthony, Sir Edmund, Will, Stephen and me. I feel a strange excitement, though so much is still obscure. Sir Anthony has ordered our trumpeters to go up on the walls to let everyone outside know the gates are about to be closed.

Will looks a lot happier now with his sword in his hand, arguing with Stephen about the best way to despatch a traitor. Sir Anthony turns to them at last, just before we reach the encampment, finger stabbing. 'You will not touch anyone unless I say so or I'll have you whipped. We're here to get answers to very important questions, not put ourselves to killing or maiming. There will be time enough for that if this man is our traitor. You might pray he is, for then our task is done.'

Will and Stephen grin behind his back, and I try not to join them.

The encampment is quiet, with most of its inhabitants no doubt outside or foraging elsewhere. The woman waits for us, less agitated now she is on her own ground. This Henry's tent is a wretched affair, more patch than cloth and bending well below any man's height in the middle. He himself is nowhere to be seen, though the woman hisses to us that we should hasten. Sir Anthony directs the others to stand outside and beckons me in with him. I look to Sir Edmund, but he just shrugs.

There is nothing much to see as we fight our way inside, the squalid roof flapping on to our faces. I feel as if I have fallen into the ocean and must push such imaginings away, even as I struggle to keep my feet on ground made slippery with the remains of unwholesome substances. There is a sack, but it is full only of rags. Pushing away the sagging roof, more in anger than with any care, I straight away see the purse, tied on to one of the stakes that attempt to keep the whole thing upright. I tap Sir Anthony on the shoulder and he quickly undoes the strings attaching the purse to the stake, turning it over and over before he hands it to me. But I do not need to see it so closely to know this is nothing to do with treachery and everything to do with murder. 'It's Alice's.' A pale green to match her favourite dress, embroidered with lilies. I hand it back to him.

'How the devil . . . ?' His shoulders crumble for a moment. 'I see. So, we still need to speak with Henry Cranston as soon as we can.'

We go outside and pass the purse around. Once it has been in every man's hand, I take it and look at it more closely in the soft grey light. I had thought it unmarked, that Alice might have lost it before the day she died. But now I see the stains, even though it looks much cleaner than anything else in this dungheap. The blood is but a series of rusty freckles now, as much a part of the fabric as the threads themselves.

'Let me look at it again.' This time Sir Anthony undoes the purse strings which, I must confess, I had not thought to do in the shock of touching something that had once lain so close to Alice when she lived and breathed. I think we all hold our breath as he struggles to unbind the strings, that we all expect him to reveal a wealth of coin. But I know he will not, for the purse was soft and yielding in my hand, though there is something inside for certain.

At last Sir Anthony pulls it open, but whatever is there will not easily reveal itself. He forces long fingers in, tugging his face into strange shapes. Slowly, he manages to pull out some folded pieces of parchment. Stephen chews on a piece of hair, Will's mouth is half open. I doubt I look any less confounded.

'What the hell?' Sir Edmund spits violently on the ground. 'All this turmoil for a couple of bloody papers. Will you open them up, man, and stop this misery.'

And he does, gently folding them out as we press close to get a better sight of them. But even as the papers lie flat and quiet on Sir Anthony's hands, I feel my head tighten and my thoughts quiver. The letters on the top sheet are perfectly ordinary, but taken together, they make no sense at all.

We all look at each other again. 'What is it?' Stephen whispers, as if the paper might hear and rise up to strike us.

Sir Anthony turns it round, then round again. 'Is it a cipher, do you think? I have heard of them but never seen one.'

Of course. 'May I have a look, sir?' The monks in the scriptorium at Gloucester occasionally wrote in cipher to amuse themselves and one of them explained the simplest of forms, where the vowels are replaced by the nearest consonant. But it does not take me long to realise that is not what has been employed here. 'It is not obvious. May I take it and try to discover the words?'

Sir Anthony hesitates, but finally nods. 'Keep it safe.' He hands it over and we look at the other paper below. This one we can read and it chills us to the bone, for here are the numbers of soldiers lodged in the town and the castle, even if they are different now from what was true several months ago when the traitor compiled them. And beneath is a description of the various places where the wall is weak.

Sir Anthony looks very pale in the misty light. 'We need to catch that knave.' He looks round each of us squires with his brows lowered and his lips pressed tight. 'And not one of you must mention these papers, do you hear? Edmund, I would ask for your silence too.'

Sir Edmund nods.

'The gates are shutting, sir.' Stephen pulls at his nose, which he always does when he's disturbed in his mind.

An old man staggers bow-legged to a nearby tent carrying firewood. He sits down heavily outside it, lamenting loudly that he hasn't had time to find much. Sir Anthony beckons over the woman who told us about the purse, but she just shrugs when he asks her where the devil Henry might be.

'Why is he not here? There's nowhere else he can be now.' Sir Anthony chews his lip. He turns to the woman again. 'What does he look like? There's no reward until we catch him, you know that?'

She shrugs again. 'Big. Bigger than any of you. But there be nothing much on him, like a stick. 'Bout your age.' She nods at Sir Edmund. 'Hair the colour of a dun horse all over his head and chin.'

I'm sure I've passed him a dozen times, but that does not help us now.

Sir Anthony tells us to go each our own way, walking through the town to look for him. I do not think this will yield anything but say nothing. There is something I want to try, though alas it means parting with more of my own money at the baker's shop. I run down, chafing at the tail of people stretched along the street and talking up rumours till they become giants and walk off by themselves. But, at last, I climb back up the hill and approach the old man still complaining outside his tent.

I squat down beside him and show him the pastry. 'I thought you might like this since you had so little time outside this morning.'

He eyes it with a tremble of his lip. Then, quick as the flick of a cat's tail, snatches it and starts eating. It is not at all pleasant to watch him, but I must be patient. He finishes and belches loudly, sending a disgusting waft of meaty air in my direction.

'Was Henry Cranston outside this morning?'

He smiles without mirth. 'Is you one o' the sojers looking for him?'

'Did somebody tell him?'

He inclines his head a little, which I understand to mean yes.

'What did he do then?'

'He don' be liking sojers.'

'Why not?'

He clucks to himself, a broad grin on his face. 'He is taking the king's money and leaving the king's army before the great battle. The king is not liking that, you see. He's not liking that at all. Henry is coming here, to be living quietly.'

'So, he went somewhere else. Do you know where?'

'Why you be asking? What's Henry done? He is a rascal of a man, right enough. Always taking people's food when he thinks you're not looking.'

'Yes, we think he took something that wasn't his and we just want to know where he took it from.'

The old man nods. 'He's not saying where he's going, just stopped his fishing and went towards the river. He used to be living over towards Scremerston. Maybe he is going back.' He looks beyond me, lines deepening. 'Or to his sister's house. In Tweedmouth. Emma, she's called. Married an Armstrong there. Henry doesn't like him, but he has tender feelings for her.'

I rise. 'Thank you.' I am almost going to say he will receive some of the reward for Henry's capture, but that is a whole other story I should not tell until we are safe again.

Chapter 11

I need to find Sir Anthony, but it is Will I uncover first, talking to some wench on the corner of Briggait. He tells me to look along the wharves without turning his head from the girl, who gazes at him with the moon in her eyes. I want to tell her to have a care.

Hastening on down through the Watergate, I dive into the noise and bustle of the riverbank. Henry would need money to get across the Tweed by boat and I doubt he had any. But the tide is only recently turned, so he could easily get across the river. I can certainly ask if anyone saw him.

I look around and at last I spy Sir Anthony talking to the burgess Walter Goswick. He sees me too and raises a hand, so I go to join them, picking my way through boxes, the hurrying of men.

I see no point in wasting time. 'Will you come over to Tweedmouth with me, sir?'

But it is Goswick who replies. 'Have you got wings under your cloak, young man?'

I smile, but inside it irks me he should think me such a fool. 'Yes, of course, sir. I mean, no, I don't. I suppose we'll need a boat?'

He turns around and studies the water, which is becoming deeper by the minute. 'That you will.'

Sir Anthony smiles, but I can see he is weary and in no mood for such an adventure. 'You have news of Henry Cranston, is that it?' He turns to Goswick. 'The man is wanted for common thievery.'

I remember to be careful with my words in front of the burgess. 'Yes. I think he went over there.' I tell my story.

Sir Anthony pats my shoulder. 'We should gather more men.'

'I think we should go now, sir, if it pleases you. He might not stay long with his sister.'

Walter strokes the length of his nose with thumb and first finger. 'The tide will not be low enough again until after dark. Sam can take you over.' He leads the way through men and merchandise down to a little craft stranded in the mud. Telling us to wait, he comes back a few minutes later with his arm around a lad not much older than Wat. But the boy is no sooner in front of us than he has manoeuvred the boat into the water and is waving us on board. I sit as low down as possible, clinging to the sides, but he is just as strong and quick in rowing us across. We are soon standing on the shore at Tweedmouth, which is but a scattering of cottages set along a knot of streets gathered round the church.

'Well,' says Sir Anthony, having made the boy promise to stay where he is, 'what do we do now?'

I feel anxious to be so far away from Berwick's protective walls, even if I can see them across the water. But it is not such a fearful prospect with him beside me. 'We are looking for a man named Armstrong, husband to Henry Cranston's sister.'

'I suppose you intend to knock on the first door and hope he answers it?'

In truth that was exactly what I thought to do, so I nod. He sighs, the creases round his eyes digging deep. We are on watch more often now, since so many men have left, and are all suffering for it. And we have this traitor to worry about. Sir Anthony is some years over thirty and suffers all the more. But he starts urgently towards the first house, half-baked in mud. A woman opens it a little way, peering at us both and blinking in the light. 'He's seeing to the sheep,' she ventures.

'We're looking for a man named Armstrong. Is there someone of that name in Tweedmouth?'

'Who is it that's asking?' She looks as if she might shut the door again, but Sir Anthony stands with his foot in the gap.

'Those who have the right to.'

She blinks again. 'John or Adam?'

I lean over. 'He'll be an older man, perhaps about his age.' I nod towards Sir Anthony. It's hard to tell how old she is, for her face is smothered in shadow.

'Aye, that'll be Johnny. Adam can scarcely grow himself a beard.' She finally pushes the door wide open and steps out of the house, revealing herself as a young woman of about my age. 'If you go around the corner there by the well, it's the one with the broken cart outside it. Mistress Armstrong will be home, I'm thinking.' She watches us go, arms folded, and I wonder how long it will take for news of our visit to pass around the village.

We walk on, the men down at the boats on the shore stopping to watch us. I start as something soft grazes my leg, but it is only a dog slinking past and into a well-fruited garden. We turn the corner into a lane that bends away from the others. Just as the young woman said, a neat, well-kept house lies next to the bones of a cart.

Without even thinking, I creep up to the hole for the window and look in. A woman sits at a table with her back to me. And opposite her, a tall man with an excessive amount of muddy brown hair holds his head in his hands. Sir Anthony tries to look in, too, but knocks over a piece of the cart. Henry's head springs up and I see in his face a terror so grim, I shiver. But no sooner has he seen us than he rises, knocking his chair to the floor with a crash that sends the woman to her feet. As she turns to look at us, Henry is already heading out of another door somewhere inside.

It seems to me that Henry will be trying to get outside, for there will be nowhere safe to hide in such a small house. I run along towards a garden gate and leap over it, listening out for anything to tell me where he might have gone. By now the woman is shrieking, presumably at Sir Anthony, which does not help me to hear anything useful.

I run through a row of fruit trees then feel the pain of regret as I trample over herbs in the physick garden. But still I cannot see Henry. As I reach the back wall and look both ways over it, I finally catch a glimpse of him to my right, far ahead of me, rushing along a back lane that separates the house plots from the fields.

'Henry,' I shout. But he does not falter for a moment. Scrambling over the wall, scraping elbows and knees, I have no earthly notion where he's going, nor where Sir Anthony might be. The lane is full of muddy pools and boulders rolled down from the fields and I don't have the strength of a man who would clearly give his life to avoid being caught. I reach the end of the lane, which leads straight into swaying pleats of barley garlanded with marigolds and poppies. He is gone, though whether he lies invisible among the corn or has gained some other hiding place, only God knows.

I stand for a moment, a throbbing in my ears. But then I hear the bees humming among the wildflowers, the larks sending their joyous song to the heavens. I open my mouth, build up my breath inside and I too – for the first time in weeks, months – lift my voice up to God. And in return am filled with His grace.

But then I fall silent, turning to the north, looking at Berwick from a distance. It seems quite untroubled from here, its trees and green places lying serene under a late afternoon sun, its walls dark and stalwart-looking, which I know is a lie. I search for Lucy's house and imagine her waving at me from her solar eyrie. I wonder what it would be like to live here in a time of peace: to give attention and strength to crops and gardens, children and wives; to keeping on good terms with neighbours and spending

pleasant hours feasting with friends, instead of polishing
the skills needed to bring death to other men.

But even as I think such foolish thoughts, I am
listening very closely. After some moments, I turn back to
face the crops just as a party of sparrows rises up with
shrill dismay from near the edge where the barley stops
and a runt of a wood begins further up the slope. I creep
quickly towards the trees and soon see a man moving
through the corn where the birds had been, half crouching.
He turns around briefly and I am glad of the cover. I must
make up my mind where he's going, so I can get ahead of
him if I can. I wonder what I will do if I catch him.

But Henry Cranston is not intent on escape. At least,
not yet. I am just about to start running as quickly as I can
through the trees when I see him rise fully out of the
barley and slip into the wood himself. I watch as he finds
a great fallen trunk and clambers on to its other side,
sitting down so that only his shaggy head is to be seen.
He rubs his face with his hands and stays there, head
bowed, for a few moments. Then he disappears entirely.

I creep nearer, breathing in the damp, secretive smells
of the wood, unsure what has become of him. A part of
me imagines he is some kind of spirit that knows of a
door to another world on the far side of that fallen tree.
I tell myself I surely blaspheme, but I hold my breath
entirely until I can peep over.

And there he is, already making a rhythmic noise with
his breathing, his face innocent beneath the great brown
beard. I always imagined a murderer, a traitor, would bear
the marks of his sin. This man does not, which leaves

me confused. But I have no time to stand and galp at such a sinner, however unmarked. I creep away until I am safely back in the lane, running down it at full tilt.

I must catch my breath again, sides heaving in the little room of Henry's sister's house, to be able to explain to Sir Anthony that he must come with me without delay. The woman begins to wail about her brother's foolishness in abandoning the army, but he did suffer most terribly from an affliction in his belly and . . .

We are already gone. I hold my heart in my hands as we move carefully towards the tree trunk, every cracking twig bringing me much anxiety, but not nearly as much as the thought he will be gone.

But there he is.

Smiling as he pulls out his sword, Sir Anthony signs with his hand that I should do the same and move past the trunk to stand on Henry's other side. Slowly and carefully, he climbs over and gives the sleeping man a good kick. Henry's eyes jump open and he cries out so loudly that all the birds in the nearby trees arise and fly away in a great wind.

I float down the lane and through the village on the wave of a mighty exultation – to think, that I should have found Alice's killer, and a traitor too! It is only once we reach the boat that I realise Henry is shuddering and shaking, crying out to the birds and the sky, to the stones on the shore, that he meant no harm by it, but it was too much to expect honest men to walk all the way into Scotland and fight those devils.

We help him in and sit crammed together opposite.

Sir Anthony leans forward. 'Henry, do you really think we'd go to all this trouble for a wayward soldier? We know what you did the other night. And we know what you did to Alice Rydale.'

Henry is silent then, though his mouth still moves through the great nest of his beard. Pulling his arms close around himself he speaks at last. 'What do I have to do with this Alice Rydale? I don't know her, and you shouldn't be saying I do.'

I want to tell Sir Anthony to be careful, not to say any more than he needs to, for fear his words will prove helpful to Henry in our questioning. But perhaps he knows this, for he sits back, arms folded, staring at our prisoner with a frown lightly traced across his brows.

We march Henry through the streets of Berwick, everyone stopping to watch, mouths open before their tongues loosen behind us. All three of us keep our silence until Sir Anthony unlocks the door to one of our storerooms on the ground floor. Only then does Henry begin to rear and foam at the mouth like a wild horse, so that I must struggle hard to contain him. Together we push him inside and lock the door again. He bangs on the other side, rattling at the handle.

Sir Anthony walks away. 'This is going to get worse before it gets better. Much, much worse.'

He goes to see Ralph Holme and, when he comes back, we gather round him even while he is eating. Sir Edmund pretends to cuff us out of the way, but he protests only a little. Sir Anthony finishes a mouthful, spins his dagger round and round on the table, staring hard at its furious revolutions. I know it will not be long before Will pokes Stephen or pulls his hair or some such petty annoyance.

Sir Anthony suddenly places his hand flat on top of his dagger and stops its rotation. 'Master Holme would make a great spectacle of this. To warn us all. The blacksmith will come tomorrow, and we will set to interrogating Henry Cranston in the courtyard. Everyone may watch who wishes. Ben, I will need you to help me, if it pleases your master.'

Sir Edmund grunts. Few remember to ask him for my services these days.

Sir Anthony turns in his chair to look straight at me. 'You do understand my meaning? This will be no gentle questioning.'

In truth, I do not really understand, but there is no doubting the ominous tone to his words. I give the faintest of nods and he gets up, bidding us a curt goodnight.

The first sign of the blacksmith's arrival is the smell of smoke. Still upright and powerful, he is not a young man. Nor is he fond of words, which has long made me smile since the warmth of the smithy offers a potent welcome to those given to idle talk. Now he labours hard to build up a fire fierce enough to glow red in a great metal pan, an iron rack hung with the implements of his trade placed nearby.

And then I do understand and run to find Sir Anthony, who is inspecting his courser in the stables. 'You cannot mean me to take part in this . . . in this . . .'

'You have no choice. Who else understands what was done to Alice? I can ask him about the Scots, but even then . . . We must work together and then it will be done quickly, and he will suffer less.' He puts his hand on my shoulder. 'Perhaps he will tell all and there will be no need to . . .' He sighs.

We walk out as Ralph Holme sweeps into the courtyard, two servants struggling with his great chair behind. He is wearing his finest clothes, a bright red coat edged with fox fur, pale blue stockings and long-tipped shoes. He sits like a judge, feet squarely on the ground, both hands clasping the ornate end of the chair arms. Some of the other burgesses hurry to sit alongside him.

The courtyard begins to fill with soldiers and townspeople alike, so that they must push and argue about who will find a place where they can keep their eyes on the blacksmith. Sir Edmund, with Will and Stephen alongside, have placed themselves close by, the look on my master's face so ferocious that few are brave enough even to stand next to them. I see Edward at the back of the crowd.

He smiles and comes over, nodding at Sir Anthony. 'So, you have caught a murderer and a traitor. You must be most relieved. I have come to give you Dame Eleanor's deepest thanks.'

Sir Anthony rubs an eye. 'Henry Cranston's guilt is not yet proven.'

I stand, hunched like a hen. 'It is the why of it that confounds me. I must speak with Dame Eleanor, to see if she knows of any reason why he should have killed Alice.'

'Certainly. Though perhaps he will tell you himself?' Edward gives us a little bow, turns as if to leave before turning back again. 'I forgot. She asked me to inquire, what made you believe this man, that he was the one?'

It is a reasonable question, but I must be careful not to mention the papers, as Sir Anthony instructed us. 'I cannot say much, but the evidence was damning. Please tell Dame Eleanor that we are . . . hopeful.'

He nods and turns, cocking his head at William Roxburgh, who is listening intently only a few feet away. Smiling, Edward goes to him, clapping a hand on his shoulder. I nod a greeting to William, who looks down, tugs his lip before looking up, his gaze flitting away from me to Ralph Holme and the other burgesses.

But now the babbling stops, all heads turning to the door from our house. Henry is in shackles, stripped to the waist and blinking in the August sun. He shuffles awkwardly alongside Sir Anthony, who holds him steady by the arm, a path miraculously appearing for them through the hissing, blaspheming crowd. I follow on behind, wishing with all my heart I was anywhere else but here. Henry is muttering to himself. I cannot make any sense of his words, if they are words.

But when he sees the blacksmith, he lets out a shriek that is the most unholy thing I have ever heard, falling awkwardly at Sir Anthony's feet. 'Please tell the king I am a wretch to desert him, and I will fight for him and gladly. Please, sir. Just tell him and I know he will forgive me.'

Sir Anthony shakes his head and pulls him up. 'For the hundredth time, Henry, we're not here to talk about that. Stay where you are and answer whatever we ask of you honestly and fully.' He puts a hand down hard on Henry's shoulder to keep him there. The blacksmith stands a few feet away with legs apart, arms folded. I pray he will not be needed. Sir Anthony jerks his head at me.

I step forward, heart pounding in my ears. 'I want to ask you about the purse we found in your tent.'

'Ah!' He closes his eyes. 'It was pretty, 'tis all. Just a pretty thing I wish I'd never seen, so you wouldn't be asking about it.'

'How did you come by it?'

''Twas there on the ground, by the tents.'

I look at Sir Anthony and shake my head, then turn back to Henry. 'Will you look at me?' He opens his eyes with a shudder. 'How long have you had it?'

'I don't know. A long time. When that girl got murdered.'

'Yes, that girl. Alice Rydale.'

And then he seems to understand. 'Is it her purse?' He whispers it.

I cannot help but whisper back. 'Yes, Henry, it's her purse.'

'Oh.' He closes his eyes again, as if he might make us all disappear.

I lick my lips, working carefully towards what I need to know. 'What can you tell me about the things inside?'

His eyes leap open. 'There was no money in it, if that's what you mean. I didn't steal nothing. I thought it was pretty. It was lost and I found it, is all.' His words run into one another and I have difficulty pulling them apart.

'That's right, there was no money. But there was something inside, wasn't there?'

'Just trash. What would a girl want with that?'

'So, you do know?'

He looks at me and shakes his head. 'It's just trash, I tell you.'

The hissing starts again and some shout at us to let the blacksmith ask the questions.

Henry clutches at Sir Anthony. 'I only found it. You must believe me.'

'How did you meet with the Scots? Was it one of Douglas's men?'

'What Scots? I don't know any Scots.'

'We know you do. What did they say they would give you? You need money or a bit of land, don't you, so you can get away from here and start living a decent life.'

Henry lifts his shackled hands as if to ward off Sir Anthony's words. 'You're mad! What would I want with the thieving Scots?'

I think Sir Anthony will hit him, but instead he beckons to the blacksmith, who seizes a pointed iron bar from the depths of the embers. The crowd whistles and jeers. Henry begins to howl, backing away, but Sir

Anthony has him and Will and Stephen rush to his side, forcing Henry down on to his knees.

I watch as if I am sliding towards an enormous hole that is blacker than the heavens on a moonless night. If I could stop myself from looking I would, but I can't. I see the tip of the bar glowing orange and still we slide towards the hole. The blacksmith does not pause, laying it gently across Henry's back, leaving it there for one second, two, all the time in the world for Henry's scream to reach Hell and back. I see his skin shrink away from the metal as the bar is removed, the wound turning angry and red and soon starting to weep. I think of our Lord on the cross and quickly tell myself to think of something else.

Sir Anthony crouches down. 'Now, Henry, shall we start again? Tell me all about how you turned traitor. And once you've told us about that, you can tell us why you killed Alice Rydale.'

Henry is panting like a dog. 'What can I do? What can I do?' Over and over, he says it. 'They'll be killing me if I say nothing and killing me if I say something. What can I do?'

As the blacksmith lifts another metal bar out of the fire I can scarcely breathe or think or even see. I know a man accused of such a terrible crime will not readily confess to it and painful means must be used to force it out of him. But I find myself afraid for Henry. Perhaps he did not know what he was doing? Or his fear of our king led him astray? I do not want him to die at the hands of the blacksmith and leave me without answers, without the understanding that brings peace. His screams no longer belong to a man, though it is flesh that rends and blood that flows. Sir Anthony's face grows so pale I fear he might swoon. But instead he turns to spit on the ground and, at last, raises a hand to dismiss us all.

The silence starts to swell as the blacksmith shrugs and turns away to clean his implements. And then the hissing starts until the men-at-arms put their hands on their swords and the courtyard begins to empty. I look down at Henry on the ground and realise there's no more to be done, for he lies entirely motionless. Sir Anthony jerks his head at Stephen, and he and Will push and pull until they can get their arms beneath him and drag him off.

I run upstairs and find my little bag of herbs, slipping into the storeroom once everything is quiet again. I make a balm of woundwort and gently smooth it on Henry's twisted skin with the back of my dagger. But he does not make a sound or move a muscle. I lean down, feeling for any rhythm of life within him and hear only a slight, fluttering breath. If he survives the night, it will be a miracle.

Chapter 12

Henry lives, though it is pitiful to watch him staring into some void only he can see. Sir Edmund and Ralph Holme are eager to press on, to bring back the smith to finish it. But Sir Anthony insists we wait until Henry's strength returns a little. And all the while rumours abound, adding to the unease within our walls. The muster of the king's army has been moved again until the middle of September, which leaves little time to accomplish anything. It is difficult to feel hope when no one I know believes anything will come of it.

But we must surely put our trust in those whose authority even the charlatan King of Scotland cannot question. This very day came messengers of the cardinals sent by our Holy Father, Pope John, to speak with Robert Bruce, presumably to chastise him. They will spend the night at the Dominican friary near the castle before venturing forth into the hostile land beyond. I catch a glimpse of them as they ride along Marygate, two tawny-skinned gentlemen swaddled in more clothes than I have ever seen on one person.

I have not yet gone to bed after being on the walls, but I do not think sleep will capture me yet, for I am much troubled by Henry's interrogation. The streets are flowing with people and clogged full of sellers and hawkers here for market day. Wat tells me I should have seen the markets of several years ago, when all the country people flocked into town to sell and buy and gawp, but since he is but a child, I don't imagine he's seen such wonders either.

It is certainly a pathetic spectacle, poor women chasing after those passing by with a clutch of eggs or some muddy piece of woollen work, their menfolk drunk on the road. As I near the narrow corner of Marygate and Soutergate, I find my way even more impeded. A cart slouches carelessly, one of its wheels off and a crowd gathered round an altercation between the driver – still stranded atop the wreckage – and a well-dressed man vehemently demanding that the obstruction be removed. I am beginning to wish I had gone the long way round by way of Eastern Lane, but I manage to slither through those who would rather stand idly than pass by such a spectacle.

And, at last, I am in Hide Hill and announcing my presence to Dame Eleanor's gap-toothed servant. I hold my breath until the boy says his mistress is upstairs and I follow him into the hall. I have not seen Dame Eleanor for quite some time and find her less haggard but perhaps a little more . . . absent.

And yet, she rises to greet me with a smile that breathes life into her eyes, taking me by the hand and pointing me graciously to a covered seat. 'I am most glad you have come now, when we might talk just the two of us.' She glances at the door. I wonder where Lucy is. I had hoped very much to discuss the cipher with her. 'Edward tells me you have been questioning a man about Alice.'

'Yes, lady.' I push away those memories. 'That is what I wanted to ask you. Have you had any dealings with Henry Cranston?'

'That is his name?'

I nod.

She draws in a long breath. 'I cannot think I have. Those people in the tents' – she waves a hand – 'I have no reason to speak with them since they cannot buy what I have to sell.'

'And Alice? Do you think she might have had some reason . . . ?'

'No. I know she was hiding something from me, but she was not a foolish girl.' She looks at me for a long moment. 'She knew what she was worth. I think that might have been why we quarrelled.'

It is my turn to draw in a long breath. 'Because you decided she should marry your steward?' I have never asked her about that. Perhaps I should have.

I see the hand nearest me jump, then roll itself into a fist. 'Yes.'

I cannot allow her to say nothing more, even if that is what she desires. 'Will you tell me why?'

She leans on her hand, watching me with a look on her face I cannot divine. Then she gives a little sigh, staring at the tiny motes of matter dancing in the sunlight from the window. 'It seemed to me better that she should stay here, that Edward might learn to occupy himself in my affairs and take some of the burden in time.'

I frown. 'But she did not wish that?'

'No.' She pushes a strand of hair back under her coif, turns her head to me and smiles. 'No, she did not. I wish I did not have to . . . did not think it best to stop her betrothal to Sir John. She would still be here, perhaps.'

I stand up. 'It is what we know now. But we did not know it then. You could not know it then.'

She nods. 'You are kind, Benedict. And is this man – this Henry – do you think he was the one?'

I know what I believe. But I need time. If Henry is not guilty, then someone else is, and it would be wise to keep that devil believing we are asking our questions elsewhere. 'It is too early to say.'

'So, he did not confess?'

'Not yet. I will come as soon as I have anything more to tell.' I want to ask her about Lucy, but do not know what to say. I start towards the door.

'Thank you. Please wait one moment.' She pushes herself up on to her feet, comes over and takes my hand once more. 'I believe you have become friendly with Lucy. That, too, is kind. She likes to speak with you. Perhaps you might walk with her on the Fields while the weather is still pleasant?'

I feel the rings on her hand digging into my flesh. I would gladly walk with Lucy, so long as we might talk, but I feel there is something more to this request and am confounded by it. 'If it is what you wish, lady.'

She drops her hand. 'Is it not what you wish?'

I stare at the wall above her head, feeling still a strange weight in her words even as I fear Dame Eleanor will tell Lucy of my reluctance. 'Please say I will walk with her as soon as we both can.' I bow and walk quickly out of the room. This time I return home along Briggait and Eastern Lane to avoid any obstacles, breathing deeply and wishing there was an end to all this perplexity.

Messages are sent to and fro our house and Hide Hill. First, Lucy is sick with a fever, then I must join a watch unexpectedly, because of a sickness among the soldiers. I spend as much time as I can sitting in the corner of our room as the others play games or wrestle around me; I am playing, too, but with the letters on the page. There is not too much of the cipher writing – only eight lines. I begin to think this makes discovering its meaning harder, not easier, for I have that much less to worry at, to move around and put to the proof. I imagine Lucy taking one look and throwing the paper back at me with a tut and a toss of her hair. Though if she really could discover its secrets, it would not matter so very much.

But one sullen late August afternoon, I find myself waiting for her in her mother's hall. She arrives, bundled into a woollen cloak, so that she looks even more of a child. Her mother rushes up to her, unfastens and refastens the cloak, and I think that Lucy's eyes will burst with fury right out of her head. But at last Dame Eleanor smiles at us both and disappears.

Lucy turns to me and we stare at each other. 'You do not have to do this.' She has not softened her face one jot.

'I do not . . . I am honoured.' I put on a smile but am fearful it is *she* who does not wish to walk with *me*.

'Is that so?'

The little maid who came to me with Lucy's message when we last met in the friary trots into the room. I feel even more irritated that we will not be alone. I had imagined that, because Lucy is scarcely a proper person, we would be allowed to walk without anyone else. I wish I was more like Will, who seems to care little or nothing for other people's feelings and is the more honest for it.

'Shall we go?' I turn away, leaving them to follow as best they can. And, though I certainly do not walk fast, I am aware they are somewhere behind me as I march up the hill. I pass the tents and try not to think of Henry.

I turn only when I have gone out of the Cowgate and am some way beyond the line of scrub and gorse. I see Lucy and Mary in the distance, just beyond the walls. When they finally reach me, Lucy carries straight on with her nose in the air. It poses no difficulty whatsoever to catch up with her, but I am astonished that she should be so ill-mannered. And still she does not stop, making her ungainly way in the direction of the sea, little Mary skipping and running at her side.

'What are you doing?' I slip round in front of her and start walking backwards.

'I'm getting some air, which my mother tells me will do me no end of good. What are *you* doing?'

'You know very well what I'm doing.'

'Do I, indeed?' She still does not look at me, turning her face slightly to the side.

'You are most ungrateful.'

She stops just as I trip over a rock lying in the grass. And now she stands over me, hands on hips, her face flushed and furious. 'Ungrateful for what? For the pleasure of your company? Well, believe me, there is none. This is not my doing. And you dare to treat me as if … as if you are ashamed. Which, of course, you are. And you promised I could help you.'

Now it is my turn to blush, and I feel tears pricking my eyes. 'Forgive me. I've been so . . . I couldn't . . .' I put my hand down to push myself up. 'Ow!'

'What? What have you done?'

'It's nothing.' I look at my hand. 'Just some nettles.'

'Stand up and let me see.'

'Ow! They really do sting.'

Mary giggles as Lucy takes my hand to look at it, smoothing her own hand gently across my palm. 'There's plenty of dock leaves over there.'

I nod but I find her touch calming.

'Go on and fetch them then,' she says. 'And you should have said no to my mother if that's how you feel.'

'It's not . . . I do want . . .' I sigh and go to pick the docks.

'Mary, stay here or I'll eat your supper myself.' Lucy is very fierce with the girl.

'But my mistress, your mother, said . . .'

'Do you want your supper or don't you?'

The girl nods miserably.

'You will be able to see us, so you needn't worry.'

I feel Lucy come to stand behind me.

'You do know what to do with them, don't you?'

'What do you take me for?' I look up at her, desperate for forgiveness.

She smiles at last. 'A southron fool who knows nothing of any importance.'

'Well, you're wrong.' I rub the leaves into my skin. 'See.'

We walk on and I offer her my arm, but she waves it away. I really wanted her to take it. And I do not want to talk of nothing. 'I really have been trying to see you for long enough, and you are unkind to speak as if I didn't.'

She eyes me warily. 'I thought it was my mother's idea.'

'That doesn't mean I hadn't thought of it myself. I was unsure how to ask to see you.'

'That is the strangest excuse I have ever heard.'

'Would you like me to think of another?' I try hard not to smile, but I see her look at me, wide-eyed, and I must laugh.

'You jest?'

'I do.'

'And you truly do not mind being seen out walking with me?'

'I do not. So long as I can talk with you, and you will help me.'

'Oh.' She turns her head away a little and it is as if the skies have turned from blue to dark grey.

'How have I displeased you now?'

'You have not!'

'I have and I do not know why.'

'I swear, you have not displeased me. I am glad you want to talk to me. Tell me about the man you arrested.'

'So long as you do not tell anyone else.'

She gives a little shake of her head, as if she finds me doltish. 'Of course.'

I explain about what was found in Alice's purse, marvelling how word of it has not spread about the town.

'Do you have the writing with you?'

I glance around, though I'm not sure what I'm afraid of. 'Yes. I keep it round my neck under my tunic.'

'It's that important?'

'I think that, because it's a cipher, it contains something that will accuse the one to whom it belonged.'

She nods slowly. 'And you have seen nothing like it before?'

'I have scarcely seen any, apart from one simple kind. When I was young.'

'But it must follow reason. It cannot be left to chance?'

'No, that is certain.'

'Then we will find its secrets.'

Already I feel many feet taller. We sit on a bank of grass among the nodding harebells. Mary sits, too, at the proper distance, and begins to make a chain of daisies.

Retrieving the paper, I spread it out on my lap and Lucy shifts so that we are joined together on one side. She lowers her head towards the lettering, so close I almost reach out to smooth away the little ridge that sits between her eyes.

'Explain the simple cipher again, please.'

I place my finger on the first word. 'Let us imagine this conforms to it. Somewhere, perhaps the second or third letter, there is a vowel, which is replaced with the consonant coming after. So, this "v" should actually be a "u". Except that clearly makes no sense.'

'No. But I understand. It looks like Latin rather than French, I think.'

'Yes, I thought so too. I have been wondering if it's a kind of safe conduct, a letter that the bearer might use to identify himself to his friends.'

She smiles at me, eyes glistening. 'And that is what you hope?'

I cannot help but match her smile. 'Yes. That would be a miracle.'

She stops smiling, stares gloomily ahead. 'But this is not the work of God, is it?'

I move my arm so that it lies across her back. 'The letter isn't. But He has brought it to us, and we will not fail. You said so yourself.'

She nods, circling a raven lock round a finger. 'And do you think, if we find the meaning in one word, that will show the way to the rest?'

I shake my head. 'I'm not sure. I have tried every combination of vowels – letters before, letters after, reversing it so that each uncovered vowel is actually the one before.'

She frowns again.

'I meant that an "a" becomes a "u", and an "e" an "a". Or the other way round. The one after.'

She retreats into her heavy cloak. 'It is harder than I thought.'

'But at least there are two of us. I am very glad of that.'

She turns her head slightly, looking at me from beneath her lids, long lashes falling on to pale cheeks. If she smiles, I cannot see it, for she has submerged her mouth within her cloak. 'I think we should go back now.' She pulls her mouth out of the cloth. 'But can we do this again soon?'

'Yes. Of course.' I leap up, offering her my hands to pull her up. This time she takes them and the three of us walk together back through the Cowgate. One of the men on the gate shouts at me. 'Are you taking that home to frighten the crows?'

Lucy marches on, lips set tight and chin high. I want to go up and thrash him till he begs her for mercy.

Sir Anthony has stopped our morning exercises beyond the walls in favour of wrestling and fighting with sticks. He has set us to compete against one another and we may take on our next adversary whenever and wherever it suits us. Apart from that and my turns on watch, I spend most of my time with the paper or with Lucy and the paper. But we are disappointed in all our efforts.

I still visit the friary, mostly now to say a prayer for Tom and light a candle. Wandering back down Soutergate, I am roughly passed by two Northumbrian soldiers coming from the Cowgate in a hurry.

As they pass, one addresses me. 'Did you know Sir Anthony has called everyone to his house? Even those on watch.'

We begin to run. 'Did you see anything when you were up on the walls?'

'A few cows and sheep.'

'That's good, then.'

Six or seven men scurry like rats, heads down, from streets and alleys, and I cannot help but feel afraid. There is already quite a crowd in our yard, with murmurings of fantastical happenings rippling through it. I find myself standing next to Peter Spalding, who nods grimly.

Sir Anthony strides out, Stephen following behind. Sir Edmund wanders out too; if any of them are worried, they do not show it. Sir Anthony begins to speak but stops as everyone mutters 'Be silent' to everyone else. Finally, there is complete quiet and stillness, as if we had all been turned to stone.

Sir Anthony clasps his hands together and begins again. 'Men, I will not keep you long, but you must know there is rebellion in the north.'

The statues come back to life, arms flying and voices raised. Sir Edmund draws his sword and yells: 'Silence!'

The hubbub dies away.

Sir Anthony continues. 'The new Bishop of Durham' – some of the men give a low growl, for I understand this Louis Beaumont does not find favour among the northerners – '. . . the new Bishop and the two cardinals in his company were attacked by forces led by Gilbert Middleton at Darlington. To add to Middleton's treachery and dishonour, it is said Randolph and Douglas and a number of other Scots rode with him.' He holds up a hand to halt the hubbub before it overcomes him once more. 'The bishop and his brother were seized and carried off. Thankfully, the cardinals were unharmed, though I understand that Knaresborough castle has now been taken out of the king's hands in the name of his cousin, the Earl of Lancaster. These dreadful deeds took place many days' ride from here, but we should not imagine we're safe. Until we know Middleton's intentions, especially if he's in league with the Scots, the danger is great.'

He looks at his feet for a moment and this time we are content to let him do so in peace. Then he casts his gaze around us all. 'As you know, the king is in York. I do not imagine he will allow such a challenge to his authority to pass unchecked, which means his army will, no doubt, be used to put down this rebellion instead of coming to help us. I cannot stop you leaving if your safe conducts run out. But no one else is to quit the garrison for any reason until I decide the danger is over.' With that, he strides back inside.

The next day, close on the heels of news of Gilbert Middleton's rough handling of their masters, the envoys of the two cardinals return dejected and forlorn from Scotland. They lodge once more in the Dominican friary before heading south the following morning. The news soon spreads that they were treated well enough in the north but could not persuade any of the Scottish lords to give Robert Bruce the Holy Father's message, because he was not addressed as king.

I ask more about their mission, though Sir Edmund certainly doesn't know, and I don't think Sir Anthony is very sure either. It is Adam Newton, the warden of the Franciscans, who finally explains. He comes to greet me every time he sees me in the church and to tell me that Tom Crory is still counted among their prayers, though we both know the money I gave him has long since been used up.

He explains that the Pope is intent on launching a new crusade against the Infidel in the Holy Land on the other side of the world. And to that godly end, he will not countenance the Scots and the English fighting each other and has written to tell them so. It is this message that the cardinals' envoys took to Robert Bruce. I wonder to Friar Adam that His Holiness imagined it would make any difference to a man who has been excommunicated these long years for a most terrible murder.

'Ah,' he says, wagging a finger at me with a smile, 'but His Holiness has ways of persuading even the most benighted of apostates. A man who plays at being king will not want his people to suffer the same sentence as himself, now would he, for they surely would not forgive him for condemning their immortal souls to everlasting Hell?'

I shiver at the thought and wish with all my heart they had been able to persuade this Robert Bruce to stop his struggle, to embrace peace. If no one will give him the name of king, then it is because he has no right to it.

The days pass. I think of what Friar Adam told me while we watch the Mass for the Feast of the Cross in the Holy Trinity, for on this day many centuries ago the True Cross was returned to Jerusalem after it fell into the hands of an Infidel ruler. Alas, it languishes still in the hands of barbarians, a symbol, surely, of our own sinfulness, that we should neglect it so.

The great door bangs open and shut as Richard Chaunteclerk comes running through it, his bootsteps resounding across the stone. He scans the company turned to gaze at him and advances quickly towards Sir Anthony. Whatever news he brings immediately impels them out of the church and the rest of us abandon our devotions to follow. We climb the steps on to the walls above the Cowgate, each sending our gaze to follow Richard's arm towards the sea. The dawn still glows a bashful pink, but we do not need the full light of day to see the ships large and small sailing headlong down from the north towards the entrance to our river.

It seems we are under siege.

Chapter 13

The men gathered in our hall talk over each other so loudly and so often that little has been accomplished this past age. Ralph Holme hammers the table with the side of his hand, while Sir Edmund paces up and down. Ralph Hoghtone, the square-built keeper of the stores, is wont to seize great chunks of his thick brown hair in his fists, pulling at it and squeaking, while James Broughton, the long-faced chancellor, insists he will agree to nothing that will bring dishonour on the king.

'How,' Ralph Holme snarls, 'will it not dishonour the king if the men guarding his last stronghold in Scotland are left to starve?'

'Hark at you,' bellows Sir Edmund. 'As if you haven't tried to starve us already, cutting our pay so that we have even less to eat.'

And so they shout and argue. At last, Sir Anthony stands up out of his chair and leans on the table. 'Let us not do the Scots' work for them, gentlemen. We all want the same thing, for it will not go well with any of us if Berwick were to fall.'

On this they do babble their agreement.

Sir Anthony walks round the table, behind each man, which seems to keep their attention. 'I have sent three messengers to Newcastle. You will understand that I could not risk sending just one, now that the Scots are paying us such strict attention, and Middleton and his rabble are doing their worst. The king must send ships to chase Douglas off. How are we for supplies, Master Hoghtone?'

The clerk wets his lips. 'We are . . . neither good nor bad, I'd say.'

Only Ralph Holme does not watch Sir Anthony's perambulations. 'We are waiting for safe conducts. We need to sail out of here before the weather turns or we will certainly be in trouble.'

Sir Anthony sits down again. 'Then we must pray at least one messenger gets through, though you don't need me to tell you it will take time for anything to happen.'

'So, are we just going to sit here?' From behind I have watched Sir Edmund's neck become redder and redder.

'Yes,' says Sir Anthony. 'That's what we do. Our job is to hold Berwick, not to win the king's war.' He smiles sadly. 'We'd need a few more men for that. But let us not fool ourselves. Just sitting here is hard enough and we must keep ourselves in as good a humour as possible.' He looks at Ralph Holme, who does not move a muscle. 'I suggest we meet again next Sabbath, and meanwhile we might all pray Douglas decides to go after easier game.'

Ralph rises slowly and pads towards the door. But when he sees me, he stops and beckons me over. 'Any news?'

I shake my head.

He turns his head to look at Sir Anthony. 'I want Henry Cranston brought before the blacksmith tomorrow. This needs to end now.' With that, he sweeps out of the room.

'Who does he think he is, giving you orders?' Sir Edmund still has a choleric look about him.

Sir Anthony does not reply, but I fear Ralph is right. We're running out of time.

I did not sleep a wink last night, finding myself floating above my bed for a few moments before coming fully to my senses and dragging myself to Mass. God feels so very far away.

Only a few townsfolk gather in our courtyard, for news of Henry's second interrogation can scarcely have had time to pass among them. But noisy knots of common soldiers swagger in, even before the smith arrives. I suppose they have little enough to amuse them when they're not on duty. I do not know what more we can ask Henry. And yet here he is, flesh encrusted with livid sores and eyes like dark mirrors, reflecting only what is out here, beyond him, and nothing inside.

Sir Anthony stamps his feet and rubs his hands, for

there is a biting harbinger of winter in the air today. Ralph Holme walks in, this time without his great chair, wrapped in a woollen cloak well trimmed with fur, a servant shivering behind him. He stands beside us, scowling at no one in particular. John Pontefract, limping slightly on his left side, comes to join him, William Roxburgh close behind. But when William sees us, he moves hastily away, and I think him a most strange man.

I pull at Sir Anthony's sleeve. 'Do you need me, sir?'

'Have you thought of anything else to ask him?'

I shake my head.

He presses his lips into a hard line. 'I will do it. But stay nearby.' He moves towards Henry, leans to speak quietly to the sunken head. Henry turns to him, lips moving, but I don't think he says anything. Sir Anthony signals to the smith and moves away, head bowed.

With the first scream, I know in my heart Henry did not kill Alice and was surely not the traitor at our gate either. And I do wonder how an innocent man can be brought to feel no pain if it is inflicted upon him here on Earth. He is made of the same flesh and bleeds if he is wounded. Can we be sure God intervenes every time we wish to know the truth about a crime? Surely He trusts us to divine the right and wrong of such matters?

So, if Henry is innocent and must suffer this ordeal, what surety do we have that anything he says is the truth and not merely designed to stop the pain? We are not all so brave that we might resist, and I can imagine even an innocent talking himself into his own execution, leaving a guilty man free to sleep well, at least until Judgement Day. I fear that is what Henry will do and we will be no better for it.

Something swims into the heavy fog in my head and I grasp Sir Anthony's arm. 'I will return shortly, sir.' He opens his mouth, but I am already running up to our chamber. Tugging at my pens and inks, they scatter on the floor and I must take a breath even as I hear Henry scream again. I scrawl something on to a scrap of parchment and run back down, a few men turning to stare at me. I take Sir Anthony's elbow and whisper in his ear.

He frowns. 'I do not see how that helps.'

'Let me try, sir. I think it may prove his innocence.'

'Why would we want to do that?'

I look at him.

'Oh, very well.' He motions the blacksmith away and the crowd growls, presses forward.

I kneel beside Henry who is whimpering to himself, curled up like a baby. 'Will you look at this paper?'

'Tell me what to say, I beg you, sir.' The darkness in his eyes pours a chill down my spine.

'That's not necessary, Henry. All you need to do is look at this paper.'

'I can't.'

'Do it, or I will call back the blacksmith.'

He looks at me, skin like wax, and slowly turns his eyes towards the parchment. He stares at it for several long moments and then he turns his face back to mine, tears flowing down the filth on his cheeks. 'I cannot, sir, not even to spare my life.'

I smile. 'I know, Henry.' I stand up and whisper to Sir Anthony. 'This man cannot read. So, he cannot have intended any mischief by the contents of Alice's purse.'

'You are sure?'

'Quite certain.'

'What did you show him?'

'I wrote that I knew he was innocent and would help him to prove it.'

He shakes his head, a slight smile on his face. 'You are a wonder and a marvel, Ben. And no help whatsoever.' He goes over to speak with the blacksmith.

One or two of the younger men push forward and argue with Sir Anthony, but Sir Edmund comes to stand by his side with Will and Stephen, so they spit on the ground and leave.

But then Sir Edmund turns on me. 'What the devil did you do?'

'He is innocent.'

'Only God knows that. But the blacksmith would have helped *us* know it.'

He is very angry, red-faced and shaking, but the Lord knows, so am I. 'We search for the truth, sir. How will it serve us to destroy a man and still be no nearer to finding it?'

He hits me then, storming off with Will scurrying after him. I can feel my jaw aching, blood seeping through my teeth, but nothing broken, I think.

Sir Anthony comes to me. 'You'd better go and speak to him.' He nods at Ralph Holme, who is nearly the only person left in the courtyard.

Ralph is angry, too, but his anger is quiet, purposeful. 'Explain and do it quickly.'

'Did Sir Anthony tell you what I did, sir?'

'Yes. But a man may be a traitor and not be able to read.'

'Indeed. But we must balance that with the possibility that Henry is telling the truth and decide which is the more likely. He cannot have written the details of the garrison and the walls, so he cannot be our traitor.' Ralph opens his mouth, but I pretend not to see. 'And I have spoken with Dame Eleanor. There is nothing that connects Henry to Alice. Which means there is a more sinister explanation that cannot be ignored.'

'And what is that?' He spits out the words.

I try to hold my thoughts together, even though my head aches almost as much as my jaw. 'If we imagine for a moment that Henry merely found the purse on the day Alice was taken out of the Cowgate, as he said he did, then it must have somehow fallen out of the sack in which she was carried.'

'Why can't it have fallen before?'

'Because there is blood on it, sir.'

He moves a jewelled hand to his mouth. 'Go on.'

'And that means – and it is so obvious I should have thought of this before, but we were so busy finding Henry and then I was working on the cipher – that means Alice was killed because she had found the traitor out. She tried to go to Sir John, on the day she died. It is such a pity she did not find him.'

'How the devil could Alice have found a traitor?'

'I don't know, sir. But it's hard to believe she would have come across him in the tents.'

'Possible, though.'

'Everything's possible until it isn't, sir.'

He nods. 'Very well. Go back to your infernal cipher. But we keep Henry here under lock and key until we know more. You'd better go to him now.' He jerks his head to where Henry still lies face down on the ground, the courtyard quite empty.

I touch him gently on the arm, casting my eye over the wounds on his back. My efforts with the woundwort have kept most of them clean, but I have more to do. 'Henry, you need to get to your feet. I can't do it without you.'

He moans. 'Leave me here, you devil.'

'I'm trying to help you. Now get up and I will see to your wounds once you're back inside.'

I do what must be done for Henry, but already my mind is far away, working on the curious arrangements of letters in the ciphered message. For there the truth lies.

The weather turns very wet, the rain bouncing off the cobblestones and whipping against windows. I grow tired of staying inside and staring at the paper until my eyes see stars. But, at last, there is a breach in the cloud and I hasten on to the Fields, though staying always only a short distance from the gate. Great seas of mud spread out before me, while out to sea, the Scottish ships perch like birds waiting for carrion.

I'm not the only one taking advantage of these moments of cloud-tossed sunshine. Schoolboys run around trying to catch each other, watched with envy by the cowherds whose charges have now gone to stand in the muddy water. Rebecca Scot and Elizabeth Belford huddle together, and I think they seem more pinched and uncertain than when I first came. No one wanders far.

I know that what presses upon all of us most heavily is something we can do nothing about. It really is very simple, though no man here will say it, even if all think it. But I can tell the grass and the sea and the sky, for I do not believe they care.

If the king does not come this year, how long can Berwick stand alone?

A wind ruffles the grass and I turn my head to watch great galleons of black cloud sailing towards us from the west. Standing up, my eye is caught by movement some distance away to the north, and I stare at the shapes, trying to make them into something ordinary. But then I think it might be riders and doubt it augurs well. I shout at the cowherds to move their beasts, if they can, as I run towards the walls. But I have not even reached the gate when trumpets sound. Those on duty on the walls have seen it too.

I turn back to run with the cowherds behind the cows and sheep, but some of the beasts are frightened and run off in all directions. 'Leave them,' I shout. The boys' faces are twisted and pale. One is sobbing and stumbling, and

I link my arm beneath his. 'We're almost there.' I worry about Elizabeth and Rebecca, but there's nothing I can do now.

The men on the Cowgate have begun to shut it, even as the beasts dash through. I see Rebecca and Elizabeth inside, Elizabeth collapsed on the ground like a sack, her friend nodding and moaning over her. The heavens open so that I am quickly soaked right down to my braies, but I run up the stairs on to the walls, see Peter Spalding leaning over. 'Do we ride?'

He turns. 'Are you mad?'

I see Sir Anthony along at the Waleysgate, one arm pointing. I catch my breath and look north again, count fifteen riders. Their horses appear so small they would excite mirth in another time, another place. But not here and now. Peter is right, though I wish he wasn't. I do not like to stand here and let them do whatever they please. I look for black-haired Douglas come to hunt us down, but he isn't there.

They stop, facing us in a line, their skill and impudence astounding. I wish I had a bow and arrow, but, after giving us a derisory bow, they are off again, deftly going after the cows and sheep, turning and weaving across the Fields until all is under their control. And with a great whoop, they turn again and go back the way they came, their message most certainly delivered.

The men-at-arms meet in our hall. Someone brings the news that we have lost thirteen cattle and twenty-nine sheep, another that a woman died of fright and I know it must be Elizabeth. Sir Anthony has notched more lines into his face and he listens with his elbows on the table and his hands to his mouth. And then he tells us that no one must leave the gates without written permission, not even the herds. They must graze the town's beasts on the broken-down land where the tents are. And then he goes off to speak with Ralph Holme.

But already I shiver, and by nightfall I shake with fever.

The fever consumes me so that night and day become one, but finally it lifts, leaving me weak. I sit in our room and think hazy thoughts. It gladdens my heart to receive a message from my sister, Elizabeth, for it has been so long, thanks to the siege. She is well, though she admits that she too suffered from a fever these past weeks and still feels as weak as a new-born lamb. I feel the distance between us, imagining her dead and me not knowing. But such thoughts are to no purpose. Her only other news is that the bailiff has run away with the miller's daughter, leaving behind an irate miller, the bailiff's equally irate wife and five quarrelsome children, who will doubtless become more so without him to chastise them. I smile at the disapproval in her words, the child's contempt for unruly grown-up hearts. And then she remembers something she does care for – her new music teacher, Sister Agatha, who is young and has 'the palest, most beautiful hands I have ever seen and that I confess draw my eyes far more often than is seemly'.

My heart lightens until I read what she has added along the bottom of her letter. I am to be married. My stepfather has applied himself at last and is very pleased with the result, for Juliana fitzWilliam will bring as her dower a portion of her father's lands at Clixby, which lie only a few miles from our manor at Howsham. Juliana is fourteen, a few years older than Elizabeth. But my sister must have made her acquaintance, whether at church or some gathering of gentlefolk, and yet she says nothing about her, which leads me to fear the worst.

And then she adds something that crawls up the side of the letter and must have come directly from our stepfather. I am not to concern myself with my clothes or gifts or any of the other accoutrements that belong to a wedding, for he will attend to all that. Rather, I should give proper consideration to the duties of a husband. I can only pray I please this Juliana – or, at least, that she will not find me loathsome. And that I might find in her a friend and comfort.

I confess that in this matter at least I am grateful to the Scots for one thing: there is no question of my leaving while we are under siege, to be married or not. They linger still at the mouth of the Tweed but have not come before our walls since the day I took ill. They don't need to. But rumours slip through doors and race through the streets. They are said to be mustering in force, though to what purpose, nobody knows for certain. Sir Anthony says nothing, as usual, but we all know he fears the worst.

Even though Ralph Holme and the other burgesses would be held responsible by the king, it would be a terrible slur on his honour if he were to lose Berwick. He walks round the walls, poking and prodding at weaknesses as if he were a veritable engineer.

But there is nothing to be done to improve them, for the burgesses say they have no money, that they have already spent what little they have on our defences, and these wars have cost them dear. If it's not Scottish pirates seizing their ships, then it's rivals in English ports who don't seem to be able to tell friend from foe. Not that they are sending any ships south anyway, thanks to the Scots lying in wait on the German Ocean.

It does not help that our king has indeed sent his army into Northumberland. But the rebellion continues and has spread to Yorkshire. I worry it might catch hold even further south and resolve to reply as soon as I can to my sister, though whether my missive will reach her, I could not say. And we still don't know if the king is sending ships to chase off the Scots.

I put Elizabeth's letter away as Will and Stephen come running in to say a fight has broken out between two of our foot soldiers and a tailor and his apprentice down in the Ness. There is nothing unusual about such fights, whether among men of the garrison or between them and the townsfolk. But this time one of the foot soldiers drew a knife and sliced off the apprentice's ear. Sir Anthony has locked the man in with Henry, who still languishes downstairs. Abandoned and fighting amongst ourselves. If only the Scots knew. Perhaps they do. I know they have every reason to press on with their fiendish designs, no matter how loud the clarion calls for peace.

Some time before I fell ill, the warden of the Franciscans, Friar Adam, left Berwick to speak with Bruce, to see if he might fare better than the papal messengers. I know he has prayed most fervently for the bloodshed to cease and that he will do whatever he can to bring it about.

He returns to Berwick at Michaelmas, when the harvest is over and the husbandmen must pay their dues to their lords. It is a melancholy time of year. The light now leaves us early again, after the long summer days, and the damp and the cold seeps into stone and bones.

The good friar must have felt most melancholy, too, for not only did the accursed leader of the Scots refuse to see him, but he was set upon and robbed right down to his last stitch of clothing on the road home. When I go to the friary I see him through the screen, lying prostrate before the altar, as if the fault was his. But I don't believe I ever thought much would come of his journey, though I understand his desire to try.

I am looking forward to seeing Lucy again for the first time since my fever. But there is nothing excited or welcoming on her face when she enters the church. Instead, she staggers forward, walks past me, turns and hobbles towards me again.

'What's the matter? Is it your back?' I try to swallow the burn of impatience, for we have work to do on the cipher.

She shakes her head violently, rubs her face. 'I don't really know.'

'Then come and sit and tell me what has brought you to this agitation.'

'Yes. Thank you. I didn't know who else to speak to.' She hauls herself down on the other side of a pillar on the far wall, pushing up her knees and wrapping her arms around them. 'I don't know how to start. It's something that has crept upon me, even as I have come to find it strangely usual.'

'Something that concerns Alice's death?'

She lowers her chin on to her knees. 'Must everything have to do with that?'

'No, of course not. I just thought . . .' I see she is most distressed, and why would she not wish to confide in me? I am her friend, and she mine.

'I just wanted to speak to you about it. Forgive me if I presume too much.' Her voice is flat and small.

'It is for you to forgive me. I spoke without thinking.'

She lifts her head, nods slightly, traces a pattern in the dust on the stone floor with her finger. 'And please forgive *me*, for it is something I have told you before and . . . you did not think much of it. That Edward . . . was master in our house, my mother always careful in his presence, though of what, I couldn't say.'

'I thought it was her intention that he should take over some of her concerns, if he had married Alice?'

She nods. 'But I do not know that any of what passes between them is at her bidding. Even the marriage with Alice . . .' Tears glimmer but she blinks quickly. 'She seems to shrink and shudder just a little when he is near to her, even when he is speaking in the way a servant should. As if she is afraid. Did I not say something of this before?'

'Not that she was afraid. I suppose it must be difficult, to be a woman and alone and mistress all at the same time.'

'I did something. I'm ashamed of it, but it needed to be done and I hope you won't think too ill of me.' The painting on the floor grows more frantic.

I smooth a hand over my mouth to hide my smile, for how much mischief could she accomplish? And how glorious that she cherishes my good opinion. 'What did you do?'

'I pretended to go out with Mary. And then I lay as quietly as if I was in my grave in the big chest in the solar. I thought they would be down in the hall, but Edward followed my mother up there. It was as if they had been speaking before and he wasn't finished.'

'What did he say?'

'You are not disappointed in me?'

'Perhaps I should be. But if you thought your mother was in danger in some way . . . Is that what you thought?'

'Not danger, exactly, but that there was some awful secret between them.'

'You haven't told me what he said.'

She frowns again. 'I must ask you something first. And you must promise most solemnly.'

'Promise what?'

'Will you keep it secret? His words, they were not . . . You will understand when I say them.'

It is my turn to frown. 'Lucy, I cannot promise when I don't know what significance they might have. Of course, I will try, but if they do have some bearing on Alice's murder . . .'

'I don't see how they can. *He* lost a prize when I lost my sister.' She twists her mouth, looking me straight in the eye. 'I'm not sure of all his words, but I think it was: "I can still tell everyone you're a whore, Eleanor. Since I can't have Alice, I'll have to wed you. I'll be a respectable burgess, and no one can throw me out. Just because Wysham's gone, it doesn't mean any of them like our kind, you know that."'

It sounds to me as if she remembers entirely. 'I don't understand.'

'No.' She says it quietly. 'I don't either. But this morning Mother told me they are to be wed. I thought she was telling me she was to be hanged.'

I say nothing for a moment, running her words hither and thither. But I cannot think of anything to say to reassure her. Taking her hand, I stroke it gently. 'He is a most enterprising fellow, this Edward . . . What is his surname?'

'Smith.'

Her hand is warm in mine. 'I imagine you know nothing about the meaning of his words?'

She looks me straight in the eye. 'You mean, why he called my mother a whore? No, I do not.'

'Didn't you tell me she was with child when she came to Berwick?'

'Yes. The Scots killed her husband. She does not speak of it.'

'What if that wasn't true? What if she was unmarried and carried a child?'

Her hand stiffens in mine, and I think she will remove it, but she does not. 'And Edward has come to know of it?'

'Yes. Though I cannot think how. He told me he'd never met her before he came to Berwick.'

She twists her mouth. 'That need not be true either.'

'I suppose. Do you want me to speak with him?'

She shakes her head. 'What could you say? And you have more important work to do.'

I'm glad she refuses, as I think the same thing. 'I'm sorry.'

'Don't be. You let me speak of it and for that I thank you.' Pushing her hair away from her face, she quickly leans towards me and kisses me on the cheek. 'Did you bring the cipher?'

'Of course.' There seems to be something sticking in my throat.

'Do you think we'll find the answer?'

'Do you?'

'Yes.'

As I pull out the cipher, I think of my marriage and feel suddenly lost at the thought of life without Lucy when I leave.

Chapter 14

And still the cipher eludes us, though we think for a moment we have found the word 'Berwick', which brings great encouragement. But if we have, then the letters do not help us find anything else. Lucy waits for her mother in the friary, and I walk home, head trailing towards the ground. Will sits by the window in our room. He watches me looking at the paper, shifting constantly. I wait for the words to fall out of his mouth, but he turns back to look out the window.

'What?'

He looks at me with a frown. 'I didn't say anything.'

'I can hear you thinking from here.'

'Well, if you're so clever, you'll know what it was.' He turns away again.

I sigh and put the parchment down. 'What's the matter?'

'Nothing.'

'Tell me.'

He clasps his hands together. 'Is Edith with child?'

I blink, wondering how he could not have noticed. 'Yes.'

A smile spreads delight across his face. 'You see!'

I remember I'm not supposed to know it is his child. 'See what?'

He puffs himself up like a peacock. 'It's mine.'

'Ah!'

He blinks, clearly expecting more.

'Are you thinking of marrying her?'

'God's balls! What are you talking about?'

'Sorry. I didn't think that's what you meant.'

'It's good for a man to have a few bastards to show he can plant good seed. I hope it's a boy. Does it look like she's carrying a boy to you?'

I shrug, perplexed by the whole conversation.

He leans forward. 'You know what you need, don't you?'

'I have no idea.'

'A good fuck. When was the last time?'

I want to lie to him, to make up some story. But he would ask for details, and I would look an even bigger fool. 'I haven't had the opportunity . . .'

He looks at me as if I have turned into something he might find on the bottom of his boot. 'By the living fiend!' He shakes his head. 'What are you waiting for?'

'I don't know.' That is not entirely the truth. I want tenderness. I want someone who will tell me everything will come to the good, who will wrap me in their love and their forgiveness.

Will shakes his head again. 'Are you a sodomite, then?'

'No, Will, I'm not. You're quite safe.' His eyes shoot up towards his eyebrows. 'I jest!'

'Well, if that's what learning does to you, I'm glad I didn't pay any attention to the old goat my father paid to teach me.' He waggles a finger at me. 'If you're not careful, your cock will shrivel up and fall off. And you'll have nothing to give to your wife and that will be the end of your line. I suppose your father has arranged your marriage?'

I was about to snort with laughter, but his last question sobers me. 'Not my father. My stepfather. He's not renowned for moving swiftly, but he has managed to do it at last. I suppose he was eager to settle the matter before I come of age in December. What about you?' The idea of marriage seems as remote and foreign as Rome, but at least I have read about the holy city's enticements in books.

He shrugs. 'My father is always looking for some plump mare with a fat dowry, but when he finds one, he imagines an even richer one, and on he goes, the old fool.'

'Not the Earl of Arundel's daughter, then?' I smile, for more recently he has moved his affections from Alice to his previous 'lady', whom he caught a glimpse of once in London.

He turns away towards the window and gently follows a raindrop down the pane with his finger. 'I would fight to the death for her. Even if she never knew I walked on this Earth, I would do it, for she is an angel. You think the world is all about your monkish mumbling and your clever questions, but that's nothing compared to what a woman like that can stir in a man.' He leans his head against the glass and stays there so long I think he has fallen asleep. But then he jumps to his feet, eyes glittering. 'I pity you.'

He takes all words out of my mouth and I let him leave, banging the door hard behind him. For a moment, I do envy him, whatever it is he feels so strongly. But I cannot bring myself to believe in it, for when I turn his pious certainties over in my mind, they seem most fantastical, if not blasphemous. And yet . . . I see his heart works harder than mine, that he moves through life to an insistent beat while I drift along quite unmoored.

I think of Alice and Tom, already turning to dust in the grave. Perhaps Will is right. It's true my questions do not bring as much illumination as I'd hoped. But they have brought death. What I don't know is whether the Dark Hunter stalks us still.

I am most surprised when the steward pops his head round our door to say Edward Smith has come to speak with me. I slip down the stairs to the hall and find Edward pacing up and down, hands behind his back.

He turns and leaps towards me. 'I heard you had a fever. I was most worried for you.' He eyes me from head to foot. 'You are recovered? Not too tired?'

'Much better, thank you.' I cannot help but smile, even as I remember what Lucy said about his strange hold over Dame Eleanor. I wonder if I'm supposed to know he is to marry her.

We sit at the table, he across from me, bringing his fingers to his lips, searching for a kerchief to wipe his face, staring hard at the contours of the wood. 'I' – he glances up at me, looks down again – 'know I've misled you and am truly sorry.'

I blink, discomfited, for I have never seen him in the least unsure of himself. 'What do you mean?'

'I have not told you the whole truth and I think now . . . I think it might help you. With your investigations.'

'That is most serious.'

'I know. I'm sorry.'

I sit back, heart racing. 'You'd better tell me.'

'It concerns William Roxburgh.'

'I thought he was your friend.'

He looks up at me with a little sigh. 'So did I. But I think he wants to silence me.'

'What does that mean?'

'It means I'm afraid.'

I frown, stare at the table myself. 'Tell me what you saw.'

'It's not so much what I saw as didn't see. I didn't see him for quite some time that night.'

'The night Alice was murdered?'

He nods. 'I think I told you I fell asleep. That's true. But I did wake up and I was all alone. I searched for him and do remember finding another jug of wine. I drank it as the bells for Compline rang and I fell asleep again. When I awoke, he was there beside me.'

I rub my forehead. 'Why did you not tell me before?'

'I really couldn't quite remember if it was real or if I'd imagined it. And I most certainly didn't think he was capable of . . . You know he is a Scot?'

'As are you.'

He purses his lips. 'Indeed. But did you know his sons were arrested for spying?'

No, I did not. I twist the cord of my purse at my waist, trying to make sense of all this. 'But you were not afraid when I first spoke with you.'

He places his palms flat on the table. 'It's his own fault. I did not think of it, being so befuddled that night. But then he kept asking and asking. "Do you not remember anything about that night? Are you sure?" And then I did and found it hard to lie to him – and I'm sure he knows.'

I think I understand. 'Let me be clear, you think William is the traitor and Alice found out, and that's why she was killed?'

He shakes his head, mouth opening and closing. 'I do not want to think it.'

'It sounds as if you already have.'

His shoulders crumple and at last he nods.

'But how did Alice find out?'

He gently rubs his fingers across his brow. 'I don't know. But Eleanor was friendly with William's wife. Took it badly when she died. Alice was ages with Roland, their older boy, and I suppose . . . I believe she visited him from time to time. With her mother's permission and taking her maid with her, of course. Perhaps . . .' He shrugs and sighs.

I nod, uncertain what to think. He stands up and I rise too. I wish with all my heart he'd told me sooner, not least to save poor Henry's skin. And now I must run around asking more of my infernal questions even as the cipher lies under my shirt, laughing at me.

As we reach the door, he pauses. 'Do you know I'm to marry Eleanor?'

I try to feign my surprise. 'Really?'

His chin juts out towards me. 'You do not approve? Or is that Lucy's opinion?'

'It is not for me to approve or disapprove.' I do not want to talk about Lucy.

'You think me mercenary, perhaps, to wed the mother so soon after being deprived of the daughter? I would not disagree.'

I say nothing, for he has it right.

'I know you're honest, Benedict, and clever too. Your good opinion matters to me. But I ask you to consider my situation. Do you think my fellow Scots will treat me well if Berwick falls? We should have gone to Newcastle when we still could.'

'Is it so easy? To set up business somewhere else?'

'No, it isn't. Perhaps that's what stayed my hand. I have already lost everything. The house my grandfather built. The land given to us by King Alexander. Brought down by Bruce's treachery and greed to become Ralph Holme's warehouse servant!' He shuts his eyes, but immediately they fly open again and he holds me in his gaze. 'Eleanor is a good woman and a rich one, if a little old for my taste. But you'd better keep those wolves from the gates, or it will all be for naught.' He nods at me, gives a taut little smile and disappears down the stairs.

I scrape my hands through my hair and wonder what to do now.

The next day, I try to keep my thoughts on the cipher, but William Roxburgh's flaccid features push their way in, so that I find myself wondering about him rather than the letters in front of me. I go on watch at Nones. But as I walk home at Vespers I know I will find no rest and I scurry along Shaw's Lane towards Walkergate.

William Roxburgh's house lies on the east side of Walkergate, which stretches from the western end of Marygate up to the Waleysgate. It is neat enough on the outside, despite a profusion of merchandise piled up in front and stretching down each side. I already know he is a widower and see, as I follow his servant into his hall, that what little he keeps inside is there for a purpose rather than ornament. A bellows sits beside the fire, the hangings are gaudy but ill-matched and the dresser is bare of all but a candle and a discarded purse. William sits with a boy of about thirteen, a book open on the table between them. He gets up with a frown and a wheeze. 'Benedict. Are you looking for me?'

I stifle the urge to wonder what else I would be doing in his house. 'If I might speak with you for a moment.'

He looks at me, mouth twisting. And then he puts a hand on the boy's shoulder, bends towards him. The boy shuts the book and leaves the room, his gaze brushing me quickly as he passes. William sits back down heavily and indicates a chair on the other side of the table. I would rather stand, so that I might leave quickly, but I have no reason to do anything other than sit. He leans an elbow on the table, cups his hand under his chin and looks anywhere but at me.

'I ...' I realise I don't know what to say even as I reason I cannot tell the truth. 'I was just wondering if you might remember anything at all about the night Alice Rydale was murdered.' I stare at the mud on my boots. 'Even the slightest thing. Are you quite sure Edward was with you the entire time, for example?'

He breathes out, stares at the wall. 'Have you . . . Do you have new information?'

I incline my head, hoping it is enough to give him room to talk.

He bites his lip then shakes his head firmly. 'I cannot tell you anything more. I wish I could.'

'And you did not leave here at all that evening?'

He swivels his head towards me then, an angry patch of red on each cheek. 'Did someone say I did?'

'I am only trying to find out if you or Edward saw something . . . anything . . .'

He frowns. 'But what about the ciph . . . ?' His mouth twitches, eyes crawling all over the wall. 'I mean, do you have nothing else to help you?'

I feel myself shrink away from him, for I know that secret has been well guarded. But I don't know if I should challenge him over it. I didn't tell anyone I was coming here. 'What is it you think might help us?'

He shakes his head, turns pallid eyes on me. 'I thought I'd heard something. From Edward, perhaps.'

I nod, stand up. I feel as if I will not be able to breathe properly until I'm outside. Edward has never mentioned the cipher. 'Thank you. I'm sorry to have disturbed you.'

He rises, too, pushing on a smile. 'You are most welcome.'

I am so eager to leave that I almost fall over my feet on the stairs. The light is beginning to draw away, but I am not finished yet. I run without stopping all the way down Soutergate, round the corner into Hidegate and on to Ralph Holme's warehouse. He stands in the middle of the floor, his men all gone home. There is so little in the warehouse, I can see the bones of its construction. He is in a sombre mood.

I look at him closely, seeing the red streaks in his eyes, the pallor chasing away what the sun has coarsened. 'Are you well, sir?'

'Do you suspect me still? Is my guilty conscience showing on my face, is that it?' He turns away.

I follow him, quite dismayed. 'No, sir. You mis-understand me. I thought you looked tired, is all.'

He sits back down heavily in his seat. 'Tired? Tired

to death.' He looks up at me, a queer look on his face. 'Don't you tell anyone I said that, you hear?'

'Yes, sir. There's much to worry about, I'm sure.'

He gently strokes the fur at his collar. 'How old are you?'

'Twenty years, sir. Nearly twenty-one.'

He nods. 'I have a son your age.'

'Robert?' I have heard he is a handsome boy with little of his father about him, so the foolish talkers say.

He nods. 'Since you have discovered every secret in this town, you'll know he is gone to York.'

I frown, for I did not know. 'For his safe keeping?'

He smiles, but his eyes do not. 'Aye, you could say that. Our boys are hostages, that we may not fail the king.'

I bite my lip. 'I see.' It's right there should be some surety that the burgesses will act in good faith. Indeed, I feel better that such a measure has been taken, for our safe keeping is a serious matter. But for all he is a bully with the pride of a peacock, he is clearly a fond father and I see how it pains him. 'We will not fail you, sir.'

'Ah, Benedict, if only every man on these walls was as innocent as you! I don't need you to make promises you might not be able to keep.' He sighs softly. 'But tell me quickly what it is you want. I need you to find that traitor.'

I hesitate, having not thought deeply about what I want to say. 'I've been told something. That is, I would like to know more about William Roxburgh.'

He frowns. 'William? Why . . . ? Oh, don't bother to tell me. You'll have your reasons.'

'Is it true his sons were arrested for spying?'

He looks at me and scratches his head. 'Yes, two or more years ago. But as I recall, it was a misunderstanding. A royal official newly come here. Didn't know William, you see. Just heard the name, which is obviously Scottish, and thought it sinister they were here.'

'But how do you know they weren't spying?'

He laughs. 'They were just lads. Out playing in the Fields when they should have been at their studies.' His face subsides into gloom. 'Who told you? Is it serious?'

I nod.

He scratches his chin. 'William's been here for years. Roland, his elder boy, is gone to be a hostage with my Robert.'

I don't know what to think.

'Mind you, he has been acting strangely recently, but I didn't think anything of it. We're all ill at ease these days. Won't meet my eye, keeps his distance.' He pushes himself out of his chair.

'Just one more question.' I know I'm being dismissed. 'What do you know of Edward, Dame Eleanor's steward. He worked for you, didn't he?'

'Not for long. He was here in the warehouse just a few months. His leaving angered me at the time. I don't like to give work to Scots, but his story was a painful one. Eleanor must have a hide as thick as a boar – the whole town could talk of nothing else but how she'd fallen for him and made him her steward. I had no idea why she did it and I still don't. I thought he was stealing from me, caught him lingering round my desk. But he dared me to find anything missing and I couldn't.'

'And now she is to marry him.'

He whistles. 'Is that right? He's done well, I must say.'

'And she fled from the Scots too?'

He nods. 'Another sad story. She lived somewhere far away in Scotland with her first husband, a corn merchant. They supplied our garrison in the town, but when it was besieged by the Scots, they were caught as traitors. They killed him and sent her away. So, she came here, where it was safe.'

I doubt she thinks it's safe now.

He stands, staring at something far away. 'Beautiful, she was then. Philip Rydale couldn't take his eyes off her from the moment she came. Married her within six months.'

I open my mouth.

He stands up. 'That's enough questions, Ben.'

The stories tally, both Dame Eleanor's and Edward's. As for William, he could be angry with the way his sons were treated. Or was sent here long ago to become one of us, ready to betray the town when the time was right. But what about his oldest boy . . . ?

Ralph puts an arm around me as he leads me to the door. 'If William's got anything to do with this, I'll choke the life out of him myself.'

I worry he might do or say something unhelpful. 'I suspect my informer is mistaken. It was not a very . . . It was only a suspicion, nothing certain.'

'Then you need to find out if it's true or if it isn't.'

I don't need him to tell me that.

I walk slowly up the road, turning over these strange
revelations. But by the time I turn into Marygate, I am
convinced of only one thing: I must not waste any more
time. It is the cipher that matters, not running around
Berwick from one scent to another.

Before I go to sleep, a sudden thought falls upon me
– that we shouldn't keep pushing and pulling at the letters
but try to imagine what the first word might be. I could
send a message, arrange to meet, but as soon as I'm free
the next afternoon I run down to Hide Hill. Lucy is very
pleased to see me, though she tells me I am still most pale
and far too thin, though perhaps she should look in a
mirror. We sit together on the window seat in the solar.
I am relieved that I need not bring out the paper, for by
now we know the letters perfectly.

On the page, the first word is written as 'Sub' with a
dot after it to indicate a shortening. Lucy leans back
against the shutter, which has been shuddering in the
wind. She picks at a mark on her dress. 'Do you think it
might be Robert, the Scottish . . . the man who leads
the Scots?'

'But that would mean the first letter is also transposed
and it's a consonant.' I clutch her arm in excitement. 'It
would certainly make sense. And the next words should
be something like "by the grace of God".' I look at her in
consternation. 'Not that he has any right to . . .'

She pats my hand. 'Let us attend to the letters and not
worry about the war for a moment.'

We both stare into the room, shifting the letters about in the air. I must admit to the cipher's cleverness, for I had assumed all this time that the first letter was the real one. The next word is written as 'eiu', which is surely really *dei* and most helpful, for now it truly looks as if the first letter in any word, if a consonant, becomes its neighbour. We also now know that 'o' is written as 'u', 'e' becomes 'i', and 'i' becomes 'o'. Crawling carefully along the line, with many missteps and sighs of frustration, we succeed in discovering: *Robert, by the grace of God illustrious King of Scots. To all who see this* . . .

And then the door opens and Edward steps nimbly through it. He smiles broadly, even as his brows furrow. 'You look most strange, sitting like that staring into nothing. I thought you were good friends, not silent strangers.'

I am truly glad the paper is hidden. 'We are both a little weary, I think.'

He nods, rises briefly up on his toes. 'How are your investigations? You will tell me if there are any developments?'

Already he speaks entirely for himself, not Dame Eleanor. I wonder when they will wed. 'Never fear.'

He seats himself in an ornate chair near the fire. 'If you will forgive me for saying so, I wonder you have time to spend here, when there's a murderer out there.'

I do not want him to doubt me. 'There's more ways than one to catch him.'

'But what you can possibly achieve sitting staring into nothing? I have Lucy and her mother to protect.'

I feel Lucy shift slightly beside me, but she keeps her gaze on her lap.

I understand his concern, for the murderer did not baulk at killing Tom Crory when it looked as if the old man might unmask him. 'I cannot say very much. But if you remember, I said we had evidence that we thought proved Henry Cranston's guilt, but it seems rather to have belonged to someone else.'

He raises his eyebrows. 'That sounds most curious.'

'Please forgive my silence.'

'Of course. May I only ask why you labour under such uncertainty, first attaching your evidence to one man, then another?'

I struggle with the right words. 'The evidence is not . . . it does not . . . exactly say what it means. But we hope to find that meaning very soon.'

He smiles gently. 'I have no earthly idea how such a thing might be true, but since I know you to be most marvellously ingenious, you will surely uncover it.' And then he turns to Lucy. 'And you, do you help with this riddle?'

I can tell she is startled, the little piece of skin throbbing at her neck. But she answers calmly. 'I have not such cleverness, sir.' She smooths down her skirts, eyes cast down.

There is a strange moment of silence and I search my mind for something to say. 'And when is the happy day? You must know I wish you and Dame Eleanor much joy.' I can only hope that, when Edward is safely wed, he will be kind to his wife.

His mouth twitches into yet another little smile. 'Soon, I hope. But I thank you. Not everyone in this town will be as kind.'

His honesty is worthy, and I cannot help but be glad his fortunes have turned to the good, given what he must have suffered. But I can do nothing more with the cipher in his presence, nor even spend a pleasant hour talking to Lucy of whatever we please.

As I stand behind Sir Edmund at supper, I try to work through more of the paper, but soon realise something is amiss. Sir Anthony's face is taut, the lines around his eyes never fading. I pour and serve, then stand back, eager to find out what's wrong.

'It's not possible to do it properly with only one at each gate, especially the ones with only a bar.' Sir Anthony swirls his goblet round and round. 'It's not safe. We know there's a traitor inside our walls and the Scots circling outside. And we must face yet another winter without any help from the king.' News has come at last that the muster has now been abandoned, as everyone said it would.

Sir Edmund sighs. 'But there will be more men elsewhere on the walls, surely?'

'Scarcely any. And not near enough after dark. That would be folly, utter folly.'

'What choice do you have?'

'The only other thing I can do is cut the men's pay. There was little enough money coming in before, but with the siege, it's . . . The point is, we don't know how long it's going to last, do we? I can hear the howling already. But if I leave each gate guarded by only one man, the entire town is at his mercy.' They sit in silence for a moment. Sir Anthony sighs again. 'I'm not going to stay much longer, Edmund. We're just sitting here like fools, and I'd rather be looking out for my own.'

'Me neither. They don't deserve us.' He beckons to me and I fill his goblet even as my hand shakes. I do not want to leave here. I might tell myself it is because I still have a murderer to find. But that is not the whole truth.

There is too much to think about and I toss and turn well into the night listening to Sir Edmund snoring and the rain beating fast and slow on the roof. The next day, he remembers that a tailor in the Ness has been making new tunics for Will and me, the first we've had since Lady Day, and sends me to collect them. The streets are still thronged after the market, though it's now well into the retreating afternoon. It is a cold day, smothered in grey but thankfully dry, roofs and cobbles glistening and many a drip catching passers-by unawares.

I am in a hurry to get back and finish making sense of the letter. But when I was awake in the night, it was Alice who came into my mind, calling me for a fool. The question that pursues me now, after all this time running after Henry and working on the cipher and turning my mind on to William Roxburgh, is how she came to have the papers of a traitor in her purse. That she should have been killed for them is now more or less beyond doubt. But how did she discover the papers? And where? Perhaps I should speak with Dame Eleanor. Ask her if Alice visited the Roxburghs in the weeks leading up to her death.

The streets are almost empty now, doors shutting firmly and a few candles visible at the windows of the bigger houses. As I turn into Hidegate, I hear a commotion up one of the little lanes leading into Ravensdowne. I peer into its narrow confines. 'Is anyone there?' I look around, but there is no one in Hidegate either. I think I hear a muffled cry. It would be foolish to go down there, but cowardly not to. No one would know if I didn't go, except God.

I take out my dagger and move slowly into the lane. There is an uncommon amount of filth and rubbish down here and I nearly stumble more than once as the light fades. I call out again but hear nothing. Turning to retrace my steps, there is a rush of movement and I raise an arm as glass shatters loudly in my ear. I fall slowly, the earth turning upside down, and someone shouts from high in the heavens. I think of the washing I will have to do to clean my hose and tunic and how sorry I am that Lucy and I cannot sing together. And then there is nothing.

The darkness comes and goes in a terrible heat and I sleep and sleep, though sometimes I wake, having been chased by a man holding a knife and singing the 'Magnificat'. People come to stand over me, then they go again. I do not care. Once, a sharp pain stabs right through me to my guts and I feel something watery slide over my forehead and down my nose. I do not think it's blood. It could be blood. I sleep on until one rainy morning when I sit up with a dreadful thirst and a great ache in my head.

'Will?' He is sitting by the window mending a shirt. 'Can I have something to drink?'

He scowls and finishes what he's doing, but at last he rises to pour me some ale. 'You've been sleeping for ever. We need to get after the dog who did it.'

I stare at him. 'What do you care?'

He stares back at me as if I were an idiot. 'You might be an ink-dabber, but you're still one of us. And if anybody touches a hair on your head, we'll get after him.'

I'm not sure if I find that comforting but I sit back and try to think. 'I only remember glass breaking. I must have been hit from behind. I thought I was dead, for certain.'

'You've got the little butcher's boy to thank.'

'Wat?'

Will's top lip curls up in a ready sneer. 'He's quite your little pet. Comes every day to ask after you. Sir Anthony spoke to him, about what they saw. Him and his master and the other one.'

'So, what did they say?'

He shrugs and moves back to the window, taking out his dagger and looking closely at it in the light. 'How the hell can this need sharpening again?'

I get up some time later and walk carefully downstairs. I find Sir Edmund in the stable and he greets me with an arm laid heavily on my shoulder, which makes me want to weep.

'Do you know what happened?' Like Will, I am now very eager to know.

'There's not much to tell. The butchers were coming home and heard you cry out. They rushed at the man attacking you, but he ran off in the other direction and it was too dark to give chase properly.'

'So, they saw nothing of this man?'

'He was well wrapped up. Neither small nor tall, which is no help whatsoever.'

As I move cautiously back to our room, I know now, beyond a shadow of a doubt, that I am very close to the truth. And that this is a fight to the death.

Chapter 15

Will and Stephen are eager to tell me all that has happened and to make sure my head continues to throb and ache. Much has changed, even if everything is really still the same. A truce between us and the Scots has been declared in London on behalf of the Pope, and even the haughty Scottish brigand will not act against it entirely. And so Bruce's ships have departed, and my heart clutches my throat at the thought I might be summoned back to Lincolnshire for my marriage. While Will and Stephen talk on, speaking against each other and cursing ever more loudly, I wonder if Lucy has mastered all the words in the paper yet. Indeed, I cannot imagine she has not done so when we had already made such good progress. I ask them if she has sent a message, but Will shakes his head, making my heart sore.

Sir Anthony arrives, chasing the other two away. He sits down heavily, the flesh under his jaw hanging loose. 'I thought we'd lost you, I confess it. But you're stronger than you look.'

I ask him if he has seen anything of Lucy, or even Dame Eleanor. He shrugs and says he cannot recall doing so but has scarcely been looking for them.

I think I have been asleep for an eternity and woken to find Berwick under a spell of despondency. 'I am sorry not to have found the traitor yet, sir.'

He nods. 'I have not had time to worry about him. It's enough just keeping men on the walls with sufficient food in their bellies to hold them upright.'

'Is it so very bad?'

He scratches his beard. 'It's been worse. But I do not doubt it is dangerous. Sir Edmund thinks the traitor has gone, slunk back among the Scots.'

'Why does he think that?'

'Perhaps because he wishes it to be true.'

Sir Anthony is a very wise man.

He sighs. 'And perhaps we have come to believe we could never find him out, even with your paper.'

'That's not true, I'm sure of it! I just . . .' I frown.

'You need your strength, Ben. Save it for your sword arm.'

I know he is wrong. 'I am surprised, sir, that Lucy Rydale did not tell you what the paper said. We had worked on it together the day before I was attacked. We nearly had it, sir.'

He looks at me for a long moment, gently stroking his cheek. 'Do you think there is a correspondence in that, you coming close to understanding the cipher and being knocked on the head?'

Is there no end to my stupidity? I had thought the

attack proved the worthiness of my quest to decipher the paper. I had not imagined the nearness of its resolution might be the reason someone tried to kill me. I spoke to Edward only in vague terms, mentioning evidence that seemed to point a finger at Henry, but now led elsewhere. William, on the other hand, knows about the cipher and my questioning him could have brought him to a pitch of anxiety. I feel a cold tingling in my blood. 'Sir, I must finish the paper.'

He sighs. 'I see you are not to be gainsaid. And we shall not mention it abroad that you are recovered. Go and find somewhere peaceful to work.'

That is certainly not our chamber. Will and Stephen will be back soon enough and whatever they do is likely to become noisy and violent. I must find them, though, for I am almost undone by the thought I do not know where the purse with the paper I kept round my neck might be. But Stephen tells me he took it off to keep safely before the physician arrived to bind my wound. My heart slows down at last when he hands it to me from among his clothes.

I steal down to the hall, where a pallid mid-winter light hovers at the window. Sitting at the table, I prise out the paper carefully and unfold it in front of me. It lies there, once more a confusion of letters, though I can still remember what the first few words say. I write them down, and the true vowels thus revealed. And I remember that the consonant at the beginning of a word will become its neighbour to the right. This takes me far longer than I would have hoped, and it is only when

Stephen comes with a candle from Sir Anthony that I realise how late it is and how much my head feels it is filled with stones.

I continue to work while they eat near me, my mind totally devoted to the slow uncovering of each word. Its form is not unexpected, the Scottish king addressing those of *his dear and faithful men who might see* – or more likely, be shown – *this letter*. It goes on: *Forasmuch as we wish to expedite certain secret matters touching on the ancient rights and liberties of this, our kingdom of Scotland, we have charged the bearer with those said secret matters. To that end, we do not wish him to be disturbed in the execution of our commands. But inasmuch as it is necessary for the bearer to conceal himself among our enemies, we wish for this letter to declare the truth.*

I look up, the knots in my stomach upsetting the drawing of my breath, to find all eyes in the room upon me. Sir Edmund comes over, leans on the table beside me. 'Can you do it, lad?'

'Yes. I will be finished soon.'

'Then I'll leave you in peace.' They pretend to talk amongst themselves by the fire, but I know they are with me and that warms my heart.

I could try to guess which words reveal the name of the bearer, but I fear that will take me longer in the end. And so I plough on, word by word.

The name of our dear friend and servant . . .

No one moves, apart from Stephen, who must go on watch.

. . . the bearer of this letter . . .

The distant bells of the Holy Trinity ring for Compline and still no one thinks to go to bed.

... *is Edward Morham, otherwise known as Edward Smith.* It is done and I am very afraid. But not for myself.

I imagine Edward would have departed from Berwick if he knew he hadn't killed me in the alley. But as everyone crowds around me, Will remembers seeing him only yesterday, riding out in Dame Eleanor's cart towards Lamberton and coming back just before the gates closed. And I remember he went there the day Alice died ... the day he killed Alice.

At the time, all those months ago, I thought him most devoted, to venture so far beyond our walls to provide for his mistress. But, of course, at Lamberton – about a league to the north of us – it would be far easier to meet with a messenger from Douglas, or any one of the Scottish leaders encircling us. Is that what he was doing yesterday, conspiring with them to make another attempt on our walls? And all the time, knowing we have the proof of his treachery. I wonder what drives him to dance so closely with death.

There is a silence, brief but full to bursting, followed by an almighty babbling. Sir Anthony speaks without being heard, his voice rising urgently until everyone quietens. 'I cannot ask men to come down off the walls and it might be dangerous to go to him tonight. We are only four.'

Sir Edmund thumps the table with his fist. 'And he is only one, Anthony. A devil, yes, but not *the* Devil. And if we wait, who knows what mischief he will manage?'

Sir Anthony sighs and nods. 'Perhaps we might tell Ralph Holme first?'

Sir Edmund gives him a stern look. 'And waste more time? Let us go now.' He looks at me. 'Are you well enough, Ben?'

'I would not have you go without me, sir.' I feel a terrible worry pressing down upon me. It is the thought that Edward has been in that house all this time and is still there now, and who knows what he will do, if he must, for he has not a scrap of loyalty to Dame Eleanor or anyone else here. I think Sir Edmund is right: that we should move against Edward before word spreads, for it will, quicker than the turning of the tide.

We strap on our swords and light torches to take us along Berwick's quiet streets. Flying along Marygate, we turn down into Hide Hill. A few shutters open, faces peering out, eyes half-shut but mouths open. 'Go back to bed,' Sir Edmund hisses, but I do not think they pay much heed. At the Rydale house, Sir Anthony attacks the heavy metal knocker grimly, the noise flooding the quiet night. That it is not answered comes as little surprise to any of us.

'There is an entrance from the garden?' Sir Anthony speaks quietly. I whisper back that there assuredly is, for Lucy and I have sat beside their physick garden when the weather was mild. 'It matters not,' he says. 'It's too late to start searching for it now. I do not see how we will gain admittance. All we've done is inform Edward that he is discovered.'

I walk back into the middle of the road, but there is only a forbidding darkness the whole height of the house. He cannot stay inside for ever, but what harm might he do before he is taken? I dare not think it. And I cannot stand here doing nothing. 'Please. I'm sure I can find my way to the back door.'

Sir Anthony looks at me for a long moment. 'If you think you must, and no harm will come by it. I want no foolishness, do you hear? Will, you go too.'

I nod, though the turmoil I feel does not make the promise feel altogether secure. If Edward has hurt Lucy, I will kill him and not think twice about it.

Will seizes a torch and we trot away down the hill, turning the corner into Hidegate. We soon reach the entrance to a narrow lane that meanders back up the slope along the bottom of the gardens of the houses on Hide Hill. I have not been here before and must hope for a gate or even just a gap in the paling to lead us into the garden and hope we have entered the right one. It is entirely dark, the moon cast out by cloud. We pass only rough ground until at last we reach a neat wall with a gate. This is surely it.

Will is too fast for me and I must be careful without the light of the torch falling in front of me. 'Wait!' My words sound too loud. I stop quickly, the powerful stench of a midden nearby. Will reappears. 'Hurry up, mumblecrust.' I cling to his tunic and we stumble on through the lumpen remains of the vegetable patch, entangling ourselves in the sticks left over from where the peas grew. The house looms large and dark ahead, so that I must imagine there is now a smothered moon somewhere giving us a little help.

I sprawl then, undone by the little hedge running around the physick garden. Will tuts. But I am unharmed and do not pause even to dust away the dirt on my clothes. We find the well-trampled path that leads to the back door and run more surely. This near to the house, I would not wish our presence to be discovered by some sort of riotous calamity.

I move my hand slowly and carefully on the door handle, turning it most gently. The creaking is terrible and obstinate, and I know in an instant it too is locked. I want to punch and kick it. I do not think I have the strength to walk away and I ask the Lord to help me.

I hear a clanging, metallic sound, and hiss angrily at Will: 'Be quiet, for pity's sake.'

'Do not chide me! I did not mean to kick it.' He holds the torch down towards the ground. 'What the devil?'

I bend towards a large metal key, scarcely believing it is real. 'Put the light on the lock.' But I am disappointed once more: the key is clearly far too big to fit. Even as I tell myself it must be old and lost, I decide it belongs in the front door instead. I could ask myself how it got here, but I am not in Berwick quite so long as to have lost all faith in miracles.

Sir Anthony takes the key from me as if it were a

holy relic. He asks me to recount the way in which the house is laid out, and I explain it as my teeth begin to chatter and my head to ache most insistently. But I would not be anywhere else. I think we all hold our breath as he lifts the key to the lock, slowly pushes it inside and turns it. There is a low grumbling, but the metal is pushed easily out of the way.

Sir Anthony turns to us. 'The danger is clear. We don't know how many are in the house tonight, but we might consider them as hostages. We don't want any of them to die, but we cannot bargain their lives for Edward's freedom, is that understood?'

I feel a lightness in my head as he turns the handle and gently pushes open the door. Sir Edmund and Will walk nimbly down the passageway, checking in all the storerooms as we climb the stairs. My heart thumps like a drum and I wish it would quieten. I worry the torchlight heralds our arrival no matter how quiet our steps might be. Sir Anthony pushes open the door to the hall but all lies silent under its blanket of darkness. He points towards the door in the opposite wall and I nod, for concealed behind it are the stairs to the solar. The pain in my head is unbearable, but I lead the way, each upward step a torment.

The solar door is shut tight. I try to still my mind, which rushes in so many directions, all of them filled with blood and chaos and death. I think I hear a moan and turn the handle abruptly, for no one can be in any doubt of our arrival. We crowd inside, the torches flaming one way and then another.

They lie or sit, arms and legs bound, pieces of cloth stuffed into mouths, Dame Eleanor on a bed, her maid Anne and little Mary on chairs. There is no sign of Edward. I search frantically for Lucy and find her lying curled on a bed in a corner, the coverings half fallen on to the floor. I leap towards her, struggling with the rope that binds her hands. I catch hold of her eyes with my own, moved to weep at the heat in her skin, the fevered shimmer in her gaze. I finally untangle the knot and move on to her feet as she pulls out the cloth from her mouth. She gasps and shivers. 'He told me you were dead!'

I seize the blanket to put close around her, sitting beside her on the bed. 'You are not well.'

'I did not care . . .' She gazes at me, puts a hand flat on my chest.

I wrap an arm around her, pull her closer and she lays her head where her hand had been.

'Where is he?' I murmur it into her hair.

She shakes her head. 'I don't know. He has done this to us night after night, and he disappears until morning. The first time I thought he did not mean to come back and only our bones would be found.'

She doesn't feel much more than bones now. I tighten my grip on her. 'Did you finish the cipher?' I ask.

'Yes. The day after you were last here.'

'Did he know?'

I feel her sigh gently. 'Yes, though he said nothing. But I knew he was watching me most strictly. When I finished it and knew it was him, I could not look at him,

knowing what he'd done. What he is. He would not let
me leave the house.'

Dame Eleanor crosses to her daughter and I stand
unwillingly so she might sit. She looks up, so that she can
hold me tight in her gaze. 'He knew for certain. He allowed
me to attend to my affairs, but he told me what he would
do to Lucy if I betrayed him.' Her skin is waxy in the
torchlight, creased and lined like an old piece of parchment.
She wipes away her tears. 'We could only pray someone
would come, even if we thought you never would.'

I look up at her. 'He tried to kill me before I could
finish the cipher. I am only just recovered. Nobody knew
if I was alive or dead.'

Sir Anthony comes close. 'We must find him.'

Lucy pulls the blanket tighter. 'Perhaps you should tie
us up again, when the dawn comes? So he will not think
anything is amiss when he comes back.'

'No!' It is not difficult to see she needs a physician and
to sleep deeply after these long, terrible nights. 'We can
catch him here without that.' I know I forget myself, so I
turn my head towards Sir Anthony. 'If it pleases you, sir.'

He nods. 'Edward has no reason to think we have
discovered him. We will leave you to sleep now.'

Dame Eleanor pushes herself up, stretches out a hand
to Sir Anthony. 'Where will you go? You cannot leave us
alone.'

'Downstairs, to the hall. You need never see him again.'

I see Lucy's eyelashes begin to sink towards her cheeks
and am glad. Sir Anthony goes down to relock the front
door while the rest of us settle ourselves in chairs in

the hall, apart from Stephen, who stretches along a bench
and is soon snoring loudly. I pull my cloak tight around
myself, feeling the chill. I know I should try to sleep, that
I might make myself ill if I do not, but I want to be sure
nothing terrible can happen. I sit near the window that
looks down Hide Hill. He may not come that way, but if
he does, I will see him and we will be more than ready.

But I soon fall into sleep, waking in dismay with a sore
neck and rising thirst. It is still dark but soon the edges of
nearby buildings start to appear, the light slowly spreading
in a golden mist. I stand near the window in the shadows.
I would never forgive myself if Edward saw me there and
ran away for ever.

I feel my guts leap over themselves when he turns the
corner out of Hidegate into Hide Hill. I run to Sir
Anthony, tugging at his sleeve to pull him back to
wakefulness. The others open their eyes, sit up and stretch.

Sir Edmund puts his hand on his sword. 'He is come?'

'Yes, sir.'

He looks at Sir Anthony. 'Will we take him here or
downstairs?'

'Here is better, I think.'

We wait for the sound of the key in the front door,
standing like statues, swords at the ready. Still no sound.
We wait. I make my way to the window, keeping out of
its full gaze. I cannot see Edward in the street. But why
does he not come in? I fear we sit in the eye of a storm,
where all is still possible, as we wish it to be, but once we
move everything might be turned up as if down.

We cannot wait for ever. Sir Edmund soon begins to

tap his foot, and Sir Anthony heaves a great sigh before striding out of the hall and down the stairs. He opens the door as we run down behind him. There is no one. We knew there would be no one. He steps outside and we follow. But as I cross the threshold, I notice a blue ribbon on the doorstep. I imagine Lucy is the only person to wear ribbons in this house, though I confess I have never seen her do so, unlike her sister. But she said she has not been out for some time and surely a servant would have found it and washed it when she was sweeping.

I pick it up and am surprised to see a flattened part in the middle. It is certainly not very clean, and I cannot think it has been used to tie up a girl's hair. Did it fall from somewhere? I look around, but there is nothing nearby apart from the door. Could it have . . . ? I measure it against the thickness of the wood, and it is a perfect match. So, its presence between the door and the jamb cannot be an accident. Since the ribbon was already on the floor when we came back down, the last person to open the door was Sir Anthony when he used the key last night. Edward had every intention of coming back in, as usual, but something alerted him to the fact that someone – in fact, five of us – had passed through the door already. The ribbon was surely arranged so he could see if it had been disturbed or not.

Will is at my side. 'What the devil are you doing?'

'I've found out how he knew not to come in.'

He grunts. 'But can you tell us where he's gone? That would be more useful.'

'Don't be an idiot.'

He sticks out his tongue. 'It would though.'

I sigh and we run to catch the others. I explain about the ribbon.

Sir Anthony rubs his forehead with both hands. 'The gates will soon be opening. We must keep them shut until we find Edward.' He sends us each in a different direction, though he takes pity on me, and I have not far to go to reach the Watergate. Peter Spalding greets me with a frown, which grows deeper as I explain we have found the traitor, though unfortunately he is at large in the town. 'They'll not be happy. And it'll be me they'll blame.' Even as I walk back up Seagate, I can hear voices raised against the closing of the gate and know he is right. Sir Anthony has gone to tell Ralph Holme of the night's discoveries and I hope he will send out the crier to tell everyone to be vigilant, to look in all their outhouses and anywhere else a man might hide. The quicker we catch Edward, the quicker we can all begin to breathe more easily and live our lives a little less fearfully.

I feel a great lightness in my head and lean against the nearest wall. Sir Anthony appears out of Briggait, and I push myself up to greet him. 'How did Master Holme take the news, sir?'

'Let's just say he would rather Edward was under lock and key. Do you have any notion where he might have gone? Would it be the same place he has been spending each night?'

That is a good question, but I have no answer.

'We must find him.' He puts a hand on my arm. 'And you must sleep, or you will fall over.'

I want to argue. I want to go and see if Lucy is recovered. But I feel as if great pieces of lead are being pressed down all over my body. I drag myself back to Marygate and curl up on the floor of our room under my cloak. If the others come back, I do not know it. I wake as the light begins its retreat and find the others in the hall. Even before pushing open the door, I know by the dull silence that they have not found him. And I see they stare into nothing, pulling apart pieces of stale bread.

'Where can that devil be, Ben? You must think hard.' Sir Edmund has such faith in my abilities I sometimes wish he thought a lot less of me, as he used to.

Sir Anthony rises, hunched like a crow with weariness. 'We cannot keep the gates closed. There will be riots.'

'Do they not know the cause of it, sir?' I sip a little ale, feel the tepid course of it run through my insides.

'Holme sent out the crier. But good reasons do not feed those who will earn nothing while we search.'

'Have you looked in Dame Eleanor's warehouse?'

'Top to bottom. And spoken with her too. But she's no wiser than the rest of us. If you could . . . If you have . . .' He shrugs his shoulders and sets off for the door. 'I know you will tell us if you think of anything.'

Sir Edmund and Will play dice and I beg a little stew from Mark in the kitchen. I try to think, but it is not as if I know Edward particularly well. We are soon all yawning and, though I have but recently got up, I already wish to be in bed under the warmth of a linen sheet and blanket. Perhaps tomorrow . . .

I wake early, an immoderate moon peeping through the window and spreading its silver light across the room. I feel most strongly that I know where Edward is, even if I have not yet put my mind on it. I must let it come in its own time. I think of all the things I know about him, which is little enough, but will have to suffice. I wonder how Alice found his papers. She cannot have known he had them, so perhaps she was looking for something else. I try to imagine her distress at having to marry him, perhaps not even understanding why. Did she threaten him? Was his journey to Lamberton that day one of his many assignations with his treacherous countrymen, or was it cover for his hasty plan to murder her? If only Alice had found Sir John. If only she had returned with Lucy and the other girl. If only she'd reached the safety of her own house when she fled from . . .

I sit straight up in bed. Sir Edmund stirs with a great grunt while Will throws his stinking shirt at me. I throw it back, but it hits Sir Edmund instead.

He growls. 'If I was awake, I'd bang your heads together.'

The bells start to ring, presumably for Prime.

'I know where he is.'

Sir Edmund groans, puts his head beneath his blanket. But then he sits up, stretching extravagantly. 'Tell us then, since you don't think we need any sleep.'

'Ralph Holme's warehouse. At the back.'

We scarcely need torches – the moon is so bright and the heavens so clear. Ralph Holme leads the way, along with some of his men, so we are a small army of nine. 'I should have thought of it.' Ralph strides out from his house in Western Lane in an ill temper, though with himself for once. 'And to think I was there all day yesterday.' He clutches the key to unlock the door between the main chamber and the passageway at the back, even though it is still attached to the belt at his waist.

We slow down as we approach the warehouse and Sir Anthony suggests we become two groups, one to enter from the front and the other to wait at the back. Ralph nods and sweeps inside with his men, so we five move quickly round its great walls until we stand waiting at the decrepit door opposite the Carmelite friary. I think of Alice and wonder if she still lived when Edward put her down here to use his key. How I hope her soul finds rest once her killer is caught.

Or soon will be.

I think we are all listening hard and soon enough we hear shouts from inside. Before we have time to draw breath, we hear a key in the lock and the door is thrown open. Edward runs out pell-mell, a dagger in one hand, keys in the other, head down like a bull.

He throws the keys to the ground and comes directly for us. Stephen is thrown out of the way but scrambles up out of the mud and I do not think him injured. Sir Edmund tries to grab hold of Edward's cloak but captures only air. Sir Anthony, Will and myself move to encircle him, but Edward is quick, darting one way and then the other. He is yelling, too, as if quite without reason, edging always nearer the road towards Hidegate and a little lane that runs straight into Ravensdowne along the walls.

Sir Anthony sees it too and moves towards the lane, yelling at us to block the other route. But Edward is quicker. Dagger outstretched, he runs straight at me and I can only leap sideways and try to grab him, the blood thundering in my ears. I too catch hold of nothing.

But Will is after him and I rejoice, for I've seen no one quicker. They slip out of sight, into the murk, and we follow. A fellow lies on the ground, the breath knocked out of him. Next to him a woman sits nursing a hand that bleeds most copiously. The lane bends, then twists again and we cannot see them.

And then we come out into Hidegate, which is full of dungheaps and people pressed against the walls of the houses. We look both ways and are just in time to see Will launch himself at Edward, who has turned round and crouches, dagger raised. I hold my breath, even as we begin to run again. They come together with an almighty yelling and roll, one on top of the other. At last, they come to a halt as we stand around them.

Edward lies on the ground looking up at us, Will wrapped around him. 'It is finished then?'

'Yes, traitor.' Sir Anthony walks towards him with a pair of shackles. 'It is most certainly finished, thanks be to God. You have led us a merry dance, but no more. Now it's time to pay.'

I lean down to look Will in the face. He grins and

I start breathing again. He leaps up and Sir Edmund pulls Edward off the ground.

Edward smiles, as he is so often wont to do, and I wonder that I ever understood it to mean pleasantness and fellow feeling. 'To whom am I a traitor? Not Longshanks's foolish whelp. He is not my king.'

Sir Edmund breathes hard. 'No? But he'll hang you for a murderer all the same.'

Edward frowns. 'She gave me no choice. I took no pleasure in it.'

Sir Anthony finishes with the shackles. 'Hold your tongue or I will tie up your mouth. There is proof enough of your treachery and you have no right to reply to that in law. The murder of Alice Rydale and the old man, they are a different case and we will decide on them soon enough.'

Henry Cranston is set free with a new set of clothes, several ells of canvas and some food. He looks confused and Stephen goes with him, back to his tent, to help him hang his new one. Edward is locked in the same storeroom, though Sir Anthony thinks to move him to the castle, if he can arrange it with Horsley. It is a good thing we have so little to store. I walk away with a great confusion in my heart, that it should be finished, what was started so long ago. Already the sky is filling with clouds, a forbidding grey that soon releases a flurry of snow. But as soon as we've eaten, I must see Lucy. I pray to God she is feeling better.

The ground crunches beneath my feet and the town does look lovely, the mud and the decay fading away beneath the white so that all becomes harmonious. The gates are open again and whatever Edward intended to do to unman our defences, the Scots will not find it done. In two days' time – on the eve of our Lord's birth – I will come of age. There is much to celebrate. I know I am fortunate to be alive and now my destiny is in my own hands. And God's, of course.

I also know for certain that which I have long been unable to admit, out of fear. Fear of ridicule from others. Fear that what I wish so fervently for myself is not shared. I do not take any pleasure in the thought that I must write to my stepfather to tell him I will not go through with the marriage he has arranged. He is a wilful, slothful man, which is a dangerous combination. But I'm sure we can agree a price for my freedom, presuming I can afford to, for I have no training in stewardship and no notion as to what my lands are worth. But how my heart sings with joy to know my dearest wish is to make Lucy my wife.

I confess to a great worry, even so. What if she thinks of me only as a kind of brother with whom she can discuss matters of substance? I am glad she has a mind that puts anything and everything to the proof most energetically. It is one of the things I love most about her. But would it not be a little . . . unsettling in a marriage, for a woman to question constantly? Or do I worry about something that causes me no disquiet, even if others might think my judgement lacking?

I reach the corner and am about to turn right into Hide Hill when a flurry of boys comes whooping down Soutergate, sliding on the snow. It is a miracle they manage to avoid those walking up and down the hill, dogs sniffing out morsels and crumbs, the stall outside the baker's shop piled high with loaves and biscuits. I see Wat and he bursts into a great smile before falling over at my feet. 'You are well, sir.' He jumps up, pushing off the snow from his clothes. 'I am most glad to see it.'

'And I must thank you for saving me.'

He hangs his head. 'It were my master mostly. But I was helping to bring you home.'

'Then you will be pleased to know we have just arrested the man who did it.'

His mouth drops open, eyes big. 'Who, sir? Do I know him?'

'I don't know. He was steward to Dame Eleanor Rydale.'

He shakes his head. 'I hope he hangs.'

'I think we can be certain of that.'

'Will it be soon?'

'I don't know what needs to be done or who needs to do it. But I will tell you when I know.'

'Thank you, sir.' He grins again and slides off down the hill.

I follow on more carefully, in less buoyant mood. I should be filled with joy at the happy outcome of our labours, not least because the part I played in it was considerable. But now, after the first ecstasy, I am become a little melancholy and I don't know why. Edward deserves to die for what he did and yet . . . I push away the strange feeling I have, for what's done is done and my current errand is a most pleasant one.

My welcome from Dame Eleanor is everything I could wish for. She rushes towards me when I enter her hall, still pale and creased, but with something of the handsome, vital woman she was when I first set eyes on her. 'He is taken?' She seizes both my hands. The room blazes with heat and light, the fire piled high and candles splashing gold everywhere.

'Yes, lady.'

'You cannot imagine how much we thought it a miracle when you came to save us. Mary still thinks you are angels, no matter what we tell her.'

'Certainly not angels, but I thought it something of a miracle myself.'

'Will you have some wine?'

'Thank you. May I ask if Lucy is recovered?'

'Not entirely. But I don't fear for her as I did.'

I wonder if I can ask to see her. Perhaps I should wait a little. 'There are some things I do not quite understand. About Edward.'

Her hand jerks and the wine spills. 'I am hoping to forget him as quickly as possible.'

I can scarcely pretend not to understand her meaning, that she doesn't want to answer any questions, and am disappointed. 'I merely want to know if you ever suspected he was a traitor. I understand there wasn't anything you could do.'

'Perhaps you would like to see Lucy? I know she dearly wishes to see you.'

That is good news, at least. It would have been unbearable if she had no use for me now. 'I would like that very much.'

'Anne, will you tell Lucy that Benedict is here?' Her maid sits near the window, mending clothes. She slowly disentangles herself from her sewing and ambles across the room, when I wish her to run.

Dame Eleanor smiles, almost as if to herself. 'May I ask – I hope you do not think it impertinent – I wondered how old you are?'

I must confess to the pride I feel at being able to tell her I am almost come of age.

She nods, tugging at the heavy gold ornament she wears strung around her neck. 'And do you intend to stay in Berwick?'

'I have not decided, lady. My master says he will go at Easter, for certain. I could join another retinue, if I chose.'

'But I suppose you are to be married soon?'

For someone who does not want to answer difficult questions, she is most eager to ask them. I nod slowly, unsure what to say. 'My stepfather has arranged it. She lives but a short distance from our manor.'

The tugging on the ornament stops, her gaze turning on me as if she sees me anew. 'And this is what you want?'

'I am not yet my own master!'

'Is she to your liking?'

'I do not think I know her. I was sent away to school in Gloucester when I was young.'

Anne returns but Lucy is not with her. I wonder how long this torment will continue and decide to put a stop to it. 'Is there some purpose to your questioning, lady?'

She turns her head away slightly, hand at her mouth. 'Forgive me. I owe you so much and yet I know you so little.' We talk about the weather, for snow is most unusual, she tells me.

The door opens and Lùcy enters at last. I rise, feeling a great yearning to go with her to the priory or somewhere quiet and undisturbed.

She looks from her mother to me, eyes shrouded, her hair unusually smooth and dress neat. 'I am glad to see you. I wanted to thank you again, for . . . the other night. I didn't think you'd come, and you did.' She jerks her mouth into a little smile and goes to sit in her usual window seat.

I wonder what has changed between us, for it does not seem to be an alchemy that works to the good. 'I am sorry it took us so long. We think he had arranged with the Scots to make another attempt on our walls. They were no doubt intending to try very soon, for Edward surely knew he had little time before we discovered him.'

Dame Eleanor flings her hands over her mouth, chokes back a sob.

I do not understand these sudden changes in temper.

Lucy struggles up, limps over to her mother. 'What ails you? Do you need the physick? Sit up, please.' She holds the wine goblet to Dame Eleanor's lips. Anne stands nearby, kneading her kerchief.

Dame Eleanor clutches Lucy's hand. 'Let us leave here. As soon as we can. It's what was supposed to happen, with Alice . . .'

'And where would we go?'

She turns her head then to look at me, and Lucy says something to her in a low voice I do not quite hear. God forgive me, I wish I were somewhere else.

Lucy shakes her head, returns to her seat, settling her skirts and lifting her chin at me. 'You found the key, I imagine? I did not manage to ask last time.'

'Ah!' I lean forward towards her and for a moment it is just the two of us again. 'It was deliberate, then?'

She nods, her smile mocking me, but I find it friendly, welcome. 'He watched me all the time, but even he must relieve himself. I hid an old key in my tunic and threw it out of that window so it would fall at the back door.'

'It was just chance that Will kicked it.'

She tilts her head, squashing her lips. 'I wasn't expecting you to come in the dark.' I see she tries not to laugh and I feel suddenly happy again, even though I must leave soon to go on watch. The snow has stopped and a little patch of blue hangs over the top of the window.

Dame Eleanor rises, pats her cap and puts on a smile. 'Please come again. If you would like.'

'Yes, lady.' I wish it were summer and Lucy and I – and little Mary, of course – might walk on the Fields among the poppies and marigolds and harebells, the sun holding us in perfect ease.

Chapter 16

It irks me, that there should be so many questions left unanswered. I could press Dame Eleanor, but it would be harsh when she seems still somewhat unsteady in her mind.

Every time I enter our house, I think of him behind the storeroom door. Sometimes I hear him singing softly, some peasant tune I do not know. I wonder that he should fear death so little. And I wonder, too, at my feelings for him. In the moment when the meaning of the cipher leapt out beneath my fingertips, there was fear for Lucy, but disappointment too. The truth of the matter is I liked – like – Edward Morham, or whoever he is. I remind myself of Alice's terrible fate at his hands, and Tom's too, that he has no right to any scrap of kindness from me or anyone else. But I did believe him when he said he took no pleasure in it. It was them or him, I suppose, even if there was evil in his being here at all.

The shortest day comes and goes, along with the anniversary of my birth and the Noel, though winter's selfish grip does not slacken. Every time I pass through our door, I tell myself I show great weakness in thinking these things and should tell Will to have him mock me. But when I hear Edward is to be sent to the castle before the end of December, I ask permission of Sir Anthony to speak with him.

Stephen locks me inside the storeroom, and I wonder how I would feel if the key turned against me in some Scottish prison. Edward watches me with eyebrows raised as I settle against an empty shelf. I clear my throat. 'I want . . . I would like . . . There are many things I still don't know.'

He smiles, the bones in his face showing much more readily now. 'And you wish for me to answer them?'

'You don't have to, of course.'

'It is a fair exchange: your company for answers. I do not thrive by myself.'

I blink. 'You cannot expect to thrive ever again.'

'Benedict, I know what is coming. I know what I have done. And God understands why. I am sorry my life is to come to an end, but I was always willing to give it in such a cause.'

'The cause of a murderer and a traitor.'

He brings up his hands to scratch his nose, the shackles hanging loose around his wrists. 'We are never going to agree on that, are we? So why waste time treading that path?'

He is right and I nod. 'Will you tell me what happened with Alice?'

He draws in a long breath, stares at the cobwebs on

the curved ceiling. He speaks quietly, still not looking at me. 'I don't know what she hoped to find. Probably something to help persuade her mother that we should not wed. And perhaps I was more unwise than I should have been. I have asked myself that many times. The letters and papers lay in an old pair of boots. She did not need to break the cipher, for she knew they were mine, and I knew she had them – for she told me she had no need to marry me now.' He rubs his face.

'And she went straight to Sir John after that, surely?'

He nods his head. 'She should have stayed there when she did not find him at home. But she was young and beautiful, and May Day is a marvellous time for such creatures. Perhaps she couldn't imagine I would touch her. It's true I had to harden my heart. I was fortunate – and she was most foolish: that she stayed by herself when the others left. I knew they meant to go to the Fields, and I went quickly to Lamberton and came back to spy on them. It was a relief and a horror to find her alone.' He stares off into that terrible afternoon. 'Anyway, the cart got stuck in the mud and I didn't have time to take her body to the Lamberton road and return to the Cowgate before the gates closed.'

'But she wasn't dead when you took her back in?'

He closes his eyes. 'No, though I thought she was. When I first approached her, she heard me coming and turned to look right at me. I think she was daring me to hurt her, and I couldn't. I asked her to forgive me and said that of course we would not be married. I suggested she come back with me in the cart, and then I hit her hard on the head as she went before me. I tried to strangle her while she lay on the ground, but I didn't do it very well.'

I am held as if under an enchantment, astonished that Alice should trust so much in her beauty and good nature.

'It became even more difficult after that. I loosened the pin on the cart, to explain the lateness of the hour and to make sure I was remembered coming in. And took the cart straight to the wright, as I told you.'

'But surely you didn't leave Alice?'

'It was a risk, I knew it was. But I was sure I'd killed her and she lay under a great pile of old sacks. The wright was in a hurry to get home that evening, so who would have discovered her? I was worried, though, I'll confess it.'

'But you went to drink with William Roxburgh.'

He smiles again. 'Yes. And no. I made a great show of my drinking, but in truth I had little, and none at all after Pontefract and the others left. I needed them to have seen me and to be able to say so with a clear conscience. But I also needed William to go away.'

He shakes his head, as if bemused and amused at the same time. 'I'd known his secret for some time. That's why I became friends with him, in case I needed someone to do things they'd rather not. He was chasing after Ralph Holme's wife and had caught her. Quite a happy pair they were, for a few weeks, until fear of Ralph crept into their bed beside them. But that was a little later. I told him to go to her, would say nothing to anyone else, was happy to doze in my cups until he got back. He didn't need me to say it more than twice. As soon as he was gone, I went back to the yard.'

He breathes deeply again. 'I'd just turned out of Marygate into Hide Hill. I saw her silhouette coming up, lurching from side to side.' He breathes hard again. 'She nearly got home. But I caught her. There was so much blood, I didn't expect that.' He looks at his hands. 'I wrapped her in my cloak and carried her down to Ralph Holme's store. You were clever to discover that. Ralph thought himself lord of everything, but he wasn't even master of his own warehouse. And then I had to come in quietly to the back of our house to change my clothes before making my pretence of drunkenness through the front door.'

'You took the key from Ralph when you worked there?'

'Yes. In case I needed somewhere to hide. So that if I needed to, I might be able to slip out of the Watergate and go back to Scotland. Of course, if I had to do that then I would have failed in my quest. There would be no songs or poems written about me.'

I touch my forehead, suddenly burning hot. And I wonder then if he does not wish to live more than he wishes me to guess, even as he doled out death so easily to us; that all these plans for escape devised so many months, nay, years, ago speak of a life somewhere else entirely that he does yearn for, perhaps even now. And then I think of how close he came to eluding us entirely, that he might indeed have made it out through our walls and away, if he'd found out that he was discovered. But in reminding me of the hiding place in Ralph Holme's warehouse, God was surely on our side.

He lets the ghost of a smile settle on his lips, leaning forward slightly. 'Perhaps I might have come back with Douglas, found a way in somehow. Berwick will fall, you know that, don't you? You cannot keep us out for ever.'

I do not wish to allow him that victory. 'We have managed this far and we'll manage it yet.'

'Yes, for what it's worth. What is it worth? To you?'

I do not know what to say. 'It is . . . I follow my master. I did not intend to come here.'

'No. It's the arsehole of the world, isn't it? Scarcely worth the trouble. And yet your king squanders his great wealth on poor little Scotland. How many English have died in these wars, do you think? And Welsh and Irish? You might have been one of them, though I'm glad now I could not finish you. How many men brought to evil deeds that now disturb their minds, all in your foolish king's name?'

'You are not one to speak of such things!'

He struggles to his feet, his clasped hands shaking the air. 'I did what I had to do. You do not have to be here. The old king stole Scotland when we were leaderless. If there is treachery, that's where it started.'

We glare at each other. And yet my heart is not in it as his is. 'You said it already: we should not talk about such weighty matters. They began before I was born. Perhaps they will go on after I'm dead.'

He snorts. 'Aye, you speak the truth there.' He leans back against the wall, slides down to sit between a barrel and a sack.

I think perhaps he wants me to leave, but I am not yet finished. 'What I most wanted to ask . . .'

'Eleanor. You want to know about Eleanor. That's why I thought you'd come.'

It is as if he can see into my mind. 'Yes. You called her a whore. That was cruel.'

He nods slowly. 'It was. And I meant it. She earned it.'

'How so?'

He looks up at me. 'Have you not asked her?'

'She will not say.'

He snorts. 'Of course not. I wonder how she would explain it.'

'Tell me.'

'As you wish. I have nothing to hide now.' He smiles and I wonder if he is glad to be himself at last, even in such a ghastly situation. 'She tells a horrible story of a husband killed and herself a grieving widow with child.'

'Yes, for having supplied our men during a Scottish siege.'

'Oh, that bit is true. But there was no husband. She saw only the advantage to herself in selling goods to English soldiers. I was little more than a child. My father farmed near to where our men put her after they caught her, and we sold food to them while they kept up the siege. I will not say she did not suffer. They took their pleasure with her, some of them, and you will say that makes them beasts. But this is not a game and she had forfeited all right to be treated gently.'

'The Scots do that whether they have reason to or no, do not deny it. Just speak to weeping girls and women in the northern dales, dishonoured beyond measure.'

'And you think your men don't?'

'I have not heard of it.'

'Don't be a fool.'

I think of Gilbert Middleton, who nearly put his hands on two cardinals and who is now captured and will die a traitor. And the hard man up in the castle, Roger Horsley, who demanded money from his own people to give them the protection he took the king's money for. There was even someone called Jack the Irishman in this very garrison who kidnapped a most important lady and did who-knows-what with her. My head begins to ache. 'So, she was sent out of Scotland and came to Berwick, claiming a dead husband to explain her child?'

'You have it right. I recognised her only a few weeks after I came here, because Alice looked so like her when she was young. Warehouse men are always first to be accused of thievery or anything else, especially if they're Scots. But Eleanor could make me respectable, especially when I thought to marry Alice. No one would challenge me, and I could go where I pleased. It would be so much easier to accomplish what I came to do.'

'You are most ingenious.'

'You mock me.'

'Perhaps.'

'It does not matter.'

I pick myself out of the shelf. 'No, it does not matter. Not now.'

His eyes follow me, fingers reaching out. 'I am sorry about the man you arrested in my place. What you did to him. Henry . . . ?'

I think he does not want me to go. 'Cranston. Yes, I'm sorry too.'

He frowns and I think we both remember the smell of burning skin and Henry's screams. Then he talks quickly, willing me to stay: 'The sack was not very robust. I worried about that. That she might . . . an arm, perhaps. That would have been difficult to explain. I didn't know she had the papers on her.'

'God was with us.'

'Was he? He wasn't with you at the battle at Bannockburn.'

It is my turn to frown. 'You blaspheme.'

'Do I?'

'You will find out soon enough.'

'Will you attend my execution? It would be fitting, I think.'

'Would that . . . would you like that?'

There is neither smile nor grimace. He is just a man before me. 'I would like that.'

I nod, disturbed in my thinking, and thump the door. 'Goodbye, Edward.'

'Goodbye, Benedict. Get out of here, if you can, before it's too late and you have a ransom to pay. Or worse.'

I don't know what to do. I yearn to go to the house on Hide Hill, but not if I must pretend to a false cheerfulness

in the face of Dame Eleanor's turbulent feelings and
Lucy's elusive ones. Sometimes, in the dead of night,
I wish she and I were still working on the cipher, heads
close together, our speech free of wiles. Now, I wonder
why I ever thought she might care for me when I was
only useful.

And yet, I cannot imagine she has let any person other
than her sister come so close to her. When I am with her
– when it is just the two of us (and Mary) – I have such a
great desire to make her smile. And not to speak stupidly.
I only wish to know how she feels. And even if her
feelings are not so very strong towards me, perhaps
I could persuade her that her affections will follow in time
if we were to be married. I have thought often about
Dame Eleanor's questions and believe she would not be
against the idea, for how else can I understand them?

But when I imagine standing before Lucy, I see myself
with a tongue tied in knots and a face redder than the
blacksmith's. Or Sir Edmund's. So, I think about writing
her a letter. Is that cowardice? But at least then I will be
able to say what I want to say, rather than stumbling
around like a drunken fool. Or do ornamented words
obscure rather than reveal? She certainly might be less
inclined to believe them. I see her in church, stealing
glances at her just like I used to do with Alice, which
seems but a childish fancy now. I have seen her look at
me, too, then turn away swiftly when our eyes meet, a
violent red scalding each cheek.

My stepfather writes to me, partly to acknowledge
I am now come of age but mostly to urge me to come

back to Lincolnshire to be wed, now that the siege is over. I tell myself I cannot go, not while men are leaving the garrison almost every day and those that remain are not always minded to stand on watch because they are no longer getting full wages.

Will and Stephen are eager to make merry in honour of my marriage. They find the very thought of it and me entirely risible, but it does afford them the opportunity to make lewd comments and to insist, if they catch me, that I buy them ale. And they chide me for not going with them to Mistress Fenwick's, for it is entirely natural to them to spend as much time with whores as possible before getting married. In truth, I cannot imagine them refraining afterwards, if they were beyond sight and sound of their wives. I try to avoid them, but it is difficult to think of places to go and things to do, for I have no wish to walk or ride on the Magdalene Fields, even when the clouds drift away and the sun washes shyly over rain-blighted ground.

At last, I see her without her mother. She stands at a clothier's stall on market day, fingering a dark green linen. I watch her speaking with the clothier before looking up and down and all around and chiding Mary for squatting under the stall to play with two whelps. She tugs at a raven tress and tucks it behind her ear, smiles at Mary who shows her something, puts a hand on the girl's shoulder. I cannot move from the doorway into which I have tried to conceal myself, even as I ache at the distance between us. They move away from the stall and walk through the throng towards me. I imagine she cannot see me, but then I think she does and lowers her head, walking as fast as her troubled gait allows.

I hear a shout and quickly turn around. Will and Stephen come rushing up. 'What are you doing? We're all waiting for you.'

I had quite forgotten, though I remembered only a short time ago. Sir Anthony still has us wrestling and fighting one another, and this time I'm drawn against one of the foot soldiers, John Ganton, who was once a tailor in York but stabbed a man in the hand. The man did not die, but Ganton thought it prudent to accept the king's offer of service in Berwick, rather than imprisonment. I know his looks deceive, for he is of modest height and girth, yet he is ferocious when roused and has already spent time locked up for brawling.

I have been dreading this moment ever since the lots were drawn. But now I set my chin and march back into the yard. Ganton is already there, beating his stick into his hand and his friends making great cries in time to it. I take off my cloak, tunic and pouch, throwing them on the ground, and Will hands me my stick. Holding it gently in my right hand a fist distance from the bottom, I see Sir Edmund and Sir Anthony standing nearby, arms folded, and others that I might call friendly acquaintances. But I am already in front of John Ganton and bringing my stick flying through the air towards him. He blinks and I move, twirling around him, hitting his stick, his hands and wrists, deflecting and blocking. I do not look but let all my feelings move me. If he hits me, I do not know it. I hear nothing but the blood thumping in my head.

I feel something pulling at me and Sir Edmund has caught my arm. 'You're done,' he says. And I look down at Ganton on the ground, blood pouring from his nose. I stagger away, breathless. Will and Stephen thump me on the back, but there is no victory. I only want to be free to do what I must. I put on my clothes, sweat trickling down my back, and run through the archway into Marygate. I don't know why I haven't done it before, for I must see her, whether she wills it or no.

The bells ring for Sext as I knock loudly on the front door of the Rydale house. The boy comes slowly, but at last he lets me in. It is dark and cool and quiet inside, and I cannot imagine anyone is at home, though the boy does not say so. I slip up the stairs and into the empty hall.

But I have been fooled before. 'Lucy,' I call quietly.

A book falls with a clatter to the floor and I feel a wave of nausea as the curtain enclosing the window twitches open.

'Ben!' For a moment, joy runs riotously across her face. But then the drawbridge goes up and my love is gone. She lifts her chin, puts her hands carefully in her lap, addresses the tapestry above my head. 'Why are you here?'

I feel a cold chill lick over me. 'Em . . . I wished to inquire if you are well.'

'You saw me in the street.'

'Yes.' So, she did see me. 'I did not think you would mind so very much if I came. Your mother did ask me to.'

'She should not have done so. Given that you are . . . you are not . . .' She frowns most alarmingly. 'I did not know you are to be married. You should have told me. I am sure you will be very happy.'

I cannot imagine she wishes it, from the pout on her lips, the fiery glint in her eye. And I curse her mother and myself, though how did I imagine she wouldn't find out? I pace the length of the room, twisting and turning through chairs and stools and books and sewing materials. I do not wish to look at her while I decide what I must say. 'What if . . . If I were free of my marriage, would you . . . would you think fondly of me?'

'You have no right to ask that.'

'No.' I feel my head droop towards my chest. I would rather go back and cross sticks with John Ganton a thousand times than do this, but I need to be sure it is not her pride speaking. She has rather too much of it, to be honest. But then, I have not discovered *she* is to be married. 'Can I beg you to answer it?'

'I will not. You wish to mock me. I do not deserve it.' She folds her arms around herself.

'I do not wish to mock you. I wish to tell you I love you and survive.' I bow my head. Wait for the blow.

'I thought you were my friend . . . What did you say?'

'I do not think I can say it again.'

'I heartily wish you would.' She frowns most energetically, biting her lip so that I fear it will bleed.

'I said: "I wish to tell you I love you."'

She sits back, a hand smearing her face. She looks at me as if suddenly afraid. 'You do not jest?' It is gently said.

I move towards her, take her hand in mine. 'I could not jest about such a thing.'

'No. No, you should not.'

'If you wish it, I can tell my stepfather I will arrange a marriage of my own.'

'If *I* wish it?'

'Lucy, what ails you?'

'What ails me?'

'Stop it. You are not at all yourself and it makes me most uneasy.'

'You just told me you loved me, did you not?'

'Yes.'

'Then allow me to behave however I please.' And then she throws her arms around me.

I feel the slender curve of her, the heat of her breath on my neck, the harsh beating of her heart. There will be many to say I am out of my mind. Or that it is her money I wish to marry. I pray she isn't one of them.

She releases me and I sit down beside her. Then she frowns and it is as if the north wind shows me no mercy. 'Do you know you're covered in bruises?'

'Ah. Yes. I had to fight a man. With a big stick.'

'Did you offend him in some way.'

'Certainly not! It is to keep us in good shape.' She still frowns. 'A form of training.'

'How strange.' She draws her fingers down my face.

I kiss her fingers as they pass my lips. 'I should have come long before this. I have been a coward.'

'I thought you had no more use for me.' The tears gather and she rubs them away fiercely.

'But you gave me no sign. I thought it was you who no longer wished for my company.'

'Then we have both been fools.

I hold her away from me and we smile. If I were a cat, I would be making a happy noise so loudly the Scots could hear me. I touch her lips with my own fingertips, and she kisses them in return.

'If I died now,' she whispers, eyes closing, 'I would be so very happy.'

I shake her gently. 'You must not say that.'

'But it is true!'

'I still don't want you to say it.'

She opens her eyes and smiles, and I want to linger there, feeling the warmth of her touch, her gaze. But I must leave this strange, enchanted moment and return to my usual life. I rise and pull her up after me. I promise I will return soon to speak with her mother. I do not know what else to say, so I kiss her on the mouth, just for a moment, taking its tender imprint with me long after I have slipped down the stairs and into the street.

By evening, my body aches as if I have been trampled by a cow. I am thinking so much on Lucy, it takes me an age to remember the fight with John Ganton. Will is in an ill humour with me, and Stephen says it's because I ran away after it. I find I have not the strength or inclination to care. I ask to leave, having barely touched my food, and fall into bed.

And yet I cannot find rest. The great joy I felt earlier, which carried me higher even than the tallest rooftops, has given way to a suffocating uncertainty. Perhaps Edward is right. The sooner we leave Berwick the better.

Chapter 17

Our food has become even less fit to eat, and I imagine the only meat to come anywhere near our broth was simply waved over it. Sir Edmund sniffs his before shoving back his chair. Stomping towards the kitchen, he demands to know from Mark how he should live on such food. The cook shouts back that it's impossible to make anything but dirty water out of the stuff we buy from the royal store.

The king's justice is come at last from Newcastle and lodges in the castle. Today he will pronounce on Edward. It will not take him long. Edward does not deny the charges and, even if he did, treason requires only that the accusations against him be read out and sentence pronounced.

Ralph Holme comes to see Sir Anthony just before sunset. He sits down heavily, jowls swaying. He tells us it is done. Edward will be hanged on the twelfth, the day after tomorrow and feast of St Aelred of Rievaulx, which he says is just the kind of spectacle to bring good cheer to everyone, townsfolk and soldiers alike. I have no doubt he is right. I wish I had not promised I would go.

The next day I hasten to see Dame Eleanor. She is in good spirits already, having heard the news. 'Will you see him hang, lady?' I look hopefully towards the curtain of the window seat, but it doesn't move. Perhaps it is better.

Dame Eleanor leans forward and smiles, though her eyes glitter like steel. 'I would not miss it, not if you offered me the entire world.'

'And Lucy?'

She shakes her head. 'I think it best she does not stand for long in this weather.' Her gaze softens. 'She told me you were here the other day.'

I place my feet at the start of the path to happiness. 'I was. And I have something to ask you.'

She settles back on her cushions, popping a sugared almond in her mouth. 'I hoped you might.'

'As you know, I am already promised in marriage, but it is my dearest wish to marry Lucy, if you are agreeable.'

'If I had not seen proof of your affection towards her, I would think your interest mercenary.'

'You know it is not. Though . . .'

She gives me a long look from under her pale eyelashes.

'I cannot deny it will make it easier to plead my case to my stepfather.'

She smiles. 'I see. I confess I never imagined Lucy would marry. I did not think . . .'

'What did you not think, lady?'

'It doesn't matter now. Have you resolved on your future? Do you stay or do you go?'

'Easter. Sir Edmund leaves then, and we will have been in Berwick a year. That is long enough. We will marry at Howsham and I hope you will travel with us.' I hear my words and marvel at their certainty.

She nods. 'I doubt it will be long enough to settle my affairs here, but I can return. You do not mind a mother-in-law in your train?'

'It will be better for Lucy, I think, that you are not far away.'

'Is Lincoln nearby? I hear it is a fair city and a goodly place to trade.'

'About a day's ride.'

She closes her eyes, gripping tight to the arms of her chair, and I wonder if I should tiptoe away. But she soon speaks, as if in a dream. 'I know I seem an old woman to you, but I feel reborn. I will be for ever in your debt.'

I think of all the lies she's told, which, I must confess, has muddied my good opinion of her. But I suppose she did not have any more choice than Edward did in deceiving us. And I do not like to think of what the Scots did to her. 'It is you who does me a great honour.'

She presses her fingertips together at her lips. 'Good. I am glad we have both been of service. I wish you and my daughter great joy. And . . . fruitfulness.'

It is but a momentary pause, but I feel it. Does she doubt our fruitfulness? She has no reason to, surely. Lucy is merely curved where we are straight. There is no internal deformity that we can know. Dame Eleanor worries for no reason, and I will not pay her any heed. I wonder what my stepfather will say when he sees Lucy. I put him firmly out of my mind and rise to my feet. 'I will bid you good morrow. I will write to my stepfather today. No doubt I will see you when Edward hangs.'

She pops another sweetmeat in her mouth. 'That will be a good day indeed.' I'm not sure to which one she refers.

Will watches me write, which does little to help the words flow. He sniffs. 'You send too many letters.'

'No more than I need to.'

'Who do you write to now?'

'My stepfather.'

'Do you have a fondness for him?'

'Not particularly.'

'You can't have anything to tell him. Nothing has happened. Nothing ever happens in this shithole.'

'You forget, there is to be an execution.'

His face brightens. 'Yes! Though I had hoped it would be more than just a hanging. I've never seen anyone sliced open.'

I have nothing to say to that.

He yawns, scratches at the wooden panelling with his dagger. 'Is it because of your wedding? Do you have word of the day?'

I eye him warily. But I cannot keep my plans a secret. I do not wish to. 'I am telling him I will not marry the girl he has chosen.'

He whistles, stops his scratching. 'My, my! That is news I did not expect. I suppose you've got a girl with child, and were stupid enough to fuck one with a gentleman for a father.'

'No, Will, I have not.'

'But she is here, isn't she, in Berwick? You've been moodier than my sister with her monthly flux these past weeks.'

I stare him full in the face. 'I'm going to marry Lucy Rydale.'

His face twists and his mouth moves without words. But he recovers himself. 'You're mad! That cripple. Has no one told you marriage is for the begetting of children?'

'Do not say any more.'

'Or what? Does Stephen know? Wait till I tell him.' He leaps straight out of the door, banging it like a child.

Perhaps he was not the best person to tell first, though I don't know what difference it would have made if he'd been the last person on Earth to find out. I wish I'd hit him, right across that vulgar, stupid mouth of his.

I hear a great clattering somewhere below and run down to the hall. The tumult comes from beyond the screen, in the kitchen, where I see Mark the cook and the rest gathered near the fire. But I cannot see why. Then more shuddering cries tear through the air and women begin to move with grim sureness, Matilda fetching a pail of water, Sarah pulling down cloths that dry in the rafters, while the cook and the kitchen boys move things out of the way. And through their labours I see Edith on the floor, her head tilted right back on to her shoulders and her soft mouth pulled taut as she wails fit to wake the dead.

I stand rigid, unable to move even as the ominous sound

goes on and on. She has disappeared once more among those crowding around her, urging fortitude or wailing in sympathy or out of fear of what is to come. I grip tight on the wooden bars of the screen. For a few moments I see Edith's face and it is almost bloodless. The wailing stops. I think she must have swooned, but cold water is splashed over her and she begins again, though more plaintive this time. I do not know how long I watch this terrible tableau, but now she breathes hoarse and fast. Cloths are taken away dripping blood, and new ones brought. And then everything stops. Edith falls to the floor even as Sarah rises carrying something swaddled in an apron. It does not move. She peers inside, struggling to hold grief at bay.

But then she looks over at me and I know I should not be there. As I trudge back upstairs, I wonder if Edith still lives and I pray she might be spared. I wonder, too, if it is for the best that the child is taken, given how it was conceived. But, in truth, I have seen the look on Edith's face when she thought she was alone, the tender smile gleaned from something pure. If she still draws breath, I know she will suffer for this most keenly, just as she suffered when the seed was planted.

I scarcely recognise him, slung between two fellows like something they've dragged from the forest and wearing only a shirt. Edward is little more than skin and bone, his legs twisted and almost useless, one eye the colour of a plum. But I am not surprised they have used him for ill. Horsley is a fighting man and yet he must sit here, impotent like the rest of us, while the Scots lord it over his lands. I wonder if Edward would do it all again now.

We stand at the top of a hill a little to the west of the town walls and the castle. The ground descends steeply to the Tapee Loch where trees cluster, bare and silent, apart from raucous rooks. It is a fair view: swans on the loch, the Tweed beyond and, further still, the hills of Northumberland encrusted with snow.

The gallows stand at the top, near the road, and a large crowd is gathered there in boisterous mood. Ralph Holme is not come, for he has gone with another burgess to our king's duchy of Gascony to get supplies for the town. But it seems as if almost everyone else is here. Masters are even content to let their apprentices watch the spectacle, though most of those have banded together in their various trades, eyeing others with swaggering bravado. We soldiers stand together, too, men-at-arms nearest the castle walls, foot soldiers vying with the apprentices for a spot nearest the scaffold. I spy Wat standing with the other butchers, arms crossed and hips thrust forward. He breaks into a smile when he sees me, letting his shoulders shudder with excitement before quickly resuming his stance.

Edward is marched through them, but they have not come empty-handed and he is soon spattered with rotten food and worse. I try to stay close to him, to keep my promise, but have no desire to stand near Dame Eleanor, who is dressed in sober silk, arm in arm with her great friend, Mistress Robson. She too seems intent on having Edward know she is there, though I'm not at all sure he sees anything.

The two men from the castle look most ill-humoured to have to hold him while the justice reads out his crimes. The crowd surges forward and I am carried with them, so that I am far nearer than I would have wished. The hangman steps forward, binds his hands and makes to place the cloth over Edward's eyes. His eyes fly open. He says something. The man shrugs and puts the cloth away while Edward stares out towards the north. It is not me he wishes to see. It is Scotland.

He is not allowed to speak or even to be shriven here. It is quite an effort to get him up the ladder but, at last, the hangman places the noose over his head. The crowd sucks in its breath. And then he falls. Or is pushed. The crowd roars and the man next to me punches the air, spittle flying on to my tunic. Edward's legs jerk, as if they are on strings. And then they fall still, a dribble of piss trickling from his limp member. I pray most earnestly for his soul, hoping that a priest saw him during his incarceration so that he could confess.

I see Dame Eleanor walk away, head held high. Does she find peace now? Some of the crowd cross themselves, but others take turns to throw what has fallen on the ground at the husk of a man hanging above us. I want to leave this place, but there is much pushing and shoving as the apprentices and the foot soldiers turn on one another as better sport than the corpse. I break free of them and run back to Sir Edmund.

'Do we leave them to brawl?' he asks Sir Anthony.

Sir Anthony shakes his head.

'I thought not.' Sir Edmund grins and we march together, using the flat of our swords to knock sense into those we cannot part any other way. The apprentices limp off, no doubt to a beating from their masters. The foot soldiers are lined up and Sir Anthony says he will take a penny from each of them. We hear them complaining with much vehemence once they are allowed to go back through the gate.

Walking back through a driving rain, Will and Stephen recount everything as if we had not been present. Sir Anthony and Sir Edmund decide to go down to the stores and I slip into the hall, poking my head round the screen, not daring to go further into the kitchen. Mark is standing over a pot. 'Edith? Is she . . . ?'

He wipes an arm across his eyes. 'Aye, she lives, though the good Lord thought about taking her. And a great confusion she made on my floor.'

'And the child?'

He shakes his head.

'Was it a boy or a girl?'

'A boy. It was a boy.' He stares somewhere else. 'With fine golden hair, just like his mother.'

I go upstairs. Will and Stephen are still chattering like magpies. 'Did you ask about Edith?' Will asks.

So, he has heard. I nod. 'She lost the child.'

'Do you know what it was?'

'A boy.' I wish it had been a girl, just to spite him.

'Ha!' He turns to Stephen. 'I told you so.'

Stephen sticks out his tongue. 'It's of no consequence if it's dead.'

I turn on my heel and bang the door shut.

Peter Spalding comes down the steps as I go up on watch the next morning at the inner Marygate. Lost in thought, he barely brings up his head to greet me. The last time I spoke with him for longer than a greeting was when we learned the king had left York to go back to London. Peter could barely contain his rage, that we had been deserted yet again. I am somewhat glad he passes me now without speaking, for what is there to say?

My candle stutters out soon enough and I stare into the western darkness. It is as if we are on an island, but one that is being swept further and further out into the vastness of the ocean. I know that somewhere out there, people live ordinary lives. Perhaps some of them even envy those of us who stand stalwart for the king, imagining we do battle with his enemies and gather honours to our names like garlands. I once thought the same, but now I know we are half-starved and wearier than a queasy mariner, circling round and round our days and weeks – and, in Peter Spalding's case, years – with only the fading memory of England's verdant beauty, her just perfection to remind us why we are here.

The light brings with it the outline of the wall in front

of me, the houses running along the road out to the far
western gate, the castle crouching beyond its left-hand
side. And beyond that, Edward's body hangs, nothing
more than a feast for all manner of winged creatures.
I walk a short way towards the northern corner of the wall
and back again, waving a hand to whoever is walking
along the northern portion, for we are reduced to one at
each gate now, despite Sir Anthony's misgivings. And
then I turn back and do it again, to keep warm. My breath
comes out in great plumes, the grassy banks leading down
towards Hatters' Lane glistening with dew.

I stand once more, staring hard towards the west.
I think I see movement in the far distance. A Scottish
raiding party, perhaps, passing like a raincloud. I stretch
and walk again, trying not to think about the passing of
time, for such thoughts only draw it out like an arrow that
is never sprung. I am once more reduced to counting the
days until we leave, but at least this time I go towards
something sweet and wonderful. Which only makes the
waiting harder to bear.

My stepfather writes at last. He begins gravely,
impressing upon me the severe difficulties my demand
piled upon him in dealing with the family of Juliana
fitzWilliam and friends and relations round about, who
all know I did not come to be married. He wishes me to
feel indebted to him, which offends me, but I cannot
deny the fault is mine.

But, in the end, he capitulates, making it very clear it
is the Rydales' wealth that swayed him. And yet he seeks
to warn me, wondering if Lucy really is rich enough to

make up for the dishonour of her low birth. I slowly put down his letter, sitting at the window of our room, for I realise that it is even worse than that. Who will believe I have long since ceased to give any consideration to her obvious infirmity and that I am not forcing myself to overlook it just so I can lay hands on her money? I feel hot just thinking about it, even as I tell myself that, so long as Lucy and I are happy with each other and she herself entertains no such suspicion, it matters naught what others think. But I know it will hurt us both.

Lucy and I long most earnestly for spring so we might walk a little outdoors with only Mary for company. Dame Eleanor is so full of advice for our future that we scarcely own it ourselves and I begin to think Lincoln is not nearly far enough away from Howsham. Lucy is sometimes so bad-tempered with her that I wish to be away from them both. But then she does pull a face to mock herself and whispers her apology, that she is no scold except her mother makes her one.

In March, we hear our king seeks a temporary peace with the Scots, but I have learned to do little more with such news than raise an eyebrow. Close on its heels come rumours that Bruce and his men are not so far away from Berwick and that our king will indeed conclude another truce with him, though Sir Anthony wonders why the Scots would agree to such a thing when we are still ripe for the plucking. But then he sees the disquiet around the table and adds: 'Of course, Berwick has survived much worse.'

He has already had to march down to the Briggait, to Master Weston's old house, to urge Master Broughton, the disagreeable Chancellor of Scotland, to hasten his investigation into disputes likely to spring up between the burgesses and the garrison, as the king has ordered. And he tells us he has gone along the walls more than once to find that whole sections have no one on them, even though he has ordered them to be manned with at least one person. He worries most particularly about the counter-keys to those gates with locks, which have been given to Ralph Holme – newly returned from Gascony – and the burgesses, and thus, as Sir Anthony put it in a letter to the king, 'no one has due care of them'. I am sure I am not the only one who catches the eye of another fellow walking up and down these streets and wonders if he has been tempted to sell us to the Scots. I find it a relief to be on watch, however uncomfortable, for then at least I know we pass a quiet night.

And yet I am not ill-at-ease in Berwick these days, for there are many who smile at me and wish me well. Even Ralph Holme is pleased enough to address me most heartily, should I encounter him walking our streets in grand state with all manner of men dancing attendance on him. We exchange little more than pleasantries and I confess I miss his coarse speech and roughness with me, for it spurred me on to ask ever more necessary questions and was at least honest. I suppose he cannot speak so plainly, now that so many require so much of him and he has only a little to give.

But on a bright March afternoon, I chance upon him coming out of his gate in the Western Lane entirely alone. He sees me and smiles, waiting for me to come closer so that he might embrace me. 'What's this I hear? Are you truly intent on marrying Lucy Rydale?'

'Yes, indeed, sir. It is my dearest wish.'

He raises his great eyebrows, but his smile is warm. 'I see. I wonder what kind of a husband you'll make. Remember, it's the wife who's supposed to disturb the peace with a plague of questions.'

I see he jests with me and do not take it ill. 'I will remember that, sir. But I have one more for you.' I have wished to ask him this for a long time, but there has never been a fitting moment.

He sighs, shakes his head. 'Go on, but quickly. I know better than to try to stop you.'

'It is about Master Weston. Do you know . . . he was your friend and I wondered if you know what happened to him?'

He pinches his nose, looks away down the muddy lane. 'Is it your conscience that asks, or do you wish to rejoice some more?'

'You know I do not.' I stare him full in the face.

He does not blink. 'Then I will tell you that he does neither good nor ill. The king has withdrawn his favour, but I doubt that will last. John is far too useful to be left idle. Many men desire to enter royal service, but not so many can serve well. And few serve admirably.'

'But he . . .'

'Hush now. I know he did. But that is not the only consideration, especially for the king. He must weigh up what might be lost with what might be gained. And there is always gain with John.' I look down at the ground and

he lays a heavy hand on my shoulder. 'Do not take it to
heart, Benedict. You too have served admirably.' And he
leans across to kiss me on the forehead before sweeping
on down the lane.

A few weeks later, on Lady Day, I arrive at the house on
Hide Hill to find Lucy most excited, waving a letter in my
face. 'It is from your sister. She is most eager to be friends.
I know she is very clever and likes to read, but I want you
to tell me everything about her you can think of.'

That is a task I am most willing to apply myself to and
we sit together, my arm around her waist. It makes me
want to weep with happiness.

On my return to Marygate, a flock of geese honk
overhead, leading dark clouds that soon spit hailstones.
I hurry onwards. Ahead, near the well at the top of Hide
Hill, Richard Chaunteclerk pushes away a small man
richly dressed but with a coarse thatch of hair. I follow
quickly after him as he strides off, seizing his arm, but he
tries to throw me off too. And then he sees who it is, and
his face opens into a great smile. 'Please forgive me,
Benedict. I am grown churlish in my old age.'

I know he jests, though only to keep from scowling.
'You seemed to be in some trouble.'

His face collapses into deep folds. 'He accused me of
not paying my bills. Me, who is most particular about

such things. I told him he had the wrong man and he eventually agreed but said it would be me soon enough.'

I pat him on the shoulder, but don't know what else to say. Back at our house, I spy the new kitchen girl, Emma, throwing out the slops in the courtyard. Edith has gone to be married to a tailor who took a fancy to her even though she bore another man's child. But he won't have her working here. Emma is not nearly as comely, but she is a happy girl, singing as she works.

We spend the rest of Lady Day quietly, our feasting reduced to a little more meat in the broth and another bottle of sour wine. Wandering downstairs before bed, I stand outside in the yard for a moment, watching the moon – waning now – cast her patient gaze upon us. The stars lie above, held up by angels. I pray that all will be well.

I hear a scuffle behind me, just inside. I go to the door. 'Who's there?'

'Leave us be,' Will mutters.

I go inside. 'What are you doing?'

'None of your damn business.'

'Let me go!' It is a girl's voice, more fearful than potent.

'Is that Emma?'

'Ben, leave us or you'll regret it.'

I move towards them. 'Let her go.' She flies out of the darkness towards me with a scream. I catch her and she runs off.

Will follows with a sneer on his face. 'I should knock your head off . . .'

I hit him, full across the face. I hear him moan and stumble as I walk away. But then he comes after me. I am already on the stairs, so I have the advantage of height and turn on him. 'Don't touch her again.'

'Says who?'

I say nothing, turning my back on him.

He does not follow. I think I hear him tell me I'll regret it, but I'm so tired I do not care.

Chapter 18

April is only just upon us, and we are in the grip of powerful winds and sudden showers: if this is spring, then there is little life to it, but at least we will be gone from here in only a few weeks. Yet, as I wake on the morning of the feast of St Ebba to the sound of yet more rain, it soon strikes me that even Scotland, with all its showers and mists and torrents, has nothing that murmurs quite so dangerously. And then the shouting and crying become more distinct and I hear the crashing together of steel on steel. I rise even as Sir Edmund is shouting at us fit to burst. We dress, strapping on our weapons, and run outside. My mind will not understand what I hear. Drawing our swords as we cross through the archway into Marygate, we stop, quite bewildered.

Everywhere men, women and children are running, chased by other men, swords and knives glinting as a blinding sliver of sun peeps from behind a cloud. Some of the intruders are throwing open doors and chasing people out, so that what is quiet one minute becomes confusion the next. They are mostly still at the eastern end of Marygate where it joins Soutergate and Hide Hill, the whole discord seeming to roll noisily down towards the harbour. But already a few have turned the corner and are making their way towards us.

'Get back inside,' Sir Anthony commands. 'There's nothing we can do. Damnation! I can't believe I'm going to have to raise another ransom.'

I stay where I am, breathing deeply, for I know I must get to Hide Hill.

'Come.' Sir Edmund tugs at me roughly before turning and running.

I linger still, but not because I hesitate. As soon as they're gone, I cross the yard. The grooms have all left, so I lift a saddle from its shelf and tie it on to Morial. I will have to manage without spurs or anything else, but I need scarcely kick my heels into Morial's sides, so eager is he to go.

Two Scots are turning into the yard as I pass. I lift my sword, but they slink back around the corner out of the way. I gallop down Marygate, scattering friend and foe alike. But Morial pulls up when we reach Hide Hill. Kicking wildly into his flanks, I force him into the tide of people coming at us from every direction. But once he is set going again, I cannot stop him, nor can I see how I might get down even if he did. As we come near to Dame Eleanor's house, I see a man brandishing a spear standing guard at the door. I turn my head as we pass but am swept on. It is all I can do to guide Morial into Briggait, which is still somewhat quiet. We turn up into the Eastern Lane, my only thought to try again. Ahead of us a group of Scots advance on foot, led by a man with jet black hair and a pale face that draws the eye.

I know that face, for I have been running from it since the day we came here. James Douglas is the taste of rotten food in our mouths. He is every fearful shape in the dark, and the sound of steel and running feet in the daylight. He lives among us in our nightmares and in every waking moment when we wish we were somewhere else. I know we give him a false shape out of all proportion to his mortal self but seeing him in the flesh again is like falling into an abyss.

A figure runs out of a gate between two houses on the right yelling fit to wake the dead, and Morial whinnies and rises up, hooves flailing through the air. I struggle to stay in the saddle but thank God I took the time to put it on. The figure turns his head, and I see it is Will. I'm not sure he knows it's me, for he immediately turns away to face the Scots without giving me any sign. Sword raised, he runs towards them with a great cry. I can see what is about to happen and shout out after him. And then they are upon him, and I hear their swords clashing and a spattering of blood surging out of the mêlée and falling like rain. Will disappears and they are coming on again.

I gather my wits and kick Morial, for we will need to be moving fast to get through them. I hear only his hooves against the cobbles, each thud matching the beat of my heart. The faces of the Scots move past us like ghosts.

We reach Marygate again and I look right, crying out too at the sight of all the people now thronging the street.

I want to scream and hit something, but then I see Richard Chaunteclerk running as fast as he can. He sees me and points down the street. 'The castle,' he yells. I pull him up behind me.

As we gallop towards the inner gate, I am dismayed to see a party of horsemen coming the other way. But then I realise their leader is Sir Roger Horsley. I slow down to greet him. 'It's useless.'

He looks up Marygate and nods. 'Ride,' Horsley says, and we turn as one. It is but a short distance to the bridge that crosses a steep ravine and leads to the outer gate of the castle. Sir Roger screams at the men behind it to shut and bar it as soon we're all through.

I jump down and join the men gathering around Sir Roger. The worst has happened, and I dare not think on it for fear I will lose my wits entirely.

A man named Richard Blackburn takes letters to the king, along with horses belonging to those who do not wish to lose them to the Scots, swimming across the Tweed. It is true we have no need of our mounts, for we have nowhere to go and they will need oats that might soon be in short supply. But I am glad Morial was not yet put in the stables when Blackburn left. I think him a brave man, for I looked at the river and felt its dark power even from the walls. Now we can only pray.

We have almost nothing to do but watch the town and my eye is constantly drawn towards the jumble of roofs that is the line of Hide Hill. A part of me wants to believe that if I only pray for it humbly, fiercely, penitently enough, I will see Lucy alive and unbroken soon. What do you want from me, O Lord, that You might grant me such a boon? I would willingly pay it and more.

And yet I know I ask the impossible, that I torture myself by even imagining I might stretch out my hand to grasp the only thing I want. She walks with me in my dreams, but soon enough they become nightmares as she is torn from my side by men with the blackest hair and the palest skin who . . . But I will not think what they might do, though when I wake, I feel such a fierce pain to realise the nightmare is still upon us.

I wonder, too, where Sir Edmund, Sir Anthony and Stephen are now and if they lie in some Scottish dungeon waiting for money to be raised to set them free. I cannot imagine Sir Edmund handing over his sword quietly to a Scot, but what choice would he have? And he will take it very badly that he must lose so much money on so ill a cause. I wonder if he wishes he had left Berwick sooner. Or never come at all? I don't think he could ever imagine the town falling, even if he were the only one left upon its walls.

And I think, too, of Will, of the strange, possessed look on his face when he dashed out in front of me. Did he mean to embrace death? Or was it a failure of imagination? Perhaps he thought he would become immortal in a song or a story about his great sacrifice. But there will be nothing sung or told about daring deeds in this sorry war, and I cannot see what good came of the ending of his life, unless – and I would like to think this – it was peace he sought, after all.

And what will become of me? I do not want the burden of a ransom before I have even spent the first revenues from my lands, but I know the king will not save us and this castle will fall. And so, we do nothing but watch, or sit and idle our time away pretending there will be an honourable end to this shameful half-life. Men talk of home, of the things they will do when they get there. But we are not done with Berwick yet and I am so weary of it. Perhaps that's what provoked Will in the end, for sometimes I imagine saddling Morial and riding through all number of Scots, killing them as easily as lifting my arm and carrying Lucy away. It is not even a dream, just a fever in the blood.

One day, many weeks after the fall of the town, a party of riders approaches the outer gate from the village of Bondington to the west, the way we came all those months ago. It is a breezy day, with long flowing clouds riding high amid the blue. We hear the distant call of trumpets first, which brings us all up on to the castle walls, and the Scots too rush to the town wall above outer Marygate to see who is coming.

It is an impressive entourage, if not especially large, pennons flapping. There is much discussion along our wall as to whose coats of arms they carry until Horsley speaks softly, arms folded. 'It's him.'

'Who?' We gather round.

'Bruce.' He unfolds an arm and points to a bright yellow pennon with a lion rampant on it.

The others stay huddled together, but a few of us run along the walls to draw level with the advancing party. I see clearly now the man they call their king, though he pays us no heed, and what shocks me most is that he is just that: a man. He rides well, talking familiarly with those around him and smiling often. He is neither tall nor short, a gold circlet catching the sun atop his greying hair. If he is wearing armour, it is not evident, which sends us all a powerful message, so confident is he in calling Berwick – and Scotland – his own. I have heard he is often ill, sometimes near to death even. But though I can see his face wears the lines of a long, hard life, he himself looks as if he will never falter.

They pass us by, and I run back towards the others even as a party of Scots comes out of the Marygate on foot. Striding at their head is James Douglas, dressed only in a shirt and hose and his riding boots, a great smile on his face and his dark hair dancing in the wind. He stops and waits for the riders to draw up. I think we must be at a theatre, though if we are the audience then the main players spare us no glances, even if a chorus of archers mounted at the back of the new arrivals watch our walls keenly.

Bruce dismounts and, arms outstretched, embraces his captain. They speak for a moment before Douglas turns to someone standing amid the welcoming party and draws him forward. A shiver runs through me, for it is none other than Peter Spalding and such a spectacle can mean only one thing: he was the one who betrayed us. I long for a bow and arrow myself to shoot through his black heart and pray fervently he does not live long enough to enjoy whatever foul reward he has been promised.

Bruce and Douglas walk together through the Marygate, the king stopping to speak with men he sees on either side. As we drift away from the walls, I do not know what to think, but one thing is certain: they will not allow us to sit here unmolested for much longer.

It begins a few days later with a loud rumbling. I stand with Richard Chaunteclerk at the easternmost corner of the castle's defences, on the top of a small tower. Horsley and his closest companions are below me, on the wall. I can hear them discussing our predicament. Horsley is very firm in his opinions, and I realise he will not risk his men beyond what is necessary. It is only the loss of the rewards for his labours that concerns him, not any slight to his honour. I understand that, but do still believe that a man's reputation, the part of him that goes abroad in his name, is not just a matter for him but for everyone. I see, too, that we live in difficult times precisely because those, from the king down, who should behave the most honourably, the most justly, are little better than liars and thieves. This I have learnt.

A great shouting accompanies the rumbling, and we all look towards the outer Marygate. A great machine is nosing its way out, brought forth on a low cart with six wheels. 'Fuck,' says Richard Chaunteclerk. We both run quickly down the steps inside the tower and on to the walls. It will be some time before the trebuchet is ready to sling rocks at us, but when it is, we will need to get out of the way.

Horsley has his arms folded, as usual, and his jaw set. But he looks around, his eyes flitting over the walls and into the mêlée of activity in the yard behind him. 'You!' He points to a big-nosed man whose name is John de la Chaumbre. 'Take as many men as you need and start moving everything you can back towards the hall.'

Richard and I run with him. I find Morial in the stables and take him and the bay in the next stall to tether them beside the southern wall. It would be best if they do not see what is to come, and I do not know if they will be safe there, but it will have to do. I join the others moving sacks of grain and placing them around the well, which lies in the centre of the yard, a little towards the west. But first I fill two buckets and stagger with them down to the hall.

We have not long begun with the sacks when we hear a cry, which causes us to stop, as if under an enchantment.

And then we see a man being helped down the steps. We run towards him, and I see it is Horsley, blood pouring down the left side of his face. 'I cannot see,' he bellows.

'Praise God the arrow scraped past you.' Sir Roger's deputy, Sir Edmund de la Mare, holds him up. 'Or you wouldn't have to worry about not seeing.'

'Find Thomas.' Horsley sits on a sack. 'And bring me wine.'

Thomas is both clerk and surgeon and comes flapping across the yard. 'God's blood, what a mess.' It is true. Sir Roger's left eye has become like a mash of egg, neither solid nor liquid, and a tangle of bruised colour.

'Well, fix it then!' Sir Roger grabs hold of the flagon of wine.

Thomas makes Horsley lie back, though he refuses to do so until he has taken his fill of wine. The last thing he says as he falls under the surgeon's sway is: 'Get back to work.' The woman he shares a bed with comes running towards him, but Thomas waves her away. 'Do not trouble us. Go look to your child.'

I am glad to be busy. Richard Chaunteclerk works beside me, and we start to move some of the blacksmith's tools into the hall. The blacksmith himself is loath to put out his furnace, but he has no choice, for fire is our greatest enemy. Everywhere men are running and shouting. The cows and goats that supply us with milk bellow as they are led down towards the southern wall. Women and children rush out of the rooms they dwell in and argue with those who tell them to go back inside.

Now this stalwart place has become unsafe, no one wants to be here, but Sir Edmund de la Mare has taken charge, standing calmly in the middle of the yard and answering any question put to him.

A few men still stand on the walls. Now they come running down and everyone stands looking towards the sky above our northern walls for a fleeting moment before turning and fleeing towards the hall. Thomas tries to help Sir Roger, whose eye is now covered with a cloth tied round his head, but he waves his surgeon away and staggers towards us. He will not be parted from his flagon of wine.

And, at last, the company falls silent. We hear the shouts of the Scots outside and then they, too, are quiet. I cannot help but imagine what is happening, though I do not understand much about these great machines. But what I do know is that a great boulder will soon be released at speed from its pouch attached to the long arm of the trebuchet.

It comes like a hunter from the heavens, a harbinger of death. The machine gives a mighty groan and the air itself cries as the boulder passes. Children scream and women weep, and I feel the urge to run, but we have nowhere else to run to. It smashes through the roof of the smithy, and I see the relief on everyone's faces.

But we do not have much time to feel thankful, for the next one comes much further, hitting the wall halfway down on the east side. It is not breached but stone flies out in every direction, hitting a few men standing nearby. There is no time for screams, but an almighty moaning rises up, blood spearing flesh and clothes amid clouds of dust.

I run to fetch water, tearing at my shirt as I go to make strips to bind wounds. Many of the injured have already walked away, but I ask them if I might look at the places where blood oozes, wiping away dirt and dust, for these are our enemies as much as the blows themselves. Only one man lies among the rubble, a great gash in his right arm and the top of his head. He is still insensible, so I pick out pieces of bone before pressing tightly down on his head wound, shouting at Richard Chaunteclerk to come and do the same for his arm, thanking God I once found the practices of the monks in the hospital at Gloucester fascinating.

The rocks fall for some time, but I find I am less aware of them if I have something else to occupy my mind. And though debris lies all around and some of the wooden buildings at the northern end of the yard are now quite unusable, we find we are beyond the reach of the great rocks if we stay down close beside the hall. I go to Morial and speak softly to him, trying to calm the fear that has him twitching and trembling. I doubt he believes me, but I check the rope that ties him to an iron ring, for that is his best protection.

And then, at last, it stops. We hear the machines being rolled away and are astonished, for this must signify that the Scots do not intend to use them again. Sir Edmund de la Mare goes up on to the wall and a few of us follow him. 'Your skills have served us well,' he says to me, seeking me out. I bow my head but am glad to have his words. We spread out along the walls, looking for damage that might lead to a breach, but are soon reassured. And then we all crowd into the little chapel as the chaplain gabbles through the Mass. I feel a great happiness rush in where fear had gripped me tightly only a short time before and I thank God over and over for His mercy.

Robert Bruce rides out a few days later, taking his leave of James Douglas with a kiss on both cheeks. That the Scottish king has a great love for his ill-famed commander is not in doubt and that it is given back freely is also clear for the world to see. I must confess to some jealousy, which surprises me. I find a corner of the wall where no one else is and I sit there until the sun goes down and the darkness covers me and my unruly thoughts.

At first, I think I must be sick, that some strange affliction has taken root in me. I feel utterly tired, as if I am as old as Methusaleh but not yet chosen to die. I miss them all, Sir Edmund, Will, Sir Anthony and Stephen. I wish our parting had not been so abrupt, for I now feel unsteady without them. I hope that Wat is safe, and that Ralph Holme and his son, Robert, will not suffer too much for the loss of the town.

I sit there, suspended above despair and am not afraid. A voice calls to me. It is Richard Chaunteclerk. I turn towards the sound. 'I am here.'

He tells me Horsley plans to surrender. I nod. It is no longer the worst thing in the world, but another step in the dance. The moon rises, showing the way. 'Will you help me?' He nods, shrugging. I untie Morial and we walk carefully down the steps to a little door that sits in the southern wall. 'I have better things to do with my money than pay a ransom.' And I will need every penny and every ounce of wit and strength to find Lucy again.

He kisses me on both cheeks and unbolts the door.

Morial and I walk on, down the steps. The Tweed lies in darkness beneath us except where the moon trails her silver gaze. I throw myself on his back and urge him on. Staggering forward, he stops. I stroke the top of his head, feeling the coarse hair of his mane, the softness of his ears. And then I press my calves into his flanks, and he trots on into sand and shallow water. We go further, the water rising. I feel its cold touch through my boots until there is nothing else, the firm ground pulled away from under us.

From high among the roofs of Berwick, Lucy watches us and smiles. For she is the moon that guides me, and I swear I will not rest until she brings me home.

Acknowledgements

It's a cliché, but an author is only the tip of the iceberg when it comes to the effort needed to produce the final words in the book that bears her name. I have wanted to write a novel, as opposed to non-fiction history, for such a very long time and have so many people to thank for their faith in me, their encouragement when I stopped believing I would ever get here, and their marvellous nursing of the text into this, a bona fide book.

The process of 'letting go' of my exclusive relationship with the fledgling novel began with those friends and relatives brave enough to read it and comment. I am truly grateful to Bill Glennie, Sheila Griffiths, John Jones and James Taylor, not to mention Nick Hanley and Margaret Watson. The fact that the final result is very different from that original version is a testament to just how useful it was to have critical – but friendly – eyes cast over it. Apart from anything else, they made me feel it was worthwhile ploughing on.

I cannot describe just how wonderful it was to receive an email from Polygon, in the depths of the first lockdown, to say that they were prepared to consider the novel. However, even that paled in comparison to the joy, several months and two iterations later, of being told it was going to be published. I owe such a debt of gratitude to Hugh Andrew, who carefully and kindly nursed me through the nerve-wracking process of getting to a contract. It has also been an absolute pleasure to have Alison Rae as my editor. Not only did she surprise me with that first email, but she has been wonderful to work with and I cannot think of anyone better to trust with my 'baby'. I also want to thank Craig Hillsley, who was both a perceptive and instructive reader during the pre-contract stage and a marvellous copy-editor afterwards. And I'm in awe of David Grogan, who designed the cover, turning what was in my head into something dramatically real. I count myself lucky to be part of the Polygon family.

But it will come as no surprise to learn that those closest to me have had the most impact. My mum, Margaret Watson, is probably the only person on the planet to have read all my books. Or at least to collect them. She has always believed in me, even when she didn't necessarily enjoy what she was reading, and I always appreciated her honesty, even when I didn't like it.

It has been a pleasure to share the highs and lows of my putative career as a novelist with Sheila Griffiths, who not only read the earliest version but has been a shoulder to cry on during the eternal process of finding a home for *Dark Hunter*. To hear her delight when I could finally say it would be published and to share a bottle of champagne (saved for that moment for *five years*!!) with her and her husband Mick was one of the happiest moments of my life.

But I know I would not be here now, with a work of fiction hitting the shelves, if it weren't for my husband, Nick. Without him there would be neither novel nor novelist. He has endured my deepest self-doubt, propped me up and sent me back into battle. I owe him far more than mere words can express. I dedicate *Dark Hunter* to him and to our son Finn, who, though certainly not priggish like Benedict nor as naïve, did inspire aspects of Ben's character, most particularly his kindness and gentle spirit, as well as a less jaded view of the world, which is yet another privilege of youth.